PRAISE FOR THE NOVELS OF

"With writing that's hilarious, profane and profound (often within a single sentence), Rudnick casts a knowing eye on our obsession with fame, brand names and royalty to create a feel-good story about getting what you want without letting beauty blind you to what's real." —*Publishers Weekly*

"A wicked good time, with moments both outlandish and touching. And as a summer beach read? Well, it's perfect."
—*The New York Times* on *Gorgeous*

"Caution: do not read in public. Will cause you to laugh (and possibly cry) out loud, sometimes at the same time. Screamingly funny and yet warmly touching. Buy multiple copies. You'll want to share this one with friends."
—Meg Cabot, #1 *New York Times* bestselling author of *The Princess Diaries*

"A culture clash on steroids. Rudnick's affection for his flawed characters lends emotional depth to his skillful satire. Hilarious, irresistible and oh so timely." —*Kirkus Reviews* (starred review)

"Totally irreverent and wonderfully refreshing."
—RT Book Reviews

"Flat-out hilarious, sort of what I imagine P. G. Wodehouse would've written after spending some time in Bloomingdale's. For sheer enjoyment, this book is a bargain."
—*The Boston Globe*

"Paul Rudnick's generous, open heart, scathing wit and encyclopedic knowledge of pop culture and droll humor is in full force with his latest creation. I absolutely adored this book and snort-laughed through the entire thing. You will too."

—Melissa de la Cruz, #1 *New York Times* bestselling author of *Never After: The Thirteenth Fairy*

"Gleefully wacky and irreverent . . . readers are treated to Rudnick's considerable gifts as a satirist as he uproariously eviscerates our celebrity-mad, class-conscious, appearance-obsessed, reality-TV-vapid culture with puckish delight—a wicked good time."

—Libba Bray, *The New York Times Book Review*

"I wish Paul Rudnick was the President, the Pope and the Surgeon General. What a gorgeous place the world would be!"

—Jane Hamilton, bestselling author of *The Excellent Lombards*

Playing
the
Palace

PAUL RUDNICK

JOVE
New York

A JOVE BOOK
Published by Berkley
An imprint of Penguin Random House LLC
penguinrandomhouse.com

A JOVE BOOK, BERKLEY, and the BERKLEY & B colophon
are registered trademarks of Penguin Random House LLC.

Library of Congress Cataloging-in-Publication Data

Names: Rudnick, Paul, author.
Title: Playing the palace / Paul Rudnick.
Description: First edition. | New York: Jove, 2021.
Identifiers: LCCN 2021001354 | ISBN 9780593099414 (trade paperback) |
ISBN 9780593099421 (ebook)
Subjects: GSAFD: Love stories.
Classification: LCC PS3568.U334 P58 2021 | DDC 813/.54—dc23
LC record available at https://lccn.loc.gov/2021001354

First Edition: May 2021

Printed in the United States of America
1st Printing

Book design by George Towne

For John Raftis

CHAPTER 1

It's still weird, waking up alone. I was with Callum for almost three years and he moved out six months ago, but this morning when I opened my eyes, for a second I thought he was just out of town on an acting job and maybe I'd have a text waiting.

But of course not. Instead I stayed under the covers and addressed my problems to the framed photo of the late, beloved Ruth Bader Ginsburg on the wall of my tiny, partitioned bedroom. Ruth keeps me on a firm, morally responsible track, and I like to think that she secretly enjoyed watching Callum and me having sex. In all matters except maybe wardrobe I always ask myself, "What would Ruth Ginsburg do?" so today as I wondered if I was ever going to fall in love again, truly in love this time, Ruth informed me, "Stop whining and go to work, you little pisher. I'm in heaven but I'm still busy." Ruth often sounds just like my equally beloved eighty-five-year-old great-aunt Miriam.

I took a shower using my new manly bodywash, which is ex-

actly the same as the female version, only with simplified graph-
ics and a steel-gray, squared-off bottle, as if it contains motor oil
and testosterone; I slathered on Kiehl's Creme de Corps moistur-
izer because a model at my gym recommended it after he glanced
at my pores with pity but then insisted, "No, they're fine, really,
you just need to think about them"; I brushed my teeth with a gel
that promised "Triple-Extreme Dazzling Whiteness" thanks to
"Gene-Spliced Wintergreen"; and then I got busy with more hair
care products than a Mormon family has children. I was pamper-
ing myself as a fan of what the mindfulness tutorials call self-
care, in order to heal and glow. But after a final check in the
mirror, I knew: none of it was working. I wasn't healed and I
wasn't glowing and a sizable chunk of my hair was completely
awry, as if it was signaling frantically for help.

"So?" asked my roommate Adam, once I'd reached the kitchen
area of our shared let's-call-it-a-three-bedroom in the budget-
friendly wilds of Hell's Kitchen. Adam's a Broadway dancer,
which means that just seeing him both cheered me up and sent
me into a body-image spiral, because he's got the lithe muscles
you only achieve from doing cardio for a living. He was wearing
the limp, colorless, shredded sweats that dancers barely cover
themselves with. "Are you feeling any better?"

He offered me a smoothy he'd concocted; he meant well, but
I shook my head no as I plunged my hand into a box of Frosted
Flakes, which made Adam look Whole Foods–judgmental but
also heartbroken on my behalf. I studied Tony the Tiger on the
cereal box and wondered if he'd ever been cheated on, maybe by
the Lucky Charms leprechaun or Cap'n Crunch.

"You people make me sick," said Louise, my other roommate,
emerging from her bedroom. Louise isn't a morning person and

she's working on her novel while contributing to a Black feminist website, which means, as she says, "I get to write about stuff that really matters without getting paid." Adam and Louise are a great balance because Adam sees life as the peppiest, most joyful musical comedy and Louise wants to strangle him, but, as she puts it, "with love."

"Here's what I think Carter should do," said Adam, stretching his hamstrings across one of our mismatched folding chairs. "I think he should find a guy who's even cuter than Callum, which I know won't be easy, but when he does, he should marry him and make a sex video and send it to Callum using the score from *Waitress*, because that's Callum's favorite."

The scary thing was that I instantly pictured myself having pounding raw sex with some mouthwateringly hot imaginary stud while a woman sang a tender ballad about rediscovering her true self.

"I think Carter should thank whatever God he believes in," suggested Louise, "for getting rid of that cheating scumbag Callum, and then Carter should buy us some sourdough pretzels on his way home."

"Everyone," I said, "you don't have to worry about me, because I've been working on myself, and last night I didn't dream about Callum, not even after I saw his Toyota ad, the one where he runs out of the surf and towels off in front of his Toyota. I'm entering a new and totally happy chapter of my life, because I've finally made a decision: love doesn't exist."

Louise nodded in agreement as Adam regarded me as if I'd slaughtered a puppy.

"Carter Ogden," Adam said firmly, jabbing at his phone, "I'm sending you the entire score of *Pippin* right now, I mean it."

CHAPTER 2

Once I'd hit 45th Street I unlocked a Citi Bike and began pedaling crosstown to my job of the day. As an associate event architect, I love the constant variety in location and clientele. But as I negotiated Midtown traffic I realized something particularly horrendous: it was Valentine's Day. Callum and I would tuck multiple cards into each other's underwear drawers and backpacks and shoes, as surprises; we'd bring each other hot pink–frosted cupcakes sprouting plastic cupids, and once I'd woken up to find my face and pillow scattered with those tiny, chalky, pastel hearts stamped with "BE MINE" or "LOVE YOU," only now they would read "FUCK OFF," "DIE ALONE" or "YOU FOOL WHY DID YOU OPEN HIS PHONE AND OBSESSIVELY SCROLL THROUGH THOSE PHOTOS OF HIM WITH OTHER GUYS EXCEPT WHY DID HE TAKE THOSE PHOTOS UNLESS HE WANTED YOU TO FIND THEM WHICH OF YOU IS THE BIGGER IDIOT?"

As I turned up Fifth Avenue I tried not to notice the many couples strolling arm in arm and then smooching goodbye on their way to work, with not a few of these people trailing heart-shaped helium balloons or toting paper-wrapped bouquets of bodega tulips. I began hallucinating a musical number in which everyone but me began to leap along the sidewalks, proposing marriage to mounted police officers, falafel cart vendors and construction workers popping out of open manholes, with everyone exchanging huge, frilly, heart-shaped boxes of Godiva chocolates. Everyone was coupled up or hugging or flirting while I pedaled glumly alone, like a chastity monitor barking at lovers to stop kissing in public.

I felt not just ignored or invisible, but like an athlete permanently benched, someone tossed out of the dating pool by a harsh blast from the referee's whistle. This would be my life: I was barreling toward thirty, I still wasn't making enough money to live in Manhattan without roommates, and while I loved my job, I knew there was something silly about it, something ephemeral and not quite adult. I helped to plan beachside weddings; Sweet Sixteens for girls who were being given Birkins and more sculpted noses; movie premieres for sequels to sequels; and gala launches of new Apple products that tracked a pet's lung capacity or reminded the user to tell their coworkers about new Apple products. This felt like a suitable career for a Ken doll, a snippy gay sidekick in a rom-com, or an heiress between stints in rehab. I needed to apply myself and maybe go back to grad school or come up with something more butchly lucrative and aspirational in one of those fields that baffled and bored me, like finance or commercial real estate development. I briefly considered tutoring people in poverty-stricken countries on creating Wonder

Woman–themed bat mitzvah centerpieces, as a form of Associate Event Architects Without Borders.

What I needed was something I'd never confided to anyone, not even my dearest friends and family members, because it was such an impossible and yearned-for wish, something that I wanted so badly it made me believe I had a soul. I wanted this one thing with such certainty that I knew it was more than a journal-entry doodle or a childhood fantasy that I needed to out-grow. It was who I was.

That's why I left my bike in the rack near St. Patrick's Cathe-dral and went inside. Even though I'm Jewish and St. Patrick's has a troubled history with New York's LGBTQ community, it's my favorite place in the city, and not just because it's strategically located between Tiffany's and Saks, although I do believe that's a sign of God's admiration for high-end retail. I love St. Patrick's because, like me, it's silly and theatrical, with its spires and but-tresses and tapestries, but it's also the home of so many people's most deeply felt longings; St. Patrick's is a form of sumptuously Gothic therapy. I head to St. Patrick's because it's inspiring and peaceful, which allows me to talk to God about what I really want my life to be, not as a negotiation, hovering somewhere between prayer and bribery, but as a conversation, as a clearing-house for my heart.

The cathedral was lightly populated with Swedish backpackers, elderly widows and a handful of scarily tough Jersey housewives, most likely here to confess machine-gunning a rival in a Stop & Shop produce aisle. I sat in a rear pew and scoped out the area for cute priests—it happens, and there's even a yearly, unauthorized Vatican calendar of the most pious dreamboats. For gay guys in New York, cruising is a formality, like checking your phone, your breath or your coat at a Theater District restaurant. I shut my eyes and took a deep, cleansing breath, as if speaking to God was a classic yoga pose. I quieted my mind to vanquish anxiety and eBay bids and thoughts of how St. Patrick's could be such a great setting for a murder mystery, a rom-com finale or a blasphemous motorcycle chase.

Dear God, I began, and I didn't worry if I was talking to myself or if God existed or what religion he favored, or if "he" was even an acceptable pronoun, or if it should be capitalized. I was talking to God because, like so many other people, I needed to, and that need makes God real.

I don't want to just keep going without a purpose, to work or the apartment or anywhere else. I don't want to keep my head down and manage my expectations and my 401(k) and call that growing up. I don't want to only feel safe. I don't want to keep obsessing over Callum and what I did wrong and whether I still hate him and wondering if we'll ever get back together, because that sort of chatter bores everyone at cocktail parties, so imagine what it does to God; God is the universe's best listener, but that's no reason to nag Him and make Him hand you Buddha's business card as He heads for the door, muttering, "Gotta get up early, nice to meet you."

I want to be like my idol, Justice Ginsburg. I want to be fair-minded and dedicated and compassionate, and look great doing it. Only, of course, without going to law school. I want Ruth's spirit of justice and curiosity and not taking any shit.

I want a big life. I want to fall in love, not like what happened with Callum, which sometimes felt wonderful but more often like an educated guess, as if while I was kissing him I needed to remind myself: this is love, right? I want to know I'm in love, no, not even know it—I want to understand why it's called being in love. I want to be overwhelmed by the miracle of another human being. Love is like God—it's the place where need and rumor and dreams become something else entirely, something sacred, something beyond questions or arguments or therapy. Ruth Ginsburg and chocolate and oxygen and God and love: the real things.

And beyond that, beyond the blissful selfishness of love, and I know that I have no right to ask for any of this, but here goes: I want more. I want to stay me, as ridiculous as that might sound, but I want to make a difference in the world and have the best time, without being torn apart by worry and fear twenty-four hours a day. I want to be of service and create beauty and see if I can convince myself that magic exists and can be shared. Not spell casting, wand-waving magic, although I'm open to anything, but the more available magic of neon-bright crepe paper and cheap tinsel and helping other people, not to forget their very real problems, which can be insulting, but to let them know that another human being cares enough about them to find the right doctor and take them for chemo and find a great playlist and simply be there and listen, without offering useless advice or ever saying "I know just how you feel."

I want what maybe everyone wants: to make being human feel like a superpower. And yes, I know that's beyond corny, but that's why I'm only telling God, who only rolls His eyes to cause thunder.

I want to stop listening to the other, snickering, undeniably sane demons, who hiss things like "I don't think so" and "Oh, please" and "Carter Ogden, who do you think you are, I mean, do you really think you can fall in love and change the world, when you still can't decide whether boldly patterned socks are ever a good idea?"

So just for now, in this resolutely private moment with You, in this prayer that can't be forwarded or downloaded or mocked by the Twitterverse, I'm asking for everything, except for the lightning bolt that smites idiots who dare to ask for everything. I'll ask, because the alternative, never asking, is sadness itself. Never asking isn't just giving up or huddling under a Slanket on the sidelines; it's admitting defeat without even trying, without daring to be a boldly-patterned-sock-wearing hero, or more likely a boldly-patterned-sock-wearing fool.

And now I'm terrified and hideously embarrassed and late for work, but I said it and You listened and—here we go!

CHAPTER 3

One of the perks of my job is getting to constantly visit new venues, because the company I work for, Eventfully Yours, promises, as its mission statement, "Vivid, life-affirming, experience-aware, visual, tactile and culinary event planning within a tristate celebration radius," which means I've helped create fiftieth wedding anniversary rodeos on Long Island, complete with bales of hay and waitstaff in gingham and Stetsons; *Game of Thrones*–themed bachelorette parties in New Jersey, with ice-sculpture dragons and crude bronze tiaras; the introduction of a "sky-high energy-plus" sports drink with out-of-work actors dressed like bottles of the stuff parachuting onto the Brooklyn Bridge; and so many more, including the after-after party for a Lincoln Center film festival where I got to help Sandra Bullock navigate the red carpet, and she was the nicest human being I've ever met. Today I was headed for the United Nations, a landmark which, like most hard-core New Yorkers, I'd brag about to new-comers but had never actually been to.

A laminated security pass on a lanyard was waiting for me, and the many security guards guided me toward a large amphi-theater paneled in sleek *Mad Men*–era blonde wood. There was a wide stage, which my boss, Cassandra Crastick, was standing on, issuing commandments.

"Bailey, please raise the banner with Prince Edgar's official portrait five inches so it's even with the photo blowup of him touring the refugee camp. No, one more inch, must I do every-thing myself? And Jesus, Carter, where have you been? We haven't even started on the flowers or your precious acrylic pan-els, whatever they are, I hope you have a decent excuse, like you were hit by a bus while riding your ludicrous bicycle, I have told you, riding a bicycle in Manhattan is basically begging the world, 'Please fracture my pelvis and give me a head injury.'"

Cassandra is not what I'd call merely high-maintenance, but a narcissistic personality disorder in a nubby cashmere poncho with foot-length fringe. She's insane, but I love her, because she's helplessly insane, as opposed to deliberately evil.

"Carter, do you have an Ambien or an Adderall or any sort of pill I can swallow, only please don't hand me a peanut M&M like yesterday, because then I'll only want more, and the entire point of antidepressants is that they're fat free. Carter, I don't know if I can say this, I don't know if my lips are capable of forming the words, but you're the only person on the planet who can possibly understand what I'm going through. My ordeal. Dwayne left me."

All five feet eleven inches plus suede platform boots of Cas-sandra had now flung itself onto me. I've learned to brace myself for these moments, and I turned my head to avoid getting slashed by the arc of Cassandra's necklace, which was several yards of huge amber beads and spiked brass discs. Cassandra's private life is always public, and often fictional or at least exaggerated. Dwayne is her doorman.

"Dwayne is on vacation with his family in Pennsylvania for two weeks," I soothed, "and I'm sure his substitute is doing just fine." I patted Cassandra on the back, or really on her cascade of multicolored hair extensions, which resembled a street fair wall hanging.

"Do you really think so?" Cassandra asked plaintively, and then, as always, her mood shifted violently, to haughty disdain: "Carter, I have to get to the Javits Center to oversee the presentation of Jasmine Tremble, that new calming shampoo, which I may drink. So I need you to finish up here and make sure everything is polished and locked down, can I trust you to manage that?"

"Of course," I assured her, trying not to remind her that after three years and countless projects, I did most of her job for her; Cassandra had trained me, which I appreciated, but she still second-guessed my decisions and took credit for my ideas, claiming the business was "a family, and families share. Well, not my family, because I don't speak to my mother, not after she slept with two of my husbands, although I suppose in a way we were sharing."

"Cassandra, I've got this, and I'm begging you, please don't steal a crate of that shampoo and use it as Christmas gifts for our staff, like last year with those dryer sheets."

But Cassandra was already on her way out, pausing at the top of the amphitheater steps and crying out, "Farewell, my children!

Give me beauty and madness!" These favorite words had been tattooed on either side of her neck and were also the names of her shih tzus.

"Okay, everybody," I told the eight members of our extremely hardworking team, "You're doing great, and Mikaela, let's get the urns filled with the forsythia branches, Sean, please center the programs on each chair, and Ryan, I'll need the cherry picker for the acrylic panels."

Everyone paid attention, because I try to never waste people's time; I believe in positive energy, and I know what I'm doing. At college I'd majored in musical theater, with vague thoughts of becoming a director or set designer, but these goals had evaporated once I'd met professionals who were actually good at them. Most of the people in the musical theater program ended up doing something else, but it had been a buoyant four years of painting backdrops, hot-gluing headdresses and learning the jazz routines I still occasionally practiced when alone in an elevator. As my great-aunt Miriam had once remarked, "So, Carter, let me understand this musical theater nonsense—you're being gay for credit, right?"

That's what college had been for me: a time to fully assemble my personality. After arriving in New York I'd interned in a publicist's office, I'd written mini-reviews of sex toys and lubricants for a website called ManBatter.com, I'd bartended in Broadway theaters, having to defend the obscenely expensive cocktails on the grounds that they're poured into sippy cups; I'd worked almost salary-free at a startup dedicated to renting scrupulously laundered luxury bed linens, which remained an off-putting and unsuccessful concept; I'd had fun as a rich lady's social secretary until her accountant had advised her to economize, so she'd fired

me, and I'd walked dogs, delivered sustainable floral arrangements (made from newsprint and recycled plastic bags), taught
Slow Pilates to seniors, and eventually began to worry that I was
drifting, embarrassing my family and coming dangerously close
to moving to California, as if that was a career.

I'd met Cassandra while cater-waitering at one of her events;
I'd been unable to resist rearranging a stack of glowing, lit-from-
within Lucite cubes into an impromptu Christmas tree, and she'd
been impressed and hired me. I'd learned the ever-shifting basics
of event planning: interviewing clients to coax out their must-
haves; drafting sketches and building three-dimensional models;
combing the city for quirky DJs, inventive chefs and off-duty ac-
robats; in short, applying my imagination to every occasion. I'd
soon realized that event planning is pure theater and that if I put
my mind to it, I could surprise and delight people who were
dreading a conference or reunion or Midtown fountain pen trade
show. My favorite moment is always overhearing a guest comment, "I can't believe it, but I'm actually having a great time!"

Today's event was a press conference for the Royal Clean Water Initiative, a charitable organization devoted to providing
drinkable water to the over a third of the world's population that
lacked such a necessity. Most of our team's work entailed filling
the stage with a podium, a sound system and restrained floral
design. So all of this wouldn't remind guests of a funeral, I'd
commissioned, as a backdrop, a series of shimmering floor-to-
ceiling acrylic panels, which, when layered and ingeniously lit,
appeared to be a glistening, tumbling waterfall, flanked by photo
blowups of Prince Edgar, who'd visited over thirty countries
helping to dig wells, construct pipelines and bring global attention to his signature cause.

I'm not going to talk about Prince Edgar, because I hate his guts, since he's perfection itself. I hate him because when I was little and I'd smear ice cream on my striped T-shirt, my parents would inevitably ask, "Why can't you behave yourself, like that Prince Edgar, who's always such a gentleman?"

I hate Prince Edgar because he's almost exactly my age and has never had, as far as I can tell, a blemish, an awkwardly timed fart, a cataclysmic breakup or not just a bad hair day but even a bad hair moment. I hate him because he's openly gay, which means every queer man in the world fantasizes, even if they won't admit it, that Edgar's their boyfriend or husband or secret when-he's-in-town fuck buddy. There aren't that many out dreamboats on such an international level; when seeking mass-media swoon material, gay men will sometimes insist that various movie or pop stars are actually gay, as if collective gossip is a form of conversion therapy.

I hate Prince Edgar because, as I stood atop the cherry picker and adjusted a banner, which pictured His Royal Perfection in a tux at a previous summit, I knew one thing for sure: I was the total opposite of Prince Edgar and I seriously wanted to slap his photo or have sex with it. But instead I signaled Mikaela to lower the cherry picker and I told the team they'd all done an awesome job and had earned a longer lunch break and could clear out, as the United Nations staff would be running the event itself.

I stayed behind to fulfill Cassandra's most unbreakable edict, which was humiliating but at least could be done without anyone watching. Cassandra had a bizarre, we-are-all-one, zen-consciousness streak, which was Cassandra combining her daily-horoscope superstitions, her rampant OCD and her needing the constant intuition that she'd pleased and befriended Marie

Kondo, Martha Stewart, Reese Witherspoon and Gwyneth Paltrow.

I stood in the amphitheater's wide center aisle and faced the stage. Everything looked good: symmetrical, dust-free and inviting. I shut my eyes and spoke Cassandra's Gratitude Prayer, which she stipulated I recite aloud, because "otherwise the universal hive-sensors will know you're cheating." But I kept the volume at a respectable level to avoid security guards rushing in and asking, "Who the hell are you talking to?"

"I am thankful for the freshness of the forsythia and the on-time delivery of all products and services. I salute the impact and grace of this event, and I bring an intersectional awareness to this day, along with providing flattering side lighting, basic but attractive stemware and effective signage. I am blessed and I bless in return."

I clapped my hands briskly three times over my head, offered three joyful shouts, and tried not to kill myself as I heard, in a distinctly English accent, "Are you all right?"

CHAPTER 4

was looking into eyes that were so radiantly blue I either wanted to faint or yell, "Just stop it!"

The eyes belonged to Prince Edgar. The Prince of Wales. The guy who was next in line to the throne. The guy who, fine, I'll admit it, I had Googled using the search terms "Prince Edgar Shirtless," "Prince Edgar Beach" and "Prince Edgar Naked" (these last photos didn't exist, but there were some amazingly undetectable fakes). The guy who made me feel like, well, a cartoon rodent or snail, especially right this second, with my hair drooping and possible sweat stains from climbing ladders and moving furniture and my shirt half-untucked but not in that casually stylish way I usually copied from Callum. And I was looking directly at Prince Edgar from only a few feet away. I wasn't just a deer in headlights; I was that deer if it had also been struck by lightning while holding an ungrounded extension cord.

"I'm so sorry," he said, "I didn't realise anyone was here. I was going to practice my speech."

I tried desperately to remember any shred of royal protocol: should I bow, nod, curtsy or helplessly scream, "I'm an American!" to justify my ignorance. Shockingly, the prince offered his hand. Like a human being.

"Edgar."

Now I wanted to not just slap him but then say, "No, just no. You don't get to look like that and be who you are and also be nice. No way."

But I didn't do or say anything because I was paralyzed with Celebrity Terror, galloping insecurity, a tsunami of lust and total brain freeze. I might very well never move again, and my rigid body would be stored in my parents' finished basement, or stationed at the end of their driveway, with a mailbox nailed to my chest.

"I . . . I . . ." I was like a primitive robot, trying to reboot its meager functions. Because in that instant, I couldn't remember my name. I didn't know if I had a name. Should I make up a name? Then my ignition turned over and I blurted, "I'm Carter! Carter Ogden!"

He smiled, which is something I'm not yet ready to describe, but I processed instantly that he was accustomed to people acting like lunatics just because they were meeting him.

"Carter. So good to meet you."

"I . . . I work for Eventfully Yours, we did the event planning for your . . . event." How many more times could I say the word "event"?

"Aha. Well done. The space looks marvelous. Especially that waterfall moment."

WHY WASN'T I GETTING THIS ON MY PHONE?

"Would you mind terribly if I ran through my opening re-marks? To get a feel for things?"

"I . . . I . . . of course. I'll just get out of your way."

As I stumbled backward, out of some dim memory of never turning one's back on royalty, I managed to ram into the seat at the end of an aisle, almost fall, kick an extra papier-mâché urn I was supposed to put back in the Eventfully Yours van, and finally steady myself as the prince studied me like a researcher tracking a mouse's journey through a maze.

"Carter?"

"I'm fine!"

"I'm glad, and this is an absurd imposition, and I'll completely understand if you refuse, but might you perhaps listen to my speech? And offer an honest assessment?"

Okay. Okay. Prince Edgar was now asking me to critique him. He was asking me to be a New Yorker. A gay New Yorker. A gay Jewish New Yorker. Trust me, I have opinions. Did he have any idea what he was in for?

"Um, sure, of course," I told him, "although I'm sure you'll be awesome." Awesome? Awesome? When did I turn into a mum-bling middle schooler, slumped from my two-ton backpack?

"Awesome would be lovely, but I'll settle for audible. I've been working on my personal presentation, as my online nicknames include the Little Wooden Soldier, Prince Plywood and His Royal Blore. And before you ask, a blore is a combination of someone bland and a bore. So I'm seeking to improve."

He was mounting the steps to the podium as I trailed in his wake, standing in the aisle below.

"And we're off. I'm introduced, to polite applause and not a few yawns barely hidden behind programs. Despite this, I begin. Ladies and gentlemen, thank you so much for allowing me to—"

"Okay," I interrupted, and I have no idea where I found the nerve to utter a single word, except that my theatrical background and event-planning DNA had kicked in. Telling people how to work a room was my business.

"You look, well, you look perfect," I began, "which is a certain indisputable form of bliss, I mean you look like your official portrait on the airport LED screen welcoming tourists to London. But that might be part of the problem you mentioned, with public perception. Try this."

I gave myself a brief shake, a blend of mild seizure and invisible hula hoop.

"Why?" asked Prince Edgar, clearly regretting having asked such a possibly dangerous stranger to stick around.

"It's a technique for relaxation and relatability. It's about allowing yourself to get a tiny bit messy. Trust me, it will only enhance your appeal. It's like, if you were a cologne, which would sell trillions of units, it could be called Slightly Rumpled Royalty. It's like a movie star with just the right amount of bedhead. Do it."

I gave myself an even more decisive shake, with my arms extended, like the Tin Man after his oil change. Prince Edgar stayed doubtful, but launched a halfway vigorous shake.

"More! Like you're alone in your bedroom and you're listening to some amazing dance mix, and then it gets even hotter. No one's watching. Go!"

I shook myself even more exuberantly, and Edgar gave in and let loose. In some loony way we were dancing with each other, like two of those inflatable air puppets outside a used car lot, flailing with joy at the one-day-only bargains. Then, out of breath, we stopped, and the prince laughed.

"This is absolutely ridiculous," he announced. "But I do feel better. Less . . ."

"Prissy? Uptight? Royal?"

He looked at me, almost glaring, and then he smiled. His face was flushed, his hair was less well-behaved, but if anything, he looked even more handsome, only approachable, which was what I'd been after.

I'm almost ready to describe his smile. Edgar had a bit of that abashed schoolboy look, but the years were lending him a man's seriousness. When he smiled, all this fell away, and he became pure joy, maybe because he didn't do it that often, and he surprised himself. His smile had a recklessness to it, which was why he held it in check. I'd made him smile, which was maybe the sexiest thing ever.

"Your Highness?" I asked, and as I was saying it, I felt like a cartoon mouse dressed as a footman in a Disney animated classic.

"Yes?" he said, as I climbed the stairs and approached him.

"May I?" I asked, reaching toward his head. "You look great, and even more adorable than in those pictures where you're feeding a tiger cub at the London Zoo, which made the entire world go 'Awww' and then donate to Save the Tigers. But you've got a flyaway—you know, a few strands of hair that might catch the light and mess up the video. So if I could just . . ."

I reached out and adjusted his naturally wavy, reddish brown hair, and while trying to stay professional, I thought, "I'm touching Prince Edgar's hair and it feels like cashmere and he's got a few freckles across the bridge of his nose and eyelashes for days and Carter, do not even look at his lips or you'll be arrested."

"There. Much better. Media-ready."

As I said this, Prince Edgar was reaching toward my own hair, and I flinched.

"I'm so sorry. I was just . . . you have very nice hair as well. But I had no right, I don't know what came over me . . ."

Our eyes locked and I couldn't breathe and I wanted to die because my life was peaking, but on the other hand I couldn't wait to see what might happen next.

My phone pinged; I'd meant to silence it and now I was shoving my hand in my pocket to find it, which never looks graceful, but as I yanked the phone free, it rang.

"Please, take it, it might be critical," Edgar said, with genuine kindness.

It was my sister, Abby, who's about to get married and calls me thirty-eight times a day for monogrammed water bottle consultations and meltdown management, which I usually love doing, only now I told her, "Abbs? I can't talk, can I call you in just a bit?"

"But I just texted you," Abby insisted, "and you didn't text me back and I'm having an epic gift bag issue—"

"Which we will totally discuss and examine in depth," I assured her, "but right now—"

Edgar was smiling at me, which almost made me drop my phone as Abby yelled, "WHAT? What are you doing that's so important you can't help me choose between miniature foil-wrapped chocolate champagne bottles and Lucite boxes of breath mints in my signature colors—"

"I'm . . . I'm . . ." I sputtered, "I'm at work. I love you and I think you should go with both the bottles and the mints and think about temporary tattoos of the bride's and groom's faces but I have to go. I'm sorry!"

I hung up and told Edgar, "My sister."

"Ah. I know the dilemma. I have a brother."

Oh my God. Oh my God. He wasn't politely excusing himself or summoning a security guard. In fact, he kept going, asking, "Is it just the two of you?"

"Yes. And I adore her, but sometimes she's, you know, a lot."

"As is my brother."

"Can I tell you something?" I said, my event-savvy instincts returning. "The way you're talking to me right now, it's so easy and appealing, and that's how you should give your speech. In fact, let's not call it a speech at all. Just make it a conversation, and pretend the audience is just a batch of friends, hanging out in your . . . castle. And remember to smile. Because your smile, oh my God . . ."

"What?" Prince Edgar asked. "What about my smile? I think it comes across as mechanical, like I'm pretending to be attentive and fulfill my duties while really I'm just activating a royal reflex or downloading my official mindless smile function. I hate my smile."

He hates his smile? Is he out of his mind? If I could smile like that, I'd spend all day looking in the mirror, smiling and sending myself selfies and begging for a date.

"Your smile," I said, firmly, "is your secret weapon. Because everyone probably expects you to be distant and formal, but when you smile . . . Okay, do it. Try it out. Let's have a test drive. Smile at me."

"I will not! That's absurd! First you make me fling myself about, and now this! I'd feel like a grinning idiot!" protested

Prince Edgar. "Smiling has nothing to do with clean drinking water or resource management or climate change!"

"You're one hundred percent right," I said. "But there are going to be Nobel Prize–winning scientists on this panel, only nobody will pay the slightest attention to them unless you're here to introduce them and unless you smile."

"So you're claiming that my smile, and my royal presence, are essential to the future of our planet? And our species? And all plant and animal life as we know it?"

I was pretty sure he was joking, but his gaze was solemn, and he wasn't giving anything away.

"Yes," I answered. "If you don't smile, the global ecosphere is doomed."

He sighed manfully, as if he didn't like it but knew what he had to do for world survival.

He paused. He readied himself, like an Olympic athlete seconds before an event. He adjusted his stance, for maximum stability. He took a deep, preparatory breath. He smiled.

I couldn't speak. I was about to faint or embarrass myself in countless other ways. Because I wasn't kidding: his smile didn't just disarm people and make them abandon any preconceptions about the prince; right now his smile was making me want to grab him and kiss him, which was something I'd probably regret from my jail cell.

"Let's see your smile," the prince demanded. "If you regard these facial expressions as so indispensable."

"My smile?" I said, trying to remember everything I'd eaten since the last time I'd brushed my teeth and whether my two teenage years of braces had been at all effective or if there was time for me to race out and have the invisible adult kind installed. Did I have a decent smile? Had Callum or anyone else ever complimented my smile? Was that left incisor still a tiny bit crooked? Should I purse my lips tightly and shake my head vigorously, no, uh-uh, sorry, I have a note from my orthodontist and I'm not smiling today?

"Do it," said Edgar, with what felt like sexual urgency.

I looked at him and couldn't help myself. I smiled, reluctantly at first and then unable to suppress a grin. It wasn't my fault or my choice: Prince Edgar of England had commanded me to smile, it was a royal decree and he was smiling right back. We were like two happy toy soldiers, having come to life and marched off the shelf at midnight, about to salute each other and then tear off our uniforms and do so much more, which was an image I definitely needed to suppress, because it was insane and pornographic and not in my job description.

"You have a perfectly admirable smile," Edgar decided. "An excellent smile."

"Should I stop now?" I asked. "I'm starting to feel like a jack o' lantern, or a frozen smiley face."

"Just one second more," said Edgar. "So I can study your smile and duplicate it."

Without thinking, we moved toward each other, and then we both stopped smiling. Something more serious was going on, and we were breathing together. Now we were close enough that I could tell how great he smelled, with a hint of what was probably some heritage custom-blended fragrance, or maybe a clean-smelling soap hand-milled by a shop that had been supplying the royal family for centuries.

"You smell marvelous," Edgar murmured, but there wasn't enough time for me to list my entire product regimen.

Our lips were inches apart and Edgar's hand was on my fore-arm and I was leaning toward him and just as we were about to kiss and cause the building to collapse, or at least set off every smoke detector in Midtown, the three sets of doors to the amphi-theater burst open and a small army of security personnel, En-glish and American, all of them speaking into earpieces, moved toward the stage, led by a tall, distinguished-looking gentleman in a dark suit with a subtly striped vest and a perfectly knotted necktie. His silver hair was not merely brushed but lacquered, or maybe threatened into place. He had the most rigid posture and immaculately polished shoes I'd ever seen. He looked like God's butler.

"Your Highness," said this person, in the sort of crisp, irre-proachable accent reserved for Mary Poppins, if she was an at-torney general. "You can't keep running off like that. No one knew where you were, and our team is now on high alert."

"I was rehearsing," said Prince Edgar. "Carter, this is James Claverack, my chief of staff, factotum and devoted manservant."

I had the feeling that at least two of these titles were a private punch line, because James, whose facial expression didn't change in the slightest, turned to Edgar and said, "For the last time: you are not Batman."

"And James, this is Carter Ogden, who's responsible for this event and making everything look so glorious."

"So good to meet you, but we're about to begin," said James, ignoring me entirely as he forcefully led Prince Edgar into a wait-ing area in the wings.

Diplomats, members of the press and staff for the prince's initiative were now filling the room and taking their seats as guards elbowed me off the stage. As I was being hustled down the center aisle, I craned my neck and caught a last glimpse of Edgar, who'd turned his head to find me. As James pulled him away, Edgar gestured helplessly, and then he was gone and I was shoved out into the hallway, where I asked myself, why was I starting to think of him as "Edgar"? And also: does he have a last name?

CHAPTER 5

S o you actually met him and you touched each other's hair and
you both smiled and you almost kissed and now you're both
hopelessly in love forever," decided Adam at our apartment that
night.

"It's so beyond repulsive," said Louise. "Royalty are an offen-
sive anachronism. They have no power but they're still not allowed to, like, criticize the status quo. They only exist to promote
English tourism and sell those big shiny European magazines that
ooze all over them. They're human jewelry."

In college, where we'd met, Louise had studied economic
theory and class dynamics, and I trusted her observations. She
charts how the world functions, and how ugly some people's mo-
tivations can be, but—Edgar had smelled so great. Which was
not a defense I could make to Louise.

"You're thinking about him, right now, aren't you?" she deduced. "Because you're drooling."

"I am not! I just . . . maybe I'm having a ministroke."

"But isn't that what love is?" Adam swooned. "If you get married, what title would you get? Would you be his Mister Prince or his Co-King or His Royal Sex Toy?"

"You are asking for so much trouble," Louise insisted. "Never get involved with somebody that uselessly rich."

"What about Arielle?" I asked, name-checking one of Louise's exes, a wafty French girl who wore sheer blouses and long velvet skirts and turned out to be an ambassador's daughter.

"You were so nuts about her," Adam agreed. "You even read the terrible poems she wrote and watched those videos where she talked to her shoes, and you didn't make vomit noises."

"Shut up!" said Louise, who has a weakness for vague, winsome women who are late for everything and apologize by handing the other person a leaf they found. "Arielle was a huge mistake!" she swore. "I was on cold medication!"

"But you loved her," said Adam. "Just the way Carter loves Prince Edgar."

"Both of you, stop it right now," I told them firmly. "Absolutely nothing happened and nothing ever will happen and no one loves anyone. It was just this deeply strange New York moment when you meet someone you could never meet anywhere else."

"It's like going to Disney World and meeting someone wearing a huge rubber Prince Edgar head," agreed Louise.

"But weirder things have happened," said Adam. "Royals fall in love with commoners all the time. And the fact that he's openly gay is just, oh my God . . ."

"Are you masturbating?" Louise asked him.

"In my mind. Except it goes way beyond that—I mean, if this was a musical, Carter and Edgar would be in different places, like

Carter would be here, and Edgar would be in his hotel suite on the hundred and fifty-eighth floor, gazing out at the lights of the city . . ."

Adam's currently seeing DuShawn, another dancer, and as foreplay, they sometimes perform the choreography from the love duets in *Carousel* or *West Side Story* and post it on YouTube, and now he was improvising a dance between Edgar and me.

"And there'd be a dream ballet," Adam announced, taking an invisible Edgar in his arms, "where they'd find each other and sing about the meaning of true love."

"And then they'd both go on Grindr and get some," said Louise.

I went to bed early because I was disconcerted and didn't want to discuss Edgar. Meeting him already felt like a blip, like it might not have happened or maybe I'd had a glimpse of him and then let my imagination embroider everything, which is something I do all the time. I'll see a guy window-shopping and he'll become a pediatrician with a collie and we'll restore a colonial farmhouse in Connecticut with an attached barn and adopt two kids until he cheats on me with a bearded male hipster nurse and I shoot them both in cold blood and a photo of me fills the front page of the *New York Post* with the headline:

GAY KILLER SAYS, 'HE HAD A MAN BUN.'

And I imagine all this within ten seconds, by which time the original guy has been joined by his wife and toddler.

Once I was in bed I told myself that I'd never think, let alone embroider, about Edgar ever again. Of course, vowing not to think about someone is the most surefire route to being up all night rolling out every conceivable outcome, from a transatlantic marriage in which I'd only wear my crown to work occasionally;

to a furtive few weekends every year, after Edgar's married a crown prince from another country but keeps texting that he only loves me; to Edgar abdicating and the two of us living off the grid in Madagascar, only my version of living off the grid always requires a marble bathroom with heated towel bars and a jetted tub along with access to American milk chocolate with almonds.

In order to grab even an hour's sleep I asked Ruth Ginsburg if she thought Edgar and I had any conceivable future. She replied, "Sweetheart, you had a momentary encounter with a prince, and if there's one immutable law of the universe, it's that princes don't end up with associate event architects from New Jersey. The proof of this is that you're under the covers in your Hell's Kitchen bedroom making up a conversation with a photograph. But maybe the universe let you meet Prince Edgar to give you a nudge and remind you to get back out there. Are you even listening to me, or are you already watching porn on your laptop? Why do I even bother?"

By the next morning I'd decided that my flirtation with Prince Edgar was officially an urban legend, like the alligators swarming the sewers or a one-bedroom apartment with lots of light renting for under a thousand dollars. Since it was Saturday, I went about the critical business of updating my photos and profile and downloading three new dating apps.

I'd been off the market for years, although after our breakup, I found out that Callum had never deleted any of his profiles the whole time we were together. As revenge, when I took new pictures of myself in Central Park, I used an advanced form of Photoshop to rework my chin, then decided not to, since I didn't want any guy I might meet to keep staring at my face, wondering, "Did it grow back?" My first profile drafts included the phrases "Bitter, angry and cheated on—how about coffee?", "I used to believe in love but now I'd like to tell you at great length why I don't" and "I met Prince Edgar, you have to believe me." After deleting all of these I went with something generic: "Let's see what happens."

Over the next two weeks, I had combinations of Starbucks lattes, dinner-and-a-movie-neither-of-us-really-wanted-to-see and not-great-what-did-I-expect sex with the following people:

- A Google product manager who was cute and sweet but slouched a lot and got very haughty about people who were still playing video games I'd never heard of.

- A bearded social worker from Bushwick who does outreach in the foster care system and was such an incredible, selfless human being that I felt like the most superficial person who'd ever lived, especially when I heard myself being very opinionated about casting options for the movie of *Wicked*.

- Two different lawyers who both liked spinning—or, as they called it, performance cycling—more than I've ever liked anything and who bragged about where they got to sit in spin class and how the hottest instructors knew their names.

- An Orthodox Jewish guy who was very eager in bed but turned out to be married with seven children, yet didn't think he was conflicted.

My main problem with all of these perfectly nice guys was that while I was with them I kept zoning out and superimposing

Prince Edgar's head, and his smile, onto their bodies. I also started doing this with my roommates and my relatives, to the point where I worried that someday I'd be found babbling in an abandoned building beside a limbless mannequin I called Your Highness.

I was so lost that I let my guard down and consented to have a meal with Callum, and yes, I can hear billions of voices, as a sort of "Hallelujah" chorus, chanting, "Oh, honey," "Really? You're back for more?" and "Then you have no one to blame but yourself—I mean it." But Callum had been texting me and sending me pictures from his arc on a Netflix limited series where he plays an Olympic swimmer suspected of killing his rivals with poisoned sports drinks and tarantulas in their Speedos. Callum had trained himself into even more phenomenal shape, and yes, there were shots of him naked in the locker room shower with the water streaming down his torso. So stop judging me.

"You look great," said Callum, sitting across from me at his favorite vegan café. As always, there was an aura about him, a golden, perfectly scruffed, shaggy blonde actor/model/bastard glow.

"You too."

"Thank you for showing up. I wasn't sure if you would, and I wasn't going to blame you. I was a total shit."

I kept my guard up. Callum could hypnotize me, using his good looks, his low, raspy voice and his ability to act as if we were the only two people on Earth. Some wildly attractive people are snobs, making sure everyone else feels inferior. Callum was the opposite; he was a born seducer, making sure everyone adores him. If I'm being honest, that's a huge part of why I fell so hard: I couldn't believe that someone as hot, easygoing and seemingly untroubled could be interested in a person as nervous and awkward as me, someone who, before leaving the apartment, tries on so many sweaters that my hair becomes a static-electricity haystack.

When I was with Callum, I felt lucky and chosen, and also that people assumed I was his frantic personal assistant. I'd worked on banishing my insecurity and imagining that we were just two people in love, a delusion that lasted until I saw the expressions on strangers' faces as they calculated, "What's that one doing with that one?" I'm not some hideous troll, and attraction isn't just about looks, but Callum had fulfilled one of my most deeply shallow fantasies: what if I was with a guy like that?

Of course, I'd found out that Callum had been busily fulfilling that fantasy for half the Eastern seaboard and several foreign countries, especially when he was on a job. I'd been terribly hurt by this and furious at myself for ignoring obvious clues, but whenever I'd almost worked up the nerve to ask Callum a question about, say, the increasingly thirsty texts from his personal trainer, Callum would gaze at me the way he was doing right now, as if we were already having sex. I can't say that Callum is a great actor, but he loves acting romantic; he's like a Hallmark Christmas movie hunk who doesn't just kiss.

"I've been thinking about us so much. And how I hurt you. I don't know why I did that, and I'm so sorry. Man, am I sorry."

Callum is one of the only guys I've ever met who can make bro-speak—using words like "man," "dude" and "bud"—sound erotic. Maybe it's part of his lifeguard-in-a-porn-video appeal. But I wasn't going to listen. I wasn't his bro.

"I know, I shouldn't make this about me, my shrink says that I never deserved you, why am I such a fuckup?"

The top four snaps on his worn denim shirt were open, and

he was rubbing his tan, rock-hard chest while looking right at me, and he could actually get away with the wristload of knotted rawhide bracelet, vintage Rolex and red kabbalah string. He could get away with anything, and he was great in bed and surprisingly generous. Right now he was aiming for an Oscar, or at least a Daytime Emmy nomination, in turning me on, and it was working. God damn him.

"I know you can't forgive me, and I would never ask you to. All I want is, I don't know, just a chance. To prove myself. Maybe start with a weekend—my agent has this amazing house in Quogue, right on the ocean, and he says it's all ours. We could hang out, no pressure. Just see what happens. Man, I can't stop looking at you."

I should never have come here. But I'd had all those depressing dates and coffees and bad sex in studio apartments with bicycles hanging over the bed, and I was starting to CGI myself into Callum's Porsche ad, sitting beside him as he steered along an Italian cliffside at dusk, wearing shades and perforated kidskin racing gloves as a saxophone wailed, which was when I noticed that Callum's gaze encompassed not just me but, for a split second, the yoga-honed ass of a nearby waiter, who was acting as if he was mildly annoyed while scribbling his cell number on our bill. Which was when my phone went off and a full-color photo of Buckingham Palace filled the screen.

"Who is that?" asked Callum, his spell broken as I held up my phone so he could see the red-uniformed guards, with their tall bearskin hats, stationed outside the wrought iron palace gates.

"Um, I think it's Prince Edgar."

CHAPTER 6

It wasn't Prince Edgar, not exactly, but James, his indispensable minder, and he informed me that he'd tracked down my contact information through Eventfully Yours and that His Royal Highness would like to have dinner with me the next evening at an exclusive downtown restaurant that I could never afford; James relayed this request in a tone that was both commanding and woefully disappointed, as if he was acting against his better judgment.

"Um, sure," I said, which brings me to tonight, when I'm presenting my hair and my outfit and my chin zit to Louise and Adam for a pre-date inspection.

"Why are you doing this?" asked Louise. "It's like going out with a statue of Queen Victoria, and I bet he's not going to tip. You're buying into the last remnants of an imperialist power structure that thinks it still matters. On the other hand, after tonight you can probably sell your intimate story to a tabloid or TMZ and make a bundle."

"I told you this was going to happen!" crowed Adam. "This is the beginning of an incredible love story, like *Pretty Woman* if you were a beautiful sex worker or *When Harry Met Sally* if Harry had a private jet. And I think you look great, although if I were you, I would shape my eyebrows just a touch."

"No!" I barked, because I'd once allowed Adam to practice threading and plucking on me, and I'd ended up like a Sharpie sketch of a frightened 1930s Hollywood starlet. Luckily, my brows had grown back; men who mess with their eyebrows are like men with bad nose jobs or beret-like hairpieces, since these alterations become all anyone can focus on.

"Carter," said Louise, taking me by the shoulders just before I left, "I want you to remember that you always have options. You can scream 'Kill the Royal Puppet People' and throw red paint on Edgar."

"Or," said Adam, "you can have the most fabulous time, end up eloping and turn slightly away from any cameras so that the totally unnoticeable teeny-tiny blemish on your chin will stay in shadow."

"Adam!" scolded Louise. "Carter is nervous enough as it is. And it's not a blemish, it's obviously his twin brother who never fully developed in the womb."

"I love you both so much," I said, "and I'm going to beg Edgar for a donation to get you the help you need."

"Just have fun," said Louise, meaning it. "And don't let the evil of a justifiably fallen empire intimidate you. You're the best."

"In your honor," Adam said, "tonight DuShawn and I are going to picture you as Cinderella in either of the last two Broadway revivals or as Sweeney Todd, who I know is a mass murderer, but he's still the star."

On the subway I experienced a first-date panic attack ultra-sized by the royalty aspect. On one hand, Prince Edgar had remembered my name and asked James to locate me, but once Edgar took a closer look he'd instantly recall fifteen previous royal engagements—and why had it taken him two weeks to ask me out? I must be sufficiently hot stuff to attract a prince, which meant that my new tricep routine at the gym was paying off, but my abs were still nowhere near as ripped as they should be, and why was I basing my entire concept of self-esteem on Instagram photos of impossibly fit guys? But maybe English people weren't as buff, so on a sliding international scale I was a catch, or maybe this whole thing was part of a scavenger hunt where Edgar had been required to find a hopeless American dweeb, or maybe I should just text him that I was flu-ish and had to cancel and then throw myself on the subway tracks so I'd be enshrined in Edgar's memory as his lost, perfect love.

Or maybe I should do something sensible, like imagining Ruth Ginsburg slapping me and saying, "You've got a date with a prince! Stop being you! And just be yourself!"

Once I'd reached the enormous plate glass doors of the five-star Tribeca restaurant Edgar had chosen, a place that had managed to remain on-trend for an unthinkable ten years, I tried to examine my reflection, but just as I was squinching my features into a sad variation on one of Callum's rugged cologne ads, the one where he'd smelled like "the savage mystery of the Sierras," the doors swung open, I leapt backward and James appeared.

"You're late—why am I not surprised? His Highness is waiting, and I'm assuming that all of your decent clothing has been stolen. Follow me."

As I struggled to keep up, James led me past a dining room filled with well-dressed, gossiping diners, all glancing up from their phones to see if I was anyone worth noticing and then jerking their heads away to make sure I knew that I wasn't. But they were also snubbing the tiny squibs of artisanal, farm-to-table delicacies on their huge white plates, so I was in good company.

"You will address His Highness solely as Your Highness, you will wait for His Highness to sit and speak first, you will ask no personal questions, your replies to whatever His Highness may ask must remain brief and modest and you must not entertain the slightest notion of becoming anything beyond an ill-advised footnote in His Highness's daily calendar. Am I understood?"

"Okay . . ."

"Okay?" James repeated, as if I'd spat on his lapel.

"Yes, sir."

James stared at me, and every part of me shrank many inches. Then, and I can't be sure of exactly how but James did something with his face that was his version of a smile, and it occurred to me that James wasn't just the most clinically English person of all time—he was gay. "Darling," he said, "don't worry. You're doomed."

Then he opened a door flanked by two security guards and ushered me into a private dining room, a hushed chamber with lustrous mahogany wainscoting, jewel-toned Venetian brocade wall coverings and a brass chandelier I'd once seen on 1stDibs, valued at twice my yearly salary.

Prince Edgar, the ultimate luxury object, was standing beside a table draped in at least three layers of fabric and set with a warehouse's worth of china and crystal. I felt like James Bond about to be offered an assignment, or maybe a handful of uncut diamonds.

"Mr. Ogden," said James, motioning me forward.

"So good to see you again," said Prince Edgar, offering his hand.

"Your Highness," I said, suppressing my instinct to kneel and be knighted.

"Edgar, please, or Ed."

James did that thing of rolling his eyes without my catching him doing it.

"Edgar," I decided, because I'm sorry, he just wasn't an Ed. Ed shows up to fix your air-conditioning; Edgar has more than one home. More than ten homes.

"Thank you, James, I think we can manage from here."

"As you wish. If you need me I'll be just outside or reachable by text. Should Mr. Ogden exhibit symptoms of violent derangement, what will you do?"

"Applaud."

"As you wish."

As James backed gracefully out of the room, Edgar gestured to the gilded chair opposite him, where I hovered, waiting for him to be seated first. He sat. I sat.

"First off, please ignore whatever nonsense James has told you. And secondly, I'm so sorry it took me such an inexcusable amount of time to locate you, but I was attending a refugee summit in Dubrovnik and then visiting an agricultural school in Somalia, and then an Australian scientist was gracious enough to demonstrate a new economically feasible desalinization system, which turned out to be quite promising but required three days in Melbourne."

"Same," I said and Edgar smiled, not his full-on heartbreaker, but a satisfying preview.

"But James worked his magic and now here we are. And don't you look handsome."

I couldn't do it. I couldn't sit across from this great-looking, well-mannered prince, this person in total command of his role in the world, and hold a conversation as if we were two guys who'd liked each other's decently accurate photos, had texted a bit, and decided to risk it, with roommates and Netflix as a backup. This wasn't normal. I felt like there was a whole other person squirming around inside my skin, so after opening and closing my mouth three times like a guppy I finally let loose:

"How? How does this work? How do I talk to you as if you're a person? Like, a person person?"

Edgar smiled, at almost full wattage but not quite, although even at, say, 8.2 on the Regal Smile Continuum, his slightly crooked grin made me levitate—I'm not kidding, I could swear that I was floating an inch or so off my chair.

"I understand. And I find that in these situations, it's best for both of us to wipe the slate clean, to eliminate any and all preconceptions and to behave simply as two human beings getting to know one another."

"Thank you. Totally." Totally? Did I have an armload of scrunchies and a troll doll sticker on my phone?

"So," Edgar began.

"So," I said. "What do you do?"

"I work for my family and we rule England."

"Okay, this isn't fair, because like everyone else in the world,

I already know way too much about you. I mean, America is obsessed. And even though I was a kid, and so were you, when your parents passed away . . ."

Edgar's smile vanished, and I knew I'd destroyed everything. He spoke in a cordial but icy tone, very this-is-my-polite-way-of-saying-fuck-off.

"It was heartbreaking and awful and yes, even though James tried to hide them, I did see the photos of the plane crash, and equally terrible and far worse things have happened to many other people, but thank you very much for your concern."

Why? Why did I do that? Why did I bring up the greatest tragedy of Edgar's life within the first five minutes? All of my paranoia had been completely justified—I wasn't just an inter-loper and a commoner and a douchebag, I was light-years out of my league.

"I'm so sorry, I'm an idiot and I've already put my foot, no, both my feet and my arms, all the way down my throat, so I'll just go . . ."

As I stood up and my linen napkin fell to the floor, I thought about grabbing it so I could thumbtack it to my bedroom wall as a reminder of how badly, and how quickly, I'd fucked up. And now Edgar was standing as well.

"Stop, please. You must stay. This is entirely my problem. Because you're right, people do know a good deal about me, and they make assumptions, which makes me back away, and I end up feeling self-righteous and snobbish and alone."

We looked at each other, more directly.

"I get it. It must be so strange, being you. And dealing with the rest of us. You're like—Beyoncé."

"Only . . . ?"

"Much prettier."

"Thank you."

As we sat back down, a formally dressed waiter appeared, announcing, "I am Louis-Pierre Roget and I shall be your initial waitperson, for the chilled appetizer, bread selection and preliminary first course options. Any decisions?"

"Carter?"

I hadn't even glanced at the menu, which was bound in burgundy leather, with calligraphy in a variety of languages, none of which I could read or speak. I'd been to fancy-ish restaurants, but nothing at this level, and even with my background in event planning, I was feeling overwhelmed.

"Okay, this place is stunning and I know that the food is five-star, and thank you so much for arranging all of this, but I'm from New Jersey, so this isn't really my sort of thing. Can I make a suggestion?"

CHAPTER 7

I knew it was a risk, but within minutes Edgar's driver was parked outside the International House of Pancakes on 14th Street, with garish photos of pancake-centric meals filling the front windows. Ever since I was a kid, IHOP hasn't been just my favorite restaurant, but one of my dream destinations. It's my home.

"And what precisely is this establishment?" Edgar asked, once we'd been led to a rear booth, with Edgar wearing a baseball cap and keeping his head down. This celebrity camouflage was futile, since we were surrounded by five members of Edgar's security team, as well as James, seated at adjacent tables.

"I can't believe you don't have IHOPs in England, because the 'I' stands for International. People say music is the universal language, but I think it's a short stack of buttermilk silver dollar pancakes."

"Go on."

"I grew up in the suburbs and we didn't have much money, so

for special occasions my parents would take my sister and me to IHOP and let us order specialties, like the Rooty Tooty Fresh 'N Fruity, where they use cherries and a pat of butter to make a face on the pancakes. And see, now they have something called Cupcake Pancakes, with frosting and rainbow sprinkles on top. IHOP is either the best or the worst of America, depending on how snooty and how hungry you are."

Edgar was inspecting his enormous, laminated menu like an archaeologist coming upon the Rosetta stone.

"They're offering something called the Harvest Grain Medley, which involves pecans, almonds, whole wheat and whipped cream. They've described it as a heart-healthy alternative, yet the calorie count is astronomical."

"Which is exactly how America deals with organic eating. Go to any Whole Foods and the shelves are bursting with cookies and candy bars, but because the packaging is boring and they use phrases like 'raw Venezuelan cane sugar,' we pretend it's good for you. Americans will give up their guns before they give up sugar, and that's really saying something."

"But that's madness."

Callum had sworn he was not merely vegan, but that he'd only eat fruits or vegetables that had fallen to the ground naturally, of their own volition, avoiding what he'd called "orchard trauma." But he'd stash those Halloween packets of Reese's Pieces in his carry-on and claim that if he ate my Dunkin' Donuts French Cruller, it didn't count, because he was saving me from myself. Vegans, like alcoholics, are accomplished liars. As far as I was concerned, the only reason to go to the gym was so I could mainline Ruffles potato chips afterward (the ones where the jumbo bag highlights "Sea Salted," which is another one of those ways Americans deceive themselves while scarfing delicious crap).

"I think," said Edgar, as I readied myself for a lecture on kale and toxins and what Callum had called Blood Twinkies, contending they were baked by child laborers, "I think this may well be the finest restaurant in the history of food. Or food-like products."

I almost passed out, but I gripped the table, because I wanted to remember this milestone, when I'd introduced His Royal Highness to IHOP. If I did nothing else with my life, this wasn't the worst legacy.

The rest of the evening went shockingly well as Edgar asked me one charming, genuinely interested question after another, about my job and my education and my family. On one hand, as a professional prince, he'd been trained to be socially adept and to make less titled people bask in his conversation. But there was something isolated and curious about him, which I've noticed in people who've been homeschooled. They have an innocence to them, because they've never experienced the schoolyard bullying and classroom competition of the real world. Edgar had been raised around prime ministers and oligarchs and visiting movie stars, but not around other kids, so his hunger for everyday information was heartfelt.

And of course, the more questions he asked, the more I chattered, and yes, it was exciting to have Prince Edgar, of all people, interrogating me about the cartoons I'd grown up on, and the plays and books that had changed the way I saw the world, and whether I'd ever been hit by another vehicle while riding my bike (yes, and both times by someone opening a car door in traffic, and yes, I'd called those people every possible name I could think of ending in stick, wad and hole).

When we'd polished off our pancakes and I at last took a breath, I was embarrassed, because I'd monopolized our date and barely asked Edgar a thing. I'd behaved selfishly, both because he'd kept wanting more details—about whether I ran outdoors or on a treadmill, whether my sister and I had gone to summer camp (yes; for soccer and theater, respectively) and whether I'd made it through all the Avengers movies (I had, although we agreed that three more had probably been released while we were eating). There was also an unspoken barrier between us; James had cautioned me about not asking Edgar personal questions, and my blunder about his parents was still fresh.

"All right, we can both feel it," Edgar admitted. "You've been wonderfully generous and amusing, although we've barely scratched the surface of your life. But I've been reticent."

"It's okay. I get it."

"Thank you. But let's try something, a small episode of trust. Ask me something. Anything. And don't be afraid of offending me, or crossing a line. Just ask, and I promise I'll be honest."

Whoa. Jesus. I'd shared incredibly intimate confessions with Callum and earlier boyfriends. But none of them was a prince. None of them could serve up steamingly authentic royal dish. I'd never had pancakes with anyone who'd be justified in asking me to sign a nondisclosure agreement.

And did Edgar really mean it? Or was this a test, of my discretion and sensitivity?

"Okay. Your life is public and pressured in ways I can't even imagine. Where do you go when you don't want to think about any of it?"

Edgar looked serious, but I couldn't tell if I'd gone too far or if he wanted to be specific.

"At the palace, there's a tiny room in a wing that's barely used. It was a nursery. I don't have that many memories of time alone with my parents. But there was a period when I was so young that I still didn't know how odd my life was. And my mum and my dad would wear old clothes, and they'd read to me, and sometimes we'd all dance to my mum's favourite disco songs. After they died, the room was closed, and all the furniture's under dustcloths. I think my grandmother, and her advisors, felt it wouldn't be healthy to let my brother and I wallow in the past and our loss. And maybe they were correct, because that room has a haunted quality. But sometimes, after I've given some precarious interview or spent an evening being blankly gracious with someone whose politics I loathe, I need to go there, by myself. Just to lie on the couch and look up at the ceiling and be completely quiet. To imagine, just for an hour, that no one can find me. And to see my parents not as tragic historical figures, but as I remember them, giggling and happy. And whenever I leave that room, I feel not just calm, but—as if I've reconnected with who I really am."

Of course I wanted to cry, and I felt honored, but even more, I was scared, because I never wanted to hurt this man, or betray him in any way. Sure, he was impossibly rich and famous in such a singular, untouchable way, but oh my God, his parents had died when he was ten years old. And he didn't seem bitter or angry, but he was understandably guarded, and sweet, and lost.

"Sorry about all that. I let things get a bit somber . . ."

"No, that room, that nursery, it sounds so special . . ."

Just as Edgar was about to say something else, which I couldn't wait to hear, I became aware of two things. First, James, at a table a few feet away, had ordered a death-by-chocolate brownie with whipped cream and a sparkler in it, to his delight. I also heard a barrage of clicks and loud whispers and chairs being moved as a pack of teenage girls descended, demanding to know: "Oh my God! Are you him!" "Olivia, I told you it was him! That prince guy! It's him! You're him, right!" "Edgar! Prince Eddie! Can I get a selfie with you? Please? I know you're gay, but can you look like you wanna kiss me, so my boyfriend's head will explode?"

Someone, or any number of IHOP patrons, had tipped off their friends, families and the paparazzi, because our table was now besieged by a growing mob, as if we'd become a Black Friday sale at Best Buy and Edgar was a half-price sixty-inch flat screen. Everyone was jostling me aside to get closer to Edgar as the guards deftly hustled him out onto the sidewalk.

"I will contact you!" Edgar promised as he was being tossed into the waiting SUV, and all I could do was say, "Please!" in a strangled voice, as I was jammed against a wall by the crowd. No one had registered my presence, so I was of zero interest as I heard more than one person asking in bafflement, "But what was Prince Edgar doing at IHOP?"

CHAPTER 8

S till nothing?" said Adam almost two weeks later, once I'd joined him after his show at a gritty theater hangout, the kind of place with paper tablecloths, dim lighting and a waitstaff, all out-of-work actors, who call everyone "honey." Adam was dancing in a jukebox musical based on the *NSYNC catalogue, and in one number the entire chorus wore curly wigs and acid-washed denim jumpsuits to portray the young Justin Timberlake's torment over leaving the group for a solo career.

"Edgar's the crown prince—he's got a lot on his plate," I ventured, but as I heard myself say it even I didn't believe it. Edgar had my contact information, but I didn't have his, because megafamous people don't just hand out their email addresses or cell numbers. Of course I'd been checking the palace website five times a day to see if I could track Edgar's schedule, but it was rarely updated and was filled with stock photos of royal gardens and a single shot of Edgar distributing medical supplies at a refugee camp in Somalia, which made me respect him and also made me wonder, don't they have Wi-Fi in Somalia?

"I warned you," said Louise, hogging the bread, "just because he's gay doesn't mean he isn't a guy. And royals are the ultimate form of privilege, because it's all inherited. They're white people whose feet don't even touch the ground. You're being ghosted by a ghost."

"I once went out with a guy who played King George in one of the tours of *Hamilton*," volunteered Adam's boyfriend, Du-Shawn, who I liked because he was, if anything, even more optimistic and theater-driven than Adam. "And after our first date he didn't call me for five weeks because he'd been hit by a car, which had also destroyed his phone."

"Exactly!" said Adam. "There could be a totally sympathetic explanation!"

"Or maybe Edgar is just a devious buttwipe with boyfriends all over the world," said Louise. "Maybe he just throws a dart at a globe."

"So I should just stop thinking about him," I said, "and going over every second of our date in my mind and trying to pinpoint what I did wrong and considering having radical plastic surgery so if we ever run into each other he won't recognize me and we could try again?"

"You are making me feel so healthy," said Adam.

"Have you thought about writing 'I Went on One Date with Prince Edgar' on a piece of cardboard," suggested Louise, "and sitting cross-legged in Times Square?"

"Or you could sue IHOP," said Adam. "Maybe they served him bad pancakes."

"There's no such thing as bad pancakes!" I protested.

"Pancakes," said DuShawn, "are filled with carbs and air and refried microorganisms, which can live on a griddle for months. And if I could have pancakes right now I would not only die happy, I would write a musical about a guy who falls in love with a plate of pancakes and petitions the Supreme Court so they can get married."

I knew I liked DuShawn.

"Carter," said Louise, passing me a chunk of bread, which meant she was being sincere, "we love you so much, and you've already been through a shitshow with Callum. You should be grateful that this Prince Edgar thing ended before you could overinvest. You deserve so much better."

"You deserve, like, Hugh Jackman," said Adam.

"Adam, for the one millionth time," I said, "Hugh Jackman isn't gay. You just want him to be gay."

"But during 'Bye Bye Bye,'" Adam countered, "when Justin leaves the group, all the dancers are bored, so we're dedicating the number to turning Hugh Jackman gay. Fifteen dancers in leather patchwork vests and newsboy caps can be very powerful."

Adam and DuShawn began harmonizing on the *NSYNC ballad "Music of My Heart," and the entire restaurant joined in, except for Louise and me, representing the people who'd recently experienced toxic relationships and just couldn't get it together and needed more bread.

I was in the ballroom of the Plaza Hotel the next morning at 7 a.m. to help Cassandra prepare a product launch for a home-wares collection from a folksy Texas couple who'd branded themselves through a makeover show on HGTV. They were building an empire based on white canvas slipcovers, cheaply handwoven throws, oversize nonworking clock faces used as wall art, and sheaves of wheat in mason jars. The couple seemed sweet enough, so I resisted murmuring "early Pottery Barn catalogue" as I stacked cans of their signature line of paint, in shades like Prairie Taupe and Tumblin' Mauve, and plumped accent pillows silk-screened with inspirational phrases like "Family Matters" and "Love Is" (I mentally finished this sentence with "a cruel hoax," "Hell on Earth" and "as fake as these faux marble eggs").

"Carter, you seem completely out of it," scolded Cassandra. "The flameless candles inside the hurricane lanterns are supposed to be in groups of three, on the battered tin trays painted with sunsets. What is wrong with you!"

"I'm sorry, I haven't been sleeping, and I think I'm dehydrated because I've been running a lot." I work out harder during periods of heartbreak, because it's one of the few things I can control. If you see somebody who's suddenly in shape, it usually means that the rest of their life is in tatters. "I promise to do better, and see, I'm putting these decorative spheres made from old license plates into these hemp baskets, just like on the show."

In truth, I'd been lagging for the past week, as I internalized the fact that I'd never see Edgar again. At first I'd wondered if I'd only had a crush on his celebrity dazzle and on the perks of being seen with him, but as a New Yorker, I worked very hard to spurn being impressed by stars. In New York, everyone acts like they're famous; there's a snob's equality. But what I really missed was making Edgar smile, and hearing about that private room in the palace, and his face lighting up as he explored the copper IHOP table caddy holding glass pitchers with four different flavors of syrup. I missed surprising him.

"Are you still pining for Prince Edgar?" Cassandra demanded, interrupting my pity party, or given the décor, my pity hoedown. "Who, I'm sorry, but I don't believe you ever actually met? You need to see someone, or take something, because your delusions are out of control. Just because you designed banners with Prince Edgar's face on them doesn't count as a date, and yes, I know you claim you had dinner with him, at IHOP, which doesn't do very much for your credibility, I mean if that doesn't define going off the emotional deep end I don't know what does. You're having a serious reality disconnect and it's affecting your work and if you don't stop lying to yourself, and especially to me, well, I'm going to have to let you go."

As I was processing this threat and preparing to either grovel more effectively or hurl a lamp made from a vintage gasoline can onto the floor and quit in a huff, a voice inquired, "Are you Mr. Ogden's employer?"

Everyone in the ballroom turned to see Prince Edgar, followed by his security team, standing near the ballroom's ornate gilded doors.

"Um, oh my God, um, yes, I am. Your Highness," Cassandra sputtered.

"Cassandra?" I said airily, causing her to fall into a wobbling curtsy as one of her wrought iron earrings unhooked and clattered to the floor.

"I'm so sorry to intrude," said Edgar, "but I was wondering if Carter might enjoy his lunch break a few moments early? If that's all right with Carter?"

For Cassandra's benefit and my own, I paused. Edgar hadn't tried to contact me in any way, and now he just showed up, as if his dramatic entrance, holding a deluxe picnic basket, would erase his neglect, or apologize for it. I gestured as if I was incredibly busy, then I checked my phone, as if I had to cancel my lunch plans with Hugh Jackman, and then I made a clicking noise with my tongue and shrugged vaguely in Edgar's direction, indicating a put-upon "Up to you."

"Of . . . of course, Your Highness," Cassandra whimpered, now clutching a table so she could remain in a half curtsy, as I bet myself that she'd repeat the words "Your Highness" three more times in the next 10 seconds.

"It's so wonderful to see you, Your Highness, and I hope our work at the United Nations was acceptable, Your Highness, and, well, what a lovely surprise to meet you, Your Highness, I'm such a fan, Your Highness."

Four times! Score!

Once Edgar and I had left the ballroom I unleashed my frustration: "What are you doing? What is this?"

We were standing in a fairly deserted outer hallway, but Edgar needed more privacy, so he dragged me into a stairwell, and I sat on the stairs as his team waited outside.

"Carter, one of the many things I most admire about you is your honesty. Which I'd like to return in kind. Because if we're to keep seeing each other, which is something I'd like very much—very, very much—honesty will be key."

"And? So?"

"I know. Once again, I've acted abominably, and I could recite my schedule and offer international excuses, but I won't. Because . . ."

He was having trouble with whatever he was about to say, trying to organize his thoughts and pacing in the very small space.

"Here it is. After our dinner, which was an utter delight, I returned to London, where I was summoned by my grandmother for what she termed a 'caring advisory,' which means everything short of my being pistol-whipped. She'd been fully briefed on your existence and our behavior, which she judged to be irresponsible and disrespectful."

When Edgar cited his grandmother, he was referring to the Queen of England. One of my grandmothers is dead and the other one lives in Vermont and sends me a cat calendar every year.

"Your grandmother was upset because we went to IHOP?"

"Because I exposed the Crown to possible rumour-mongering by placing myself in a far too public and down-market setting with what she kept referring to as a 'questionable stranger.'"

I was stung. I was from New Jersey, and I had an unneccessary job, and I'd distracted myself from the Edgar situation by adding a silvery-gray streak to my hair, but being a "questionable stranger" made it sound as if I hung around schoolyards at recess.

"I know. I told her that you were gifted and smart and funny, but she got this look, it's like a dinosaur with gout, it's so unpleasant and intimidating—here, I'll show you."

He fished in his pocket for a five-pound note with a picture of his grandmother, Queen Catherine, etched on it in a dried-blood red. I saw what he meant.

"And then she had a proposal. She said that if I really wanted to continue, and that if our relationship held genuine promise, it could weather a test of time. She said I should wait a year, and if I still wished to see you, she might allow it. We bargained. I brought her down to one month, and she agreed, as long as I made no attempt to communicate with you. But after two weeks

I couldn't stand it anymore, and I was so ashamed of my spine-lessness, and I'd been so rude, that I jumped on a plane and here I am. And I apologise, which is feeble. And now you know precisely how cowardly and constrained I am, so if you'd like to head right back into that ballroom, you have every right. Because I . . ."

He was searching for exactly the right damning word.

"I am an asshole. Or as we say in England, an arsehole. But I prefer asshole, because I'm being one in America."

This was new. I'd never been vetted, and found wanting, by the Queen of England before. And I'd never seen Edgar so tormented. And I was feeling interestingly powerful.

"Say it again."

"What? That I'm an asshole?"

"Yes."

He paused and opened the stairwell door, calling out, "James?" James stood in the doorway.

"James, what am I?"

"An asshole, Your Highness."

"Were you just guessing?" I asked James. "Or is that his, like, Scotland Yard code name?"

"I was listening at the door. And his code name is Fuckhead."

This sounded especially elegant in James's Mayfair accent.

Edgar stared at James, who added, "But it's being changed, because everyone kept guessing it."

"Thank you, James," said Edgar. He turned to me: "Your decision?"

CHAPTER 9

By the time Edgar and I had reached a secluded clearing in Central Park, James had set out our picnic lunch on a blanket in the royal tartan. There was fine china, champagne, neatly trimmed sandwiches and, artfully spilling out of the wicker basket, a selection of Hostess Yodels, boxes of Mallomars, canisters of Pringles and every variety of M&M, poured into Wedgewood bowls. I was starting to forgive Edgar, because this wasn't a generic feast; this was aimed at me. The way to my heart lies through my future dental work.

"So," I asked, as we dug in, "do you have to run every decision past your grandmother?"

"She would like me to. She's always been overprotective, and I understand her position. With our parents gone, she was all Gerald and I had. She wants to be certain that in all matters, we present a united front. I love her dearly, and I also admire her. She never whines or feels sorry for herself, even with all the constant criticism, from Parliament and the media and what she calls 'all those people at their computers who've decided they have something to add.'"

"Jesus. It's like she thinks she's the Queen of England."

"Fine. The time has come. Just do it. Let it out. All of your royalty jokes. As if I've never heard them before. I'll give you five minutes to exhaust yourself, and then I'll dissect America."

It was a challenge: should I act as if none of these terrible jokes had ever crossed my mind and I was above all that?

"When you play checkers, do you say, 'King me'? Do people ever comment, 'That Edgar, he's a prince of a guy'? When you listen to Prince songs, do you tell yourself, 'He's good but he's not a real prince'? When you watch Disney movies, do you admit that all of the princes seem gay? Do you take any responsiblity for that? When Snow White sings 'Someday my prince will come' do you giggle? Have you ever said 'Yaass, Queen' to your grandmother? Do you think 'Royal Flush' sounds like a premium toilet paper? When Leonardo DiCaprio yells 'I'm the king of the world' in *Titanic*, do you always mutter, 'I don't think so'? In America, Prince is a popular dog's name—if someone yelled, 'Here, Prince! Here, boy!' would you turn around?"

"Time's up. Is American cheese redundant? When you sing 'God Bless America' do you secretly add, 'and no other countries'? Is there a reason why all American tourists wear cargo shorts on airplanes, and everywhere else? Does your entire country have a fear of clothing that doesn't resemble oversize T-shirts, leggings or prewashed blue jeans with stretch? Did your Congress declare using a napkin illegal? Does everyone in the American South share a single pair of ill-fitting dentures? Is the real American dream a recliner with a heated massage function and a built-in beer tap? Was there truly a need for the return of *American Idol*? Are your nation's greatest achievements AstroTurf used indoors, water parks with safari adventure themes, and those ride-on scooters that perfectly healthy people use for travelling from the blackjack tables to the slot machines in Las Vegas?"

For a moment I wondered if I should be horribly offended by Edgar's unjust stereotypes. But he had a point. "Yes," I replied.

"But why are you laughing?" asked Edgar. "After I've just savaged your homeland in the crudest possible manner?"

"I'm laughing because your mouth is covered with Hostess Yodel cake crumbs and cream filling."

James stepped in instantly, with a premoistened wipe, confiding, "Sometimes we change His Highness's shirt five times a day."

"I think we need to walk," said Edgar. "At least a bit."

We stood up and headed toward a nearby pond. And while they were silent and maintained a respectful distance, I was acutely conscious of the security guys keeping a protective cordon around us and monitoring all passersby. James had packed up the hamper without a wasted gesture and trailed us by a few yards.

"Does it ever bother you?" I asked. "Or do you not even notice it?"

"What?"

"Your team. The surveillance. The fact that we're out in nature, and having a great time, but we're never really alone?"

Edgar sighed. "Of course. But you must understand, security is necessary, and I'm extremely grateful to the men and women who protect me. Because this isn't about me as an individual— they're protecting a symbol and an institution. And so if my freedom is curtailed, I mustn't complain. And James isn't merely an employee, but a treasured friend, with only my best interests at heart—he's raised me. And all of this, it's a situation I've experienced since birth, so it's simply—my life."

We'd been walking for some time and Edgar had only grown more earnest, laboring to convince himself as well as me.

"So," I said, "do you really believe all that?"

"Excuse me?"

"Do you believe that you're some delicate artifact, a rare orchid or a Fabergé egg that gets placed gently into a velvet-lined trunk and carried through the streets under armed guard?"

"You really are, what was that American word?"

"An asshole?"

"No."

"A nasty little brat?"

"Getting warmer . . ."

"The voice of truth and reason?"

"No—a douchewad. That's the word."

We'd left the park and were heading west, through the city. I retrieved a membership card from my wallet to unlock a Citi Bike from a nearby stand.

"What are you doing?"

"These are Citi Bikes, and I'm using my membership to get a bike for each of us. Come on. You can ride a bike, can't you? Prince Powderpuff?"

"Of course I can ride a bike. But where would we go?"

"I need to show you something. It'll change your life. Right now."

"But we mustn't, James will have my head, and the team—"

"It's just for a few minutes. A temporary prison break. Over the wall."

"I can't. Really."

"Chickenshit. Which is another American word. It means you."

"I am not—any form of chicken! I served in the military for two years! I've piloted medivac helicopters in Afghanistan!"

"Then come on, soldier," I said, handing him his bike.

"Your Highness!" James called out from half a block away.

"You're a dreadful influence!"

"I put that on my tax return."

For a second Edgar debated between duty and mischief, or as I liked to call it, me. I'd already straddled my bike, and as I pedaled across the West Side Highway, Edgar was right behind me. We picked up speed and made it across many lanes of traffic just as the light changed, stranding a fuming James and the security team, who were busily trying to unlock bikes of their own, without any luck; they could defuse a bomb or take down a squad of kidnappers, but New York transportation was a very different challenge, and I bet none of them had MetroCards either.

"This is so beautiful," said Edgar as we cruised along the bike path beside the river. It was a gorgeous April day, and the view stretched for miles, bounded by trees and grass and not-too-fussy flower beds; sometimes New York gets it just right.

"See over there, across the Hudson? That's New Jersey, where I grew up."

"It's like the White Cliffs of Dover."

"With Walmarts."

We pedaled faster and faster, reaching a speed that allowed intervals of effortless gliding, and I could see Edgar relax; he was so tightly wound that each micro-moment of surrender became visible, like an enhanced video of a flower blooming or a baby chick hatching and blinking at the world. Edgar was still ridiculously handsome, but his smile was becoming more genuine and less professional.

Two bike messengers, a man and a woman, pulled up beside us. They were true New York athletes, in customized spandex and ragged leather, with battered canvas bags slung across their backs. I've always admired these messengers, in their *Mad Max* couture, as they swerve in and out of traffic, outraging drivers, terrifying pedestrians and laughing at gridlock, young enough so that being underpaid and sexy becomes a fabulous drug.

This pair didn't seem to recognize Edgar and would never admit it if they did. They pulled even with us and nodded, or their neon goggles and aerodynamic praying mantis helmets nodded, at the path ahead.

"Oh, it's on!" said Edgar, and the four of us started racing, leaning over our handlebars. Edgar was fiercely competitive, because he had to spend most of his time being selfless and polite. I could barely keep up, but Edgar cutting loose gave me rocket fuel, along with awarding myself a few thousand extra cardio points.

While Edgar was an experienced cyclist, he was no match for the messengers, who outpaced us, laughed and waved as they headed back across the highway.

"Good God," said Edgar, as he stretched out his arms and turned his face to the sun, drunk on thinking about nothing but fresh air.

"We're here," I said, because we'd hit lower Manhattan, right across from not just my favorite vista but my favorite anything: the Statue of Liberty, who seemed almost within reach.

"She's magnificent," Edgar said as we dismounted and walked our bikes to the railing.

"When I was little I thought she was real and that she waded through the river and stood there every day, to welcome the world to America."

"And while I know she was a gift from the French," said Edgar, "I've always felt there was something terribly English about her. Something utterly dignified but with a touch of wickedness around the eyes. Very Helen Mirren. She's alluring."

Edgar faced me and I felt breathless and so turned on and like crying, all at the same time—it was an unexpected tremor, as if introducing my cherished landmark to a crown prince was way too much emotional activity for one lunch hour. I could tell Edgar was feeling the same thing, because he was bending toward me, only he paused, as if some inner alarm had been triggered. He stepped back, leaving me helpless and confused and hurt.

"What? What is it?"

"I . . . I need to be cautious."

"Why? You're out, you're single, who cares?"

"I know, and I so wish I could, I wish I could stop remembering everything that's been drummed into me, except—look around. What do you see?"

"People. Tourists. Nannies with strollers."

"And they're all pretending not to recognise me. And they all have phones."

"I get it. Pictures. Which they can sell. Of Prince Edgar and some guy from New Jersey. It might seem a little trashy. A little, what's that word? Common. And I understand. Your life is very different from mine. And I don't envy you. But thanks for the picnic and the bike ride and I guess—I was about to say I'll see you, but I bet I won't. This was all, I don't know, a footnote. A bubble."

I walked my bike to a nearby rack, and as I was locking it back into place, I felt a hand on my shoulder, which in New York is usually a signal to scream for help, but before I knew it I'd been spun around and I was surrendering to a shockingly passionate kiss and two wonderfully strong arms embracing me and a moment of such pure happiness that it made me stop being a person and turn into an essence, into a paint chip or a fragrance strip labeled "Pure Happiness," into something that all the stories and products and sequined T-shirts are based on.

Don't do it, I told myself, *don't faint and don't be such a pushover and don't ever stop kissing him, and don't try to remember every detail of this moment so I can describe it to Adam and Louise and my sister*—something I really didn't need to worry about, because I'd never forget it, and then, before I could even begin to stop my brain and other parts of my body from bursting, it was over, and Edgar's face was a foot away from mine and he was grinning triumphantly.

"What did you call me? Chickenshit?"

"Your Highness?" said James, who was standing a few yards off along with the security team, as if they were five powerfully built bridesmaids in matching dark suits, white shirts and narrow black neckties. They'd found us so quickly, and it occurred to me that Edgar was probably equipped with a chip or wire that enabled a royal tracking device. This was a dismaying possibility but with a definite logic; our kiss had most likely already been noted, logged and reviewed. I hadn't just been kissing a person but, as Edgar had mentioned earlier, "a symbol and an institution." This would take some getting used to. I felt like I'd been caught shoplifting at Cartier or Bergdorf's by store detectives.

"I need to see you again," said Edgar. "I've got an embassy reception tonight—it will most likely be endless and dreary, but would you like to attend? I'm sorry, I don't think I've made that sound especially appealing."

"I would love to go, but I've got a rehearsal dinner for my sister's wedding."

"Which will undoubtedly be joyous. I'm leaving the States on Sunday. Will tomorrow be at all possible?"

"Shit shit shit. No, I mean, not shit, it's going to be really great, but that's the wedding, in Piscataway."

"Might I come? As your date?"

CHAPTER 10

Okay. Okay. The crown prince of England had just asked if he could be my plus-one at Temple Beth Israel in Piscataway, New Jersey, for Abby's wedding. This shit was getting real.

"Okay," I said, "but before I say yes, I need you to know what you'll be getting yourself into."

"I'm certain it will be delightful."

"Have you ever been to Piscataway?"

"Is that a real place?"

"It's a suburb, and it's very nice, it's fine, but I need to warn you: if my sister sees you, she's going to explode. And I don't mean, oh, she'll be impressed, or she'll fangirl all over you, or she'll get pissed that you're upstaging her big day. I love her and I know her, and I know how she feels about celebrities, let alone royalty. Have you ever seen footage of like, the birth of the cosmos or an avalanche swallowing an entire Swiss village or a van filled with crash test dummies hitting a brick wall at a hundred and fifty miles an hour?"

"And those things are like your sister?"

"Those things are jealous of my sister."

The next morning we took a huge, shiny, black SUV along the Jersey Turnpike, with Edgar and I in the back seat and James up front beside the driver. "And now we're passing a metropolis called Secaucus," said James, noting an exit ramp.

"Secaucus is a really great town," I told him. "Even if years ago it was filled with hog rendering farms and there was a big sign reading 'The Pig Capital.'"

"James," said Edgar, before James could say a word.

Everyone peered out at the acres of swampy landfill belonging to another community.

"Isn't this marvelous," James commented. "It's like one of those dystopian films which teenagers so enjoy, where much of civilization has been destroyed. And that sign said we're in a city called Elizabeth, which is undoubtedly named after one of our most beloved monarchs. And you've memorialised her with piles of rotting truck tires, the rusted shells of abandoned vehicles, lakes of iridescent green sludge and a rather pungent odor. May I ask, and only from curiosity, at this wedding—will there be zombies?"

"James!" said Edgar.

"I'm so very sorry," said James, "that was rude and uncalled for. But—zombies?"

"It depends," I said, "on which table you're sitting at."

We reached Piscataway in a little over an hour and pulled into the parking lot of the temple where I'd been bar mitzvahed, a large brick building with a soaring A-framed chapel and those sort of modern stained glass windows that resemble expensive crafts projects.

"I went to Hebrew school here for about ten minutes because my parents wanted me to appreciate my heritage, but then I told them, I'm sorry, but I'm not going to regular school and then another school."

"Is your family deeply religious?"

"I'd say we have a chatty relationship with God and appreciate a decent buffet."

We were late, and as we left the SUV, a second van pulled up and the security team emerged, fanning out to investigate entrances and exits.

"If I were you," I told the team, "I'd keep my eyes on the bride and my great-aunt Miriam."

"This is so exciting," said Edgar, "I've been to more than my share of weddings, but they've always involved cathedrals and processionals and shrieking choirs. This feels so much more, what's that expression, user-friendly."

I almost ran, escaping across the parking lot and past the 7-Eleven and over the many lawns to my childhood home, where I could hide in my old room for the rest of my life, clutching Paddington Bear and gorging on ice-cream bars and Tootsie Pops, in hopes that no one would ever find me. *Stop it*, I scolded myself. *This is your family and you love them and if they embarrass you until you wish you were dead, well, so be it. Shut up. You're an adult. Gay up. Maybe there'll be a freak tornado.*

"Just remember I warned you," I told Edgar as we moved through the lobby and into the synagogue.

The room was packed with women wearing everything from lacy pastel sheaths with matching coats to skintight bandage dresses to more subdued silk pantsuits with simple jewelry; growing up, I had loved to watch my always perfectly dressed mom sizing up our more flashy relatives, studying their plunging necklines (revealing tattoos of butterflies or roses) and wobbly spike heels while murmuring, "I wish someone could explain that."

The men mostly wore dark business suits or pressed jeans, blazers and open-neck shirts, and the squirming children and ostentatiously bored teenagers had on whatever compromises their parents had agreed to: "I don't care, I'm sick of arguing about it, wear whatever you like, I'll just tell everyone you're a heroin addict."

While I'd offered my services, Abby hadn't asked me to oversee her wedding: "Because I don't want you to have to work and worry about everything. I want you there as my guest and as my brother and to deliver your sacred cosmic gay blessing." I'd been grateful for this gesture, but now I had a whole new level of anxiety to deal with.

An usher escorted Edgar and me to a pew in the front row on the bride's side, putting us on full display. During the few times I'd brought Callum to family gatherings he'd caused a minor stir, since he was so good-looking in such an obviously gentile manner, and because certain family members recognized him from his commercials and would shout "SUBARU!" or "LYRICA!" as if these words were his first name.

But this was different. This was a whole other category of mob rule. As we passed each pew, one person would spot Edgar and execute a double take, as if their eyeballs were on springs.

This person would violently nudge whoever was sitting next to them, unleashing a viral nudge moving from aunt to cousin to nephew, accompanied by fervid whispers of, "Is that who I think it is?" "Or does it just look like him?" "No, it's really him!" "What's he doing here?" "Why is he with Carter?" "Take a picture! Take a picture!" and inevitably, "Is he Jewish?"

As the entire congregation leaned toward us like a flying wedge, I hustled Edgar into our pew, inserting myself between him and my mom. At that exact second, the string quartet segued from "My Heart Will Go On," a song that I'd tried to discourage my sister from using, since it's essentially a dirge, into a percolating medley mixing "Uptown Funk" with "Rockin' Robin" and "Crazy In Love" as a formally dressed bridesmaid and groomsman somersaulted down the center aisle and golden glitter rained down. The other paired bridesmaids and groomsmen followed, performing exuberant, fist-pumping, boogying, leap-frogging choreography and tossing more glitter in my sister's signature colors, magenta and powder blue. I loved all this, because I think any event should reflect the spirit of the participants, and my sister Abby wanted, as she'd told me, "a cross between a flash mob, the finale of a reality show singing competition and Mardi Gras on Mars."

I glanced at Edgar to see if he was appalled, but his shoulders were bouncing happily to "You're the One That I Want" from *Grease*, for which the quartet had added an electric guitarist and a horn section. Then, as a syncopated "Wedding March" began, Abby appeared, on my father's arm. Abby has devoted her life to the following items: her family; her career as a pediatric surgeon; her circle of friends, who'd voted on a collective shade of spray tan; her search for love, which had arrived at Dane Lefkowitz, a jock-ish, affable attorney and golfer; but above all else, her wedding gown. At the age of two, Abby had swaddled a Raggedy Ann doll in toilet paper and married it to our dachshund, in a bowtie and yarmulke.

Abby was no amateur bridezilla, slicing pages out of magazines in dental offices and curating a Pinterest board of lacy options. She'd submitted a thousand-signature petition to her Girl Scout troop to have Gown Research ranked as a merit badge. At sixteen she'd asked for a custom-crafted dress form to be installed in her bedroom to wear muslin mock-ups. As an intern she'd cheered up desperately ill children by asking them to vote on front-running options, as a welcome distraction.

While I wasn't Abby's wedding planner, since birth (I'm two years younger) I'd willingly served as her designated gown consultant. I'm not saying that having my G.I. Joe tell Barbie, "I hate leg-of-mutton sleeves—you look like a linebacker" had made me gay, I'm just saying the research hasn't been done. Abby and I would watch rom-coms together and howl at the stars to wear a decent corset. We'd both use shower curtains as practice trains. It got so that, when we'd attend actual weddings together, only a fraction of a glance would convey "The strapless yanking-it-up mistake," "Flesh-colored mesh inserts never flatter anyone" or "Your veil shouldn't make you look like a piece of patio furniture being weatherproofed over a long winter."

Abby had one other all-consuming addiction: celebrities. She had alerts on her phone for hundreds of models, pop stars, Bachelorettes, Real Housewives and the occasional female criminal, especially if she'd killed more than one husband. We can gossip for hours about famous people we'll never meet because, as Abby once explained, "They're more interesting than us, they can afford to make themselves more attractive than us, they have sex with other famous people, but we don't have to really worry about them. I spend all day making sure kids with terrible diseases get every chance they can, so when I get home I like to think about Kim Kardashian's new line of shapewear."

Whenever my job took me anywhere near a star, Abby would pummel me: "Was Sandra Bullock genuinely nice, or I-want-everybody-to-like-me nice? Has she had her eyes done? How tall? After that last marriage can she ever trust any guy ever again?"

As for royals, of course we'd scrutinised and ranked them, but Abby was intimidated: "They're the purest form of celebrity, because they're born into it. They don't have to pretend to be anything except famous. They're the only reality stars who don't end up doing laxative ads and reunion specials. If Queen Catherine ever looked at me I'd turn into a little pile of incredibly overeducated dirt."

When Abby made her bridal entrance, the congregation swiveled from staring at Edgar to adoring Abby. She was preceded by four flower girls, who were tossing magenta and powder blue rose petals. Abby was beyond gorgeous, glowing with the assurance that after decades of cross-referencing every available ensemble, she'd made the indisputably right choice. Her gown was elaborate but classic, sleeveless but high-necked, a cascade of white satin subtly worked with shivers of gold scrollwork and the tiniest pearls. As Abby had triumphantly concluded during her final fitting: "Yes. Audrey Hepburn if she liked dessert."

Seeing Abby look so beautiful and so happy was thrilling; we were a lifelong team, and I knew how much this day meant to her. It was a fulfillment, and a celebration of her love for Dane. Sometimes weddings can drown in preparations and overspending and unreachable expectations, but Abby was equal to her event. She was sharing her happiness and having a blast, which made me start to cry, and I worried that I'd embarrass Edgar. But instead his hand found mine as he murmured, "She's stunning. What a lovely moment." I couldn't be sure, but I think Edgar's voice cracked just a bit; was he also susceptible to all of this wonderfully over-the-top romantic theater?

Abby's eyes swept the room, aware of a buzz not entirely centered on her. She laser-focused on Edgar. She looked at me. What had I done? I hadn't told Abby that I'd even met Edgar, because I hadn't wanted to add to her prenuptial stress or turn the spotlight anywhere near me. I was also superstitious; Abby and I were ultraserious about dating and kissing and the prospect of love, so once I told Abby about a guy, his name would be inscribed in our mythology, and she, of course, would sit me down with an exhaustive checklist ("Okay, so tell me about his neck") until she knew everything. I trusted Abby's opinion, so I didn't want Edgar to appear on her radar until there was a reality to analyze. And on a practical note, I knew that Edgar's schedule could be variable, so I didn't want to promise Abby that Edgar was coming to her wedding and then have something interfere and disappoint her.

Beyond all this, on a wickedly selfish level, a tiny part of me thought of Edgar as the ultimate wedding gift, as a special guest star with the potential to stun and delight Abby. But had I been wrongheaded? Was bringing Edgar going to mess with Abby's agenda and her vision of synagogue splendor? I'd rather die than hurt Abby in any way, and now I was petrified that I'd ruined her bliss for the sake of my royal arm candy.

Abby stared at me and at Edgar as her eyes grew wide and her breathing intensified. I could feel her neurons recalculating the moment, assembling data and churning toward a decision. She opened her mouth to say something, couldn't, then mustered her full resources and declared:

"OH MY FUCKING GOD. I LOVE IT!!!"

She swooped toward us and kissed me and then Edgar as if we were her human good luck charms. Edgar blushed, smiled and, with what I can only call amazing grace, nodded Abby toward the altar, where Dane, her befuddled groom, awaited. Abby sailed toward her husband-to-be as the rabbi was explaining to him, "He's Prince Edgar of England," and then, helpfully, so Dane wouldn't feel jealous, "Gay."

CHAPTER 11

The reception was held in a ballroom, one of many, at the nearby Grande Park Chateau Reception Arena and Conference Center, a rambling catering hall designed in an architectural style best described as "Neoclassical Jersey Mob Boss," which meant columns, fiberglass statuary and floral arrangements sent to colonize Earth.

Edgar and I were seated at the bridesmaids' table, at the take-no-prisoners demand of six thirtyish women wearing not-terrible magenta and powder blue gowns, by which I mean they didn't resemble 1950s Chevrolets, along with rhinestone headbands bisecting their foreheads, as if they were all recovering from some glamorous, matching surgery. They'd been devoted to Abby since preschool, and were now marketing analysts, dermatologists and CEOs of companies that bedazzled sports bras. Like Abby, they were sharply perceptive, rowdy and not in any way shy.

"First off," said Kaitlynn Blatt, a team leader at Amazon, to

Edgar, "Are you absolutely one hundred percent sure you're gay, because you are so incredibly cute."

"Edgar," I interrupted, "you don't have to answer that—"

"Shut up," Kaitlynn informed me. "We're not talking to you. We're talking to him."

"Thank you so much," said Edgar, "but I'm afraid I'm a one hundred percenter. Although if I were not, I would hope to be placed at precisely this table, among so many supremely appealing young women."

"Ooooo," the bridesmaids whooped in unison, as Kaitlynn told Edgar, "You're good."

"Moving on," said Ginnifer Warston-Brasnow, a hospitality services coordinator for Hilton. "So how long have the two of you been dating? Is it serious? Are you monogamous? Are there rings? Have you been in counseling? How many times have you broken up?"

"Ginnifer," said Edgar, who I'd noticed was able to remember every stranger's name instantly, "those are all fascinating and important questions, but let's just say that Carter and I have only known each other a short while, but we're having the very best time."

I joined in the resulting swoon, because this was Edgar's first public acknowledgment of our relationship, and while "the very best time" was diplomatic, it made my heart soar.

"But someday," said Shannyn Weiner, who sold huge novelty wineglasses etched with the phrase "Mommy-Size" online, "and I'm not just talking about Carter, but it could be Carter, do you want to get married?"

There was a pause, during which I strove to seem nonchalant or even bored, but the question had transformed me into a seventh yearning bridesmaid, hungry for any crumb of commitment.

"Very much so."

When Edgar said this, I not only froze, I pretty much blacked out, because the truth is: I am my sister. Times a billion. Because when we were growing up and I became her bridal assistant, I spent an equal amount of time imagining outfits, honeymoon islands with suites set on pilings in the bluest oceans, and sexual positions for Ken and my G.I. Joe, who for some reason I named Drew. Gay marriage hadn't yet become legal, but I'd bypassed that fact without hesitation, because I'd believed in true love, which called for a wedding of tasteful yet still *Moulin Rouge* production number glory, meaning Ken would enter the Great Hall of the Metropolitan Museum of Art astride a unicorn to wed Drew in his suit of armor on his motorcycle.

I know that some gay kids are forced to disguise both their true selves and their most dearly held fantasies, but I was lucky: thanks to a supportive family and a stubbornly romantic nature, I'd refused to be anyone but myself. Which, when it comes to grown-up love, can become incredibly dangerous.

My years with Callum had confirmed what I'd been suspecting: love is unstable, unknowable and a trap. Callum had said he'd loved me and we'd talked about marriage and even indulged in daydreams of sharing a seaside cottage years down the road (although since he hated cottages, Callum had opted for a Hamptons glass and steel box). But when Callum had lied and cheated on me and we'd fought, I hadn't been surprised because I wasn't enough—handsome enough, smart enough, sexy enough or seductively mysterious enough—to justify another human being's love. I was too weird, too aware of surfaces, too anxious about everything and, finally, too frightened. I was a bad bet, hopelessly damaged goods, nothing special or not special enough. I was me, and that would always be the unfixable glitch. I was an associate event architect, never an event. I was the person who could assist other peoples' happiness, I could frame their joy and celebrate their great good fortune, but not my own.

So when Edgar expressed such an enthusiastic interest in marriage and the bridesmaids hugged themselves and relied on me for agreement, and to ratify their own most heartfelt dreams, I did what I always do. I looked around for my mother.

"Your Highness," she said, her hands on my shoulders and directing the royal title to me. My mom had been waiting her whole life to use this particular joke; she loves a good punch line almost as much as she loves me. On some level she considers me her finest punch line.

"So are you going to introduce me, or are you too ashamed?" she asked.

"I pick too ashamed."

"Shut up. Prince Edgar, hello, I'm Sarah Ogden, Carter's mom. Has he mentioned that he has one?"

"Ms. Ogden!" said Edgar, leaping to his feet and shaking my mother's hand. "What a pleasure. I've assumed that from his personality and fine manners, Carter must have an extraordinary mother."

"He does. And it's wonderful to meet you . . ."

"Edgar."

"Edgar. I like that. Look at you two. How did this happen?"

"Mom!"

"What, I'm not allowed to ask a question?"

"I imagine that Carter's been discreet," said Edgar. "But we met at the United Nations, and I begged him to allow me to be here today and meet as many Ogdens as possible."

"Then we need to talk—about so many things. And I have photos."

"Excuse me, but I'm sitting right here," I insisted.

"It's always about Carter, isn't it?" said my mom, shaking her head.

"Tell me about it," agreed Edgar as they hugged.

My mother often scolds me about only identifying her as my mother, since she's a full, multifaceted person with a successful career as a personal shopper at high-end retail throughout New Jersey and online, where her website is called SarahStyle. My mom has fabulous taste, as she's currently enlightening Edgar, and she's given me a lifelong interest in books, movies, theater and compassionately judging other people. ("Maybe that woman is wearing those hideously creased white pants because they were a gift from a beloved relative with Alzheimer's; you never know.") My friends revere my mom, and her desire to guide every aspect of my life is mostly a blessing and only sometimes a reason I wish she'd never learned how to text. She's Dr. Frankenstein, if he'd known over five hundred ways to tie a scarf, and I'm her creature.

"So, Edgar, may I sit down, oh look, I'm already sitting, I've always been a huge fan of your grandmother's wardrobe, she really makes bold color her friend, and I hope you're enjoying my daughter's wedding, which let's just say is pure Abby. I'm so proud of both of my children, and you don't have to tell me if you're having sex with my son, unless you'd like to."

As Edgar and my mom leaned their heads together and I overheard the words "IHOP," "Citi Bike" and "skin care," I wondered if, just maybe, Edgar having grown up without a mother made him take such an immediate and fierce interest in mine.

"So you bought Carter his first Tom Ford suit from a resale

shop but you could tell it was brand-new because of the tag under the lapel—that's so wise. I'm hopeless about fashion, James brings me to our tailor and makes all the decisions."

"And he's doing a marvelous job, but if you'd like a second opinion, I'll give you my card."

"I would love that!"

"Carter?" said my dad, who'd extricated himself from a debate over Baltic politics at a nearby table. "Is this indeed His Royal Highness?"

"Edgar," said my mom, "this is my husband, Peter, and yes, his muted paisley tie and coordinated houndstooth pocket square were my idea."

"Mr. Ogden, first of all, you look superb, and beyond that, it's so very good to meet you. Carter tells me you're a professor at the state university."

"Indeed," said my dad, who I love because he's kind and generous and deeply enjoys using words like "indeed," "wherewithal" and "everlastingly." "I teach world civilization, and if you'd like, I can provide some fascinating lore regarding your ancestor, the first King Edgar in 959, and his alliance with the thanes of Mercia and Northumbria—"

"Who helped him introduce Benedictine Rule to the monastic communities."

"'Tis true!" said my dad, thrilled at discovering a fellow scholar. While I'm not a history buff, my dad and I have sought common ground by occupying our couch in stained sweats, guzzling microwave popcorn and binge-watching the most moronic sitcoms together, just to outrage my mom: "Why are you two laughing like idiots at those people wearing striped polo shirts and polyester windbreakers?"

"CARTER YOU FUCKING TRAITOR I THOUGHT YOU WERE MY BROTHER I GUESS FUCKING NOT," said Abby, standing six feet away, with her hands on the hips of her gown and her glorious mountain of hair almost reaching out to choke me. Abby has naturally abundant hair and often forces strangers to yank on it to prove she never needs extensions. "We spent our lives figuring out this wedding and what do you do? You bring His Royal Fucking Highness Prince Fucking Edgar as your date! AND YOU DON'T GIVE ME A FUCKING HEADS-UP!"

"Edgar," I said, "meet Dr. Abigail Ogden."

"GET OVER HERE!" Abby commanded, and Edgar bravely stood as Abby cannonballed toward him, enveloping him in white satin and nearly lifting him off the ground.

"You are the loveliest bride I've ever seen," gasped Edgar, still in captivity.

"And today I'm the only bride in the entire world with you at my ceremony and reception." And then, addressing the room, while clutching Edgar's hand: "I want everyone to remember that! I want you to tell your children and your grandchildren!"

"So it's okay?" I asked, as Abby hugged me and Edgar simultaneously and decreed, "It's way beyond fucking okay!"

She took Edgar's hand and dragged him toward some available chairs in a more private corner, and I followed them, both excited by their collusion and checking around for steak knives to cut my throat at whatever Abby was going to say next.

"Okay," she began, to Edgar, "first of all, you're adorable and you look just like in your pictures only a little bit taller, so yay! Second of all, we need to talk about your grandmother's dogs and a thing I read online that said you were dating Matt Bomer, which made me very worried, because I thought he was happily married to another guy."

"As I believe he is," said Edgar. "And I've never met either of them."

"Good," said Abby. "Because here's my bottom line. Carter, come over here."

"I am over here."

"Edgar, you see this unbelievably cute guy, even if he doesn't think so? He's just been through a total nightmare trainwreck with a person we will not even name, because I'm a surgeon, so he's lucky I haven't cut out his despicable nonexistent heart and made it look like an accident. But he treated Carter like garbage, I won't go into details, but one word: cheating bastard."

"That's two words," I corrected.

"Shut up. So, Edgar, I'm going to tell you one thing: if you hurt my brother in any way, even by accident, even for a second, I will hunt you down, and all I can say is, your brother will become king and your body will never be found, not even as diced onions made of royalty."

I've always loved that, for a doctor with infinite benevolence for children, Abby has the most luridly violent inner life of anyone I've ever met.

"So Edgar, Your Highness, whatever, we'll figure out what I'm going to call you later, but right now I need to hear it, from your royal lips: are you going to be good to my brother?"

"I would very much like to try . . ." Edgar began.

"Trying isn't doing. Are you going to be good to him, and treat him with the caring and sweetness and respect that he deserves?"

Edgar glanced at me without moving his head. I made a helpless I-have-no-power-here gesture.

"Yes," Edgar said, forcefully.

"Yes?" Abby asked, not giving an inch.

"Yes, ma'am!"

"That's what I wanted to hear!" Abby exclaimed, going for another bear hug as I offered Edgar a good-job thumbs-up.

"Honey?" said Dane, Abby's new husband, strapping and square-jawed in his tux with a magenta-and-blue rose on his lapel and a magenta-and-blue yarmulke embroidered with "Abby & Dane" and the date.

"Dane," said Abby, "this is Prince Edgar of England, who's just sworn on his life not to treat Carter the way you-know-who did. And Edgar, this is my husband—I love saying that! This is my husband, Dane Lefkowitz, who's the most incredible man I've ever met, and I love him to pieces."

When Abby said this I knew that, given Abby's recent remarks, Edgar and I had both just visualised Dane in cornflake-size fragments.

"Good to meet you, dude," said Dane, shaking Edgar's hand—did anyone in England ever call the crown prince "dude"?

"You're the luckiest fellow," Edgar told him.

"I am!" Dane said, his arm around Abby.

"He really is," Abby averred wholeheartedly.

"And Abbs," I said, gently but firmly, "unless you have something you need Edgar to sign, in blood, isn't it time for cake?"

There were two cakes, one an eight-tiered, powder blue and magenta rosettes-and-lilies, buttercream-and-rum super structure, and the other only three tiers of a gluten-free, nondairy alternative. And I'm not even mentioning the table with those Christmas-tree-like wire stands stacked with magenta and powder blue cupcakes.

"Not yet," Abby told us. "First we're gonna dance!"

As the evening progressed I observed the following things:

• For a guy who'd resisted loosening up at the UN, Edgar was a surprisingly out-there dancer. When we joined Abby, Dane and what my mom termed the "younger people" on the floor, Edgar moved like someone determined to break a sweat and let his limbs do whatever they pleased. I like to think of myself as a great dancer, but Edgar's what-the-hell whirling made me rethink my patented club-trained cool. We danced like people at a New Jersey wedding, which was much more fun.

• Edgar was willing to eat things I'd never go near. Royals, like politicians, are availed upon to at least sample every possible food and feign enjoyment, but Edgar devoured Abby's socially aware delicacies, including a meatless sirloin, a cucumber lasagna and flourless mini-donuts decorated to resemble wedding rings. These last items offended me on a primal level, because they tasted like children's aspirin mixed with construction paper. "They're actually quite tasty," Edgar insisted, "if you've never had food."

Edgar was really good at his job. Before the cakes were served, I toasted Abby and Dane, raising my glass of champagne and declaring, "I have the best sister in the entire world and I'm so glad she's found the perfect guy. And they can never get divorced, because Abby will never be able to find a more incredible wedding gown!" Abby stomped her feet and whistled, and then she surreptitiously jabbed Edgar with a fork, to indicate that he should make a toast as well. He obliged, saying, "I've only just met the beautiful bride and her dashing groom, but I'm in awe. Some of those in attendance today may have seen coverage of various royal weddings, but I can only say this: America, and specifically Abby and Dane, do it so much better!"

The crowd, naturally, went berserk, and I had a flash, from Abby's eventual video album, of His Royal Highness standing beside me and beaming. How was this in any way my life? I'd known Edgar such a short time, and he was already scoring a huge win at my sister's wedding, and he'd just put his arm around my shoulders. My immediate response was a brain-bomb of trepidation: I knew I'd fuck this up; the only questions were how and when. My mom shot me a look, because she could tell I was spiralling, and she mouthed the words, "Stop it!"

After a trip to the restroom to pull myself together, I couldn't find Edgar, until James approached me and confided, "I believe His Highness is engaged in conversation with your great-aunt Miriam. I've served in two wars, dealt with the media and wrangled Her Majesty Queen Catherine. But I will say only this: Miriam scares me."

My great-aunt Miriam is maybe four feet tall in the flesh-toned patent leather pumps she buys in bulk, with a towering, shellacked hairdo tinted a shade my mom calls Ash Blonde Eternity. I've never seen Miriam with her hair even slightly relaxed, so it may be a permanent achievement, much like her rice powder makeup accented with unblended circles of rouge and lavishly applied red lipstick. I love the way Miriam looks, because it's not based on anything human; she's going for German Expressionism or Kabuki sheet cake. She's always very well-dressed in stiff, glittering brocades reminiscent of Miami Beach hotel bedspreads, with coordinated handbags the size of steamer trunks. Miriam's handbags seem to be handcuffed to her birdlike wrists, due to her armloads of bracelets in Italian gold, Mexican silver and Home Shopping Network Ping-Pong ball pearls.

Miriam had sequestered Edgar in the lobby, possibly at gunpoint, and sat facing him, both of them on gilded bamboo chairs, their knees touching, the interrogation lacking only electrodes and snarling Dobermans.

"So someday, when your grandma dies, God forbid, kina hora," Miriam was saying, and then she mimed spitting on the ground three times by saying "Poo poo poo" to keep the evil eye away—this was a Yiddish expression she used, and who's to say it doesn't work? "Then you'll be king, Mr. Big, all the marbles, am I right?"

"Yes, that will be the line of succession," said Edgar. Miriam grabbed his hand and looked into his eyes as if she was about to deliver a psychic prophecy.

"Being the king is a tough job. My late husband, Morty, may he rest in peace, he ran a carpeting business, he was the Broadloom King of Ronkonkoma out on Long Island, so it was a similar responsibility, only it was maybe even harder, because I bet no one ever asks you for a fifteen percent friends and family discount on wall-to-wall in a wool/nylon blend, am I right?"

"That's very true."

"So let's cut to the chase. Eddie—can I call you Eddie? You're a nice-looking fellow, and you're gay, which I think is just dandy, and do you know why? Because my first cousin Frieda was a lesbian, she flew cargo jets in World War II, because they wouldn't let her into combat, and then she lived with her ladyfriend, this pretty young schoolteacher, until the day she died. They couldn't have been happier, and when somebody would make a remark, I would tell them, so Frieda wears slacks, just like Katharine Hepburn, what's it to you? So when Carter told me he was gay, do you know what I said? I told him, Carter, since you were five years old you've kept a scrapbook of table settings, do you think I'm blind? And Eddie, look at you, you're single, you have a nice career ahead of you, you're English, but I'm not holding that against you, I enjoy English people, I dated Churchill, I'm kidding, I don't date married men, but let me ask you, and I'm talking about your relationship with Carter—what are your intentions?"

This question was exactly why I'd worried about bringing Edgar to the wedding, both because it was wildly unfair to put Edgar on the spot and because I was longing to hear his answer. Edgar's session with Abby had been intense, but this was Final Jeopardy. So I jumped in, exclaiming, "Miriam! It's so great to see you, and have you heard that they're about to distribute the centerpieces?"

Miriam's face twitched, because during the waning moments of the reception, all guests would lift their dinner plates, seeking a parchment card embossed with the happy couple's initials. This card entitled the owner to claim their table's elaborate floral centerpiece and they'd later carry it to be stowed in the trunk of their car. Arriving early for just this purpose, Miriam had already moved the card from beneath the plate of an outlying niece to her own, because, as she'd told my mom, "I'm sure that Lauren would want me to have the centerpiece, because it would look terrible with all of her IKEA furniture, which I'm not criticizing, but why does she want to live in a Swedish dorm room?"

Miriam knew that Lauren, as a vindictive, recently divorced life coach, was more than capable of moving that card right back, so she stood, saying, "Eddie, it's been a pleasure, and I hope I'll be seeing more of you. You shouldn't feel nervous just because Carter comes from such an accomplished New Jersey family, or because you're a gentile, which is sad, but it's just like having poor posture or a ketchup stain on your shirt—we'll all pretend not to notice. And I should mention, I'm a semiretired CPA, so if you'd like me to take a look at your taxes, let's stay in touch."

Miriam handed Edgar a business card, which was laminated ("In case anything splashes") with her name, email, and a 3D picture of her face emerging from a red rose, beside the slogan "Miriam Yansky, CPA—Helping Your Assets Flower."

"I'm so sorry about that," I told Edgar as I steered him toward the exit and the parking lot, "we don't have to stay, you've been unbelievably great and I owe you."

"Don't be ridiculous, I've been enjoying every moment, and we're not leaving without proper goodbyes and a centerpiece."

An hour later, after Edgar had been thoroughly kissed, hugged and pinched and Miriam had tucked dinner rolls into the pocket of his suit jacket ("As a nosh, for when you're on the road"), James placed our centerpiece in the rear of the SUV and we all climbed inside. As we hit the Turnpike, Edgar asked me, "What is wrong with you?"

CHAPTER 12

He went on: "You have an utterly delightful family, yet you work yourself into fits of embarrassment over a group of people who love you with near-hurricane force. Your heavenly if slightly ferocious sister only wants you to be happy, and your parents would battle a marauding army to bring that about. And as for Miriam, while her handbag may contain weapons of mass destruction, I fully intend to contact her on behalf of the British economy. Why are you such an unnecessary mess?"

I could tell that not only Edgar but James and our driver were eager for my answer. I took a shot at the truth: "Okay. You're right. I spend too much time worrying about what my family thinks of me, and trying to predict their opinions, and getting scared that I'm turning into them, although that's already happened. But here's my real problem: I don't want to disappoint them. They're fine with my being gay, and they sort of get why I'm an associate event architect instead of a neurologist or the next Mark Zuckerberg, but when they think about my love life, the jury is still out. Abby fixed me up with three different guys, all doctors she works with, but then she showed up on the dates and told the guys to leave because she thought I could do better. My mom volunteered to go into therapy with me in case she was holding me back, and my dad keeps sending me profiles of different Shakespearean characters he thinks would be great matches for me. And Miriam once texted Callum, my ex-boyfriend, asking him to describe our sex life so she could give pointers. And because she was doing his taxes for free, he did it."

"And what was her advice?"

"I can't repeat it, because I only glanced at her bullet points, which included 'water-based lube' and 'advanced nipple play.' The real point is, my greatest and totally justified fear is that they're right and I get in my own way and I talk myself out of happiness and I'm barely holding it together. So when I brought you to the wedding, I knew that everyone would be ecstatic beyond belief, and that there'd be enough kvelling to make God complain about the racket."

"'Kvelling'?"

"It's a Yiddish word," said James, "describing extreme and vocal good wishes. As when your grandmother greets her corgis."

"Yes, but even beyond the kvell factor, I know they were all looking at you and thinking, 'How did that happen? He's too good for Carter,' and most of all, they were probably placing bets on 'How is Carter going to fuck this up?'"

Realizing what I'd just said and how far I'd overreached, I was about to open the SUV door and hurl myself onto the turnpike.

"So in other words," said Edgar, "if I understand this correctly, you're being you."

"Yes. So if you'd like to drop me off at a rest stop and head for the airport, I wouldn't blame you. And I'm still being selfish, because when I was little I loved turnpike rest stops because they have gift shops."

"No. Because first of all, we're driving you home."

We sat in awkward silence for the next forty-five minutes, until the SUV pulled up in front of my building. James opened my door, and I assumed Edgar would stay inside, but he stepped out as well. We faced each other in front of the brownstone's corroding steps.

"Carter," Edgar said, as I stuck out my hand for a farewell handshake.

"Yeah?"

"You're a strange and confused person. But before I leave for London there's something I would very much like to do. May I come up?"

"Come up? You mean, to see my apartment?"

"Among other activities."

"You mean you want to . . ."

"If you'd like to."

"But is that really a good idea?"

Edgar turned to his security detail, saying, "Carter, I've been incredibly rude. You haven't been properly introduced to my superb team. Please meet Ian Hoagland, Charles Wintermore, Clark Dartley, Terry Winton and Lucky Bartle."

"You guys are amazing," I said.

"Yes, they are," said Edgar. "They're the finest security force not merely in London but in the world. So let's ask their opinions. Gentlemen, do you think I should accompany Carter up to his apartment?"

The men scrunched up their faces, as they decided.

"I'd say absolutely," offered Clark.

"We've been discussing it among ourselves for days," said Ian. "What're you blokes waiting for?"

"Maybe you're not really gay," suggested Terry.

"Miriam asked me about it," confided Charles.

"Otherwise you're just wasting our time," concluded Lucky, who had an impressively broken nose.

James sighed and addressed both of us: "If you must."

As we climbed the five flights I channeled my mother, racing through a to-do list: was the apartment and especially my bedroom anywhere close to tidy, or at least nontoxic, were there clean towels and non-budget toilet paper, and had Edgar ever been in a rent-controlled apartment where the tilting bookcases covered the cracks in the walls, and oh my God, because this was my mom's greatest terror, beyond plague or earthquake, would there be any visible bugs? Sometimes, just to upset her, while I was on the phone with my mom I'd pretend to be scolding the bugs, telling them, "Hush, it's Sarah, we'll play charades later."

"Stop it. Stop worrying," Edgar told me.

"You mean stop breathing?"

"If necessary."

Clark and Ian took up their posts in the hallway; the other guys were grabbing coffee from a nearby Starbucks. All I could think was that, like raising a child, having sex with a crown prince took a village.

"Hello?" I said, pushing open the front door.

"HIIII!" said Louise, Adam and DuShawn, lounging on the couch.

"Edgar, these are my friends and roommates Louise and

Adam, and that's Adam's boyfriend, DuShawn, and they're all about to head into their own bedrooms and be very, very quiet."

"Good evening," said Edgar. "It's so good to meet all of you, and please don't mind us."

"We figured you might end up here, and we think it's wonderful," said Adam. "You have our blessing."

"Mazel tov," added DuShawn.

"And out of respect for Carter," said Louise, "I'm not going to bring up England's economic meltdown, bigoted treatment of immigrants, or ancient yet ongoing class wars."

"And I love you for that," said Edgar. "And we've brought you a centerpiece."

"And we've prepared an offering as well, to welcome you," said Adam. "And Louise even helped."

Louise hefted a gift basket and removed: "A jar of Prince spaghetti sauce."

"Two cans of Royal Crown Cola," said Adam.

"A paperback romance novel called *Royal Pursuit*," said DuShawn. "I've highlighted all the juicy parts, as a how-to guide."

"And if that doesn't work," said Adam, "here's a sex toy I bought on Amazon called the Royal Reamer."

"And most importantly," said Louise, holding up two flimsy golden cardboard crowns with printed-on jewels.

"We got them from Burger King," Adam explained.

"We told them it was your birthdays," said DuShawn.

"Edgar," I asked, "if you killed them you couldn't be arrested, right, because of diplomatic immunity?"

"But I wouldn't do that," said Edgar, "because I think these are the finest tributes I've ever received. I like them even more than the oil painting of a llama I was given by the envoy from Peru."

"And now we're going away," said Adam.

"And we're not going to crouch outside Carter's door," promised Louise, "and record whatever noises we hear on our phones."

"Or shout 'Nice one!'" said DuShawn, "or 'Do it!'"

As the three of them retreated I heard Adam whisper, "Beyond cute," and Louise reply, "Nice white boys in heat."

"We are going to mentally delete all of that," I told Edgar, herding him into my bedroom. As I did this and shut the door behind us I had two explosive thoughts: first, that I was most likely the only person on Earth to bring a future king of England into a room containing a framed photo of Ruth Ginsburg and a set of mugs from Broadway hits, and secondly, that I was about to have sex with someone I actually cared about, which could result in both extreme joy and many shipping containers' worth of panic attacks.

Adam and DuShawn could be heard crooning "Tonight" from *West Side Story*; DuShawn had danced in the most recent, heatedly sexual revival. I cracked open the door and told them, "If you don't stop that and go to your room I'll make you watch the sequel to *Mamma Mia!*"

There was a gasp and the sound of scurrying and a slamming door.

"All right," said Edgar, sitting on the Danish linen duvet I'd purchased at cost following a showroom event, accessorized with throw pillows from Bed Bath & Beyond; as my mom always says, "It's about taste, not money." Edgar turned away.

"Did I do something wrong?" I asked. "Would you like a snack? We can just talk if you want."

"No, it's just, when I look at you, you make me so happy, and I . . . I would like that to continue. But it can't."

"Why not?"

"Because everything I've been accusing you of, and haranguing you about, like apprehension and shame and nervousness about your family—I'm so much worse. Which is why I'm hopeless about sex or intimacy or even the simplest pleasures."

I sat beside him. "What are you talking about?"

"As you might imagine, being raised in the palace didn't provide any sort of . . . romantic education, for either my brother or myself. James and my grandmother did their best, but I've remained inept and fearful. Which is why I've only enjoyed, if that's the correct word, three relationships."

"Edgar?"

I almost took his hand, but he wasn't after polite comfort.

"I'm trusting you. We've only been together for such a brief time, but somehow—I believe that you're an entirely decent person."

Was I? I hoped I was.

"My first was a mad crush on a boy at school. We were wild for each other, or really wild for having sex in all sorts of unlikely places. Storage rooms. A corner of the library. We were finally apprehended in the gymnasium at midnight, and my grandmother was notified, although God bless her, all she did was tell the headmaster, 'They're two English schoolboys—isn't that what they do?'"

"She said that?"

"It was one of her finer moments. But the boy and I were separated, and he transferred to a different school, and when I encountered him years later, he was married and losing his hair. My second spasm involved another soldier while I was in the military, in Afghanistan. It was all very rugged and clandestine, until Scotland Yard documented that he'd been approached by several tabloids and was in negotiation to sell his exclusive story of torrid royal lust. With photos."

I was starting to understand that Edgar wasn't inhibited and maybe inexperienced—he had good reasons for keeping his distance, from even the possibility of love.

"I felt much like you: that I was disappointing everyone, severely. Because ever since I can remember, there's been only one unthinkable sin, and that was disgracing my family, and my country, in any way. I was being held to a different standard, which I agreed with. I had one job: to represent the royal household and to make England proud, and I was a calamity. So even the briefest affair, even a questionable friendship, began to seem—irresponsible. Not befitting the Crown. Far too risky."

"So are you supposed to just be alone? And shut down?"

"No. I'm supposed to be aware, at all times, of the dangers involved. So in certain ways, yes, I'm a prisoner, a necessary prisoner, of expectations."

Edgar's eyes were shining with tears, which he didn't acknowledge in any way.

"But you said there were three relationships?"

"The last was two years ago, with a docent from the British Museum. His specialty was the architect Augustus Pugin and the Gothic Revival, so we bonded over our mutual crush on the House of Lords and Westminster. He was erudite and level-headed and quite handsome. A swimmer."

I was instantly jealous, envisioning every actor who'd ever appeared shirtless in a BBC miniseries as a chauffeur or a stable boy or a country parson revealing a trim torso, often while skinny-dipping in a Shropshire pond.

"So what happened?"

"He was lovely, almost fictional, which should've been a red flag. Long talks. Shared interests. Modest. Until after a drunken argument, over nothing, he shouted his intention of writing a book, exposing everything I'd told him about my childhood and my grandmother and my sessions with a therapist. The worst part was his justification—he said the world needed to know how damaged I was. He said I should be made an example of why the monarchy should be abolished."

"Oh my God."

"He was quite serious, and this had been his motive all along. He'd hired a literary agent and provided video, which I never knew existed. When I tried to reason with him, things became physical, but if I'd brought charges, it only would've made everything worse. The Palace legal team stepped in, a great deal of money exchanged hands and—here I am. The poor little prince sobbing over his absurdly privileged and extravagant life."

He stood.

"I should go. You don't deserve this, you're far too kind, and I've begun to believe that I curse people. That I plunk myself down not merely with baggage but with a sign around my neck reading 'Beware—No Fun At All.'"

I was standing too. We were equal. He was destined to become the king of England, and I was a nice Jewish boy from New Jersey; we both knew what we were supposed to be doing, but we were fighting it. When it came to emotional stability, neither of us had a prayer. Maybe in some way, everyone feels inadequate and broken and ashamed of being so needy. Even Callum had once confessed to me that he was letting the world down when he didn't maintain his blonde highlights and facial scruff at what he'd classified as "peak stud."

Edgar's eyes. He was looking at me from across an ocean, across centuries of his family's history, and his own romantic fumbles. I had to do something, not just to help him and show him how worthy he was of being loved, but to get both of us naked.

"Edgar . . ."

"Yes?"

"I heard everything you just said, and I get it. And we're both incredibly fucked up. And there's only one thing we can do about it."

We lunged for each other and I couldn't stop kissing this gorgeous man and ripping his clothes off and trying not to glance over his shoulder at Ruth Ginsburg and tell her, "He's a prince, so he really doesn't need a chest like that, but he's fucking got one!"

CHAPTER 13

The sex was:

Wonderful and heartbreaking, because at first we were both trying way too hard to be good at it, and then we laughed and had a much better time not acting like reality show judges were holding up grades as if one of us could be eliminated before the next round.

Wonderful because Edgar was voracious and take-charge, and I decided that he was making up for lost time and proving that he wasn't coasting on his title so I wouldn't think, "Pretty good, for a crown prince." Also, some of the most courteous and deferential people can get roaringly liberated in bed. Edgar was one of those people.

Wonderful because an English person talking dirty can be very hot, as if a Jane Austen character snarled, "You really like that, don't you? Why don't you beg me."

Wonderful because for long stretches I forgot who he was and who I was, although I'll admit I did tell myself, *I'm having sex with the cover of People magazine!* If I tried not to think about this I'd fall apart, so I reasoned that maybe Edgar was thinking, "I'm having sex with a commoner!"

Wonderful because there was a moment when we looked into each other's eyes and got scared because we were starting to understand each other, physically and otherwise. Sex can be fun or boring or a million other things, but it can also be an introduction to something true about the other person. Something we were both being trusted with.

Wonderful because for the first time in my life I felt like I was exactly where I was supposed to be with exactly the right person.

Terrifying because of that last observation.

Exhilarating because after going to my sister's wedding, exchanging deeply personal information and having sex for the first time, we fell asleep in each other's arms, which is something that usually sounds good but is actually cramping and uncomfortable and makes getting up to use the bathroom difficult, but in this case, maybe because we couldn't get enough of each other's bodies, it worked.

CHAPTER 14

Edgar's phone started blowing up while we were having breakfast the next morning at IHOP. His face went very pale as he listened and said, "I didn't know . . . I have no idea . . . Calm down . . . I'll be right there."

"What? What's happening?"

"I'm not quite sure but we need to visit the British Consulate. Immediately."

The Midtown British Consulate was as stalwart and stuffy as I'd expected, but I didn't ask Edgar if he stayed there or just used it for meetings, because he'd swung into his Responsible World Leader mode, which I'd only caught glimpses of. He'd become extremely solemn and preoccupied, and I didn't want to get in his way.

We were ushered into a conference room with mahogany paneling and framed photos of British landmarks, and I tried not to think, *Ralph Lauren ad without the sailboats and three-thousand-*

dollar cashmere sweaters. James was waiting, along with two other people: a man in his fifties wearing a board of trustees–style blue suit and a younger blonde woman in a plum-colored shirtwaist dress, her Liberty of London scarf knotted with military precision.

"Your Highness," said the man.

"This is Marc Bracegirdle, my grandmother's equerry," said Edgar, "and Alison Talbot, the Palace media liaison."

"I'm Carter," I said, but before I could add my last name, Alison cut me off: "We know who you are."

"A situation is developing," said Marc, "which is causing Her Majesty great concern. It seems that a photo has been released and gone viral with global momentum. A compromising photo of the two of you."

Shots had already popped up online of Edgar and me kissing along the Hudson with bridesmaid selfies from Abby's wedding, but Edgar hadn't appeared to be bothered. "Let me see it," he told Alison, who offered her tablet with an image of Edgar and me in bed, shirtless and smiling, wearing our Burger King crowns.

"Who took this?" demanded Alison. "And who leaked it?"

"I took it," I said. "This morning. But I only sent it to Edgar, and there've been other pictures of us together, so what's the problem?"

"This is an extremely intimate portrait," said Marc.

"The other photos," added Alison, "were unfortunate, but you were both clothed and in public places. This verges on the pornographic."

"But you can't see anything!" I insisted. "And we just look happy!"

"And worst of all," Marc continued, ignoring me, "His Highness appears to be mocking the dignity of the Crown itself."

"So sorry I'm late," said someone instantly familiar, entering the room.

"My brother, Gerald," Edgar told me, but I'd already recognized Gerald, in his crisp blue shirt, blazer and gray flannels. Unlike Edgar, Gerald had typecast himself as a glossy young royal, meticulously groomed and proudly obedient. While two years younger than Edgar, Gerald seemed older; he was the child a teacher might put in charge of the classroom while she left to make a call, confident that Gerald would enumerate all infractions. I suspected that Gerald owned a large and exhaustively researched wristwatch with countless functions, including an orbital moon phase display. He stretched his arm so this watch peeked out from his French cuff, with a cuff link enameled with the royal crest. I didn't mean to pigeonhole him, but Gerald reeked of trying-too-hard.

"How could you let this happen?" Gerald said forcefully. "Especially after so many previous incidents."

"This isn't the same," said Edgar, but he sounded unsure.

"This photo has been viewed over fifty-eight million times," reported Alison, "and has appeared on the front page of the Sun, the *Daily Mail*, the *Guardian*, the *Observer* and on websites around the world. And as for the comments, well, you can just imagine. The two of you are being referred to as the Burger Kings, the Burger Boys and the Burger Queens."

Someone stifled a giggle, and I had the feeling it was James, which made me like him.

"I take no issue with your homosexuality," said Gerald, "but I'm extremely upset by your exposing our family, and especially Nana, to open ridicule. This photo is salacious and adolescent and demands an immediate response."

Of course I wanted to ask Edgar, "Do you and your brother call the Queen of England 'Nana'? Do you ever have to say 'Your Nanaship' or 'Your Nananess'?"

"I've drafted an official apology," said Alison. "And a statement referring to Mr. Ogden as merely a misguided acquaintance with an unfortunate history."

"As what?" I asked.

"We've come to believe that your phone has been hacked," said Marc, "and additional photos have begun circulating, including shots of you and a group of friends dressed as Lady Gaga at various stages in her career, along with a gallery of you and an actor named Callum Turner wearing almost nonexistent swimsuits and a Halloween portrait of you costumed as Princess Leia."

"The Jabba the Hutt metal bikini?" James inquired.

"The white sheath," said Alison disdainfully, "with the braided pastry hairdo."

I opened my mouth to say something, anything, in my defense, but quickly closed it. Most of these photos were souvenirs of my summers sharing a house on Fire Island—at the Gaga theme party I'd been wearing a subdued Star Is Born shag and white tank top, and sure, Callum and I had owned Speedos. I wasn't embarrassed by any of this until now, because the pictures had been sent to a batch of friends, the only people who'd cared.

But I felt slapped in the face by a fundamental contrast between my life and Edgar's. He was under tabloid surveillance every second of every day. I could stroll to Starbucks in my sweats or wear a rainbow jockstrap and tutu at a Burning Man party without a second thought. Edgar could never attempt any of this, not without an instantaneous worldwide backlash from strangers dissecting everything he wore or said, everyone he stood next to and, God forbid, anyone he had sex with. His warning from our night before was becoming a neon billboard.

"I . . . I'm so sorry," I sputtered, "I had no idea. I was so happy, and I wanted to remember the moment, and share it with Edgar."

"And you're a civilian," said Gerald, "which is a luxury Edgar cannot afford."

Edgar had been silent and watchful, weighing his response. While we hadn't done anything wrong, I'd betrayed him. He'd told me about his awful and particular problems with his past relationships, so often centering on privacy. I'd listened, but with the ear of a tourist or an Instagram follower, hungry for details of a celebrity's life and misfortunes. I was like most people, because I'd supposed that an invaded life and exposure to the relentless bitchery of a cruel and thoughtless public were simply the price to be paid in exchange for multiple castles, private air travel and gluttonous helpings of adoration. I'd considered this a fair trade: stardom for scrutiny.

But sitting here, as Edgar dealt with my mistake, and with his family and his country, I couldn't let him shoulder this or make excuses for me or be as generous and sympathetic as I knew he'd be. It wasn't fair.

"Okay," I said, "this is all my fault. I've been having such a great time, without thinking about fallout or consequences. So I'll bow out. I don't want to keep messing everything up, especially not for Edgar. I'm sure that you're all amazing at your jobs, so please fix this, and if there's anything I can do, please, please tell me, but the best and most helpful move I can make is to disappear, forever. And put my phone under the wheels of a truck. And I'm so sorry."

As I moved toward the door, Edgar said, "Carter," but I waved him off: "No, please, you've been—I can't even say how wonderful you've been, and you were so sweet to my family, and this is how I repaid you. So please don't be nice. Goodbye."

I left as fast as I could, and when I was at least five blocks away and out of breath, I leaned against the wall of an apartment building facing a small park. I hadn't let myself deconstruct the situation or have a breakdown or call anyone, not yet. But of course I'd known this would happen. I'd met an incredible guy and I'd fucked it up. I almost thought "royally," but stopped myself, because maybe someday, a few centuries from now, I'd be able to make jokes about my totally unlikely whirlwind royal tryst and how I'd sledgehammered it into oblivion, but not right now.

All I could think was *I want to die or vanish or rewind my life since birth and change everything so I'd never know this degree of heartache.* But my mom always told me to learn from my mistakes, "especially shredded jeans," so I told myself, there it is, absolute confirmation, the verdict is in without the slightest chance of appeal: I was never meant to fall in love. I was alone, again, like I should be. I was Carter You Fucking Idiot Ogden, and now a little girl, standing with her nanny, was staring at me as I crouched down, trying not to cry.

The girl asked the nanny, "What's wrong with that man?"

"Oh, honey," I muttered, as I stood up and started walking, "don't get me started."

CHAPTER 15

And he didn't try to stop you?" asked Adam, once I'd returned to the apartment. "I mean, shouldn't he have chased after you on the street and taken you in his arms and renounced the throne in the name of love?"

"But that wouldn't be productive," countered Louise, "because then he'd just be another useless unemployed pretty boy hanging around our kitchen and eating our food. He'd be Callum."

"He's not Callum," I said, tilting a family-size bag of chips to send the final dust tumbling down my throat. I wasn't just eating my feelings; I was pushing for a crap-induced coma to punctuate my did-I-do-the-right-thing nosedive. I'd silenced my phone to dodge the nonstop texts, voice mails and emails from reporters, bloggers and everyone I'd ever known, all thirsty for—what? The inside smut on dating Edgar? To punish me for detonating such a golden opportunity? To shame me for befouling the royal family?

There'd been a horde of paparazzi waiting for me outside our building, yelling fairly obscene questions, as if I was a low-level felon on my courthouse perp walk, handcuffed with my coat draped over my head. I'd absorbed an especially painful fact of Edgar's life: his emotions, from the dizziest happiness to the most profound grief, had to be polished and performed for public consumption. Like it or not, the world would always be watching, so even someone merely celebrity-adjacent had to construct an attitude, either toughing things out or playing for wide-eyed, caught-in-the-crossfire pity.

I got why stars repeat an identical pose in all photographs, with their legs adroitly angled, their chins down and their palms placed to shield any less-than-ideal body parts. They're controlling the narrative, at the cost of a grim sameness; they're turning themselves into blandly almost-smiling, faultless brand ambassadors.

Louise handed me her phone; it was my mom. "Sweetheart, I know you've got your phone off but I just needed to know that you're okay. I saw the photo of you and Edgar and I thought you both looked adorable, a little pasty, but like such a cute couple. And it was so nice to meet him, and I'm just going to say this, he's a big step up from Callum, who I never trusted, ever since I figured out he was wearing blue contacts."

There was a knock at our front door, and Adam checked the peephole: "It's him. Edgar. Do you want to see him?"

"Don't do it," advised Louise. "It might be a trap. He probably has his goons with him to shove a bag over your head and drag you to England to be put on trial for looking better than him in the picture."

"That's not true," said Edgar, from behind the door. "I don't have goons and we both looked good."

"Let him in," said my mom, still on the phone, just to me. "At least hear him out."

I nodded and Adam opened the door and there was Edgar. I couldn't read his expression, because he'd adopted the gracious, noncommittal, official mask of his public appearances. But he clearly had something to say, a speech he'd been refining on his way over, and maybe he'd run it past James.

"I must apologise," he began, "for how abysmally and inhumanely you were treated by my staff. None of this was your doing; you hadn't been prepared for—a royal uproar. And the stranger thing is, neither was I. After all these years and so many mishaps, you'd think I'd have developed a protocol, or a thicker skin. But I did what I always do under pressure: I retreated. I locked my emotions in a strongbox, in the smallest room of the highest tower, where I could look down on the world without participating. But that needs to end. And so I have a proposal. First, I'll ask you to become more aware—of certain parameters, of the detours I've invented for sidestepping constant exposure. But far more importantly, I have an unequivocal demand."

"A demand?"

"I've met your family, which began to explain so much about you. So I insist you meet mine."

Adam and Louise exchanged a not-uninterested glance, and my mom, thrilled to be eavesdropping via the phone, said, so only I could hear, "I'm liking this. I'm intrigued. Tell him to keep going."

"How?" I asked Edgar. "How would I meet your family?"

"Well, you've skirmished with Gerald, and not at his best. So I'm inviting you to travel, as my guest, to London, for a week or however long you'd like, to stay in the palace and tangle with the most bizarre and unhinged creatures on Earth—the royal family. Who, if they weren't absurdly wealthy and impossible to fire, would be found working in a carnival or in jail."

"Wait," I said. "You want me to stay at Buckingham Palace and meet . . ."

"The Queen of England," my mother hissed in my ear.

"Your grandmother," I translated.

"Yes," said Edgar.

"If you don't do this," my mom continued, "if you don't give Edgar a chance, you'll regret it for the rest of your life. Hand him this phone."

I passed Edgar the phone and he listened patiently, saying, "Yes . . . Yes . . . Of course . . . You as well . . . Yes, it's spotless . . . No, I would never do that . . . All expenses paid . . . Of course. I'll tell him."

Edgar hung up and told me, "Your mother says you should pack twice as much clean underwear as you think you'll need and that Miriam believes English aspirin is better than American so you must bring back five bottles, and Miriam also says that if I do anything to bring shame on the Ogdens, she will, and I believe her exact words were, 'come over there.'"

"Watch out," I said.

"What I'd prefer is this," Edgar went on. "We were having such a lovely time, and I don't want that interrupted. If you disagree and have deduced that I'm a bonehead, a jellyfish and a rotten deal overall and that you're lucky to have fled my pampered royal clutches, I can't argue the point. Although I might add that your mother did request guest soaps from a palace loo, that you remember to wear the russet suede jacket which she likes so much, and which she gave you, and that you follow your heart. What I'm saying is, let's find out where this goes. Let's try to circumvent the world and the media and all of those prying eyes and chattering voices."

"Do we get a vote?" asked Louise.

"I vote yes!" said Adam, vigorously raising his hand, "and Du-Shawn's at rehearsal, which means I have his proxy, so that means two votes yes!"

"Louise?" asked Edgar.

"Well, I think you're the enemy of equality and human rights and any halfway decent form of socialism. And that in a perfect world you'd be forced to get a job without health insurance or sick days or parental leave. And you'd sell the crown jewels and donate the proceeds to the homeless, Black Lives Matter, that fund for women candidates of color and buying me a new MacBook."

"And you also have to find Louise a new girlfriend," Adam improvised, and Louise concurred wholeheartedly.

"So that's a yes?" asked Edgar.

"Yeah," said Louise, still skeptical. "But only because Carter really needs to get laid more often, and from what Adam and DuShawn and I overheard, it sounded like you guys were at least getting started."

"Carter?"

The millions of voices in my head had launched an epic election-year-caliber debate, bellowing opposing positions regarding self-respect, guarantees, the feeble odds for love and the ironclad certainty of catastrophe. But I came across an emotional override function, which might've just been installed as an upgrade. I looked into Edgar's eyes and saw that his smile was being held in check until I'd answered. I couldn't be responsible for imprisoning that smile, and I had feelings for Edgar that were so strong I couldn't go anywhere near them, not yet, and I argued that whatever happened or didn't happen, I could always blame my mother.

Adam gave me his phone. It was Abby, FaceTiming me from her honeymoon on Bali. Behind her were palm trees, miles of white sand and Dane in sunglasses and board shorts with zinc oxide on his nose.

"Mom just filled me in on everything," she said. "And I saw the pictures online, and everyone in Bali agrees that both of you guys should at least think about self-tanner, but we all agree Edgar's shoulders are to die for."

Dane raised his ice-blue tropical cocktail with a pineapple wedge and a hibiscus.

"And Edgar asked you to go to England, right," Abby continued, "and meet his family, which is a good sign, because it means you're not just a hookup, and right now you're driving yourself crazy with self-doubt and social anxiety and trying to decide what to do. So please hold up the phone so Edgar and everyone else can see me."

I did as I was told.

"YES!!!" Abby howled as Dane pumped his fist in the air. Then Abby added, "And I can't believe we're talking about any of this when everyone should still be gushing about my dress."

"Your dress was exquisite," Edgar told her. "Recalling your dress was the only way Carter and I achieved orgasm."

Abby yelled "YES!!!" at a volume that made me hold the phone a yard from my ear. Because the crowd, on two continents, had spoken, I closed the comments section and asked Edgar, "When do we leave?"

CHAPTER 16

Cassandra put up a fight over giving me a week off, ranting about her busiest season and the L'Oreal Sizzling Shades of Summer product launch and the Dapplemans' *Frozen II*–themed brunch for their daughter's graduation from preschool, until I played the royalty card and handed Edgar the phone so he could tell Cassandra, "Darling Cassie, it's Edgar, and I'm so sorry, but I need to borrow our boy for just a spell, which we'll tell you all about at a very private dinner once we return, thank you so much, and yes, I will make certain my grandmother takes a good long look at your website, including the recently rethought section covering pre-engagement hayrides."

A few hours later a car picked me up, along with my tired black nylon wheeled duffel, which everyone has, and to which I'd knotted a rainbow ribbon for identification on the luggage carousel, like everyone does. I'd imagined we'd be leaving from JFK, but the car soon pulled into a small private airport and drove directly onto the tarmac, parking beside the royal jet, where James was waiting by the stairs.

There was no malfunctioning electronic check-in with an additional charge for my second bag.

No winding, double-backed line for passport control.

I didn't have to remove my shoes and belt, or deposit my keys, wallet and loose change in a bacteria-clogged plastic tub.

I wasn't patted down or wanded or told to put my devices in a separate bin.

I didn't trudge for miles, while one of the wheels on my luggage broke off, before someone told me I was in the wrong terminal.

I didn't juggle my backpack, my phone and whatever Starbucks was calling a muffin these days while I searched for my boarding pass.

I didn't sit in a packed waiting area beside screaming babies and strangers falling asleep on my shoulder, for hours, until the flight was delayed and then canceled.

I didn't have to browse through purple velour, foam-filled neck pillows at a kiosk, because I'd finished my reading material, twice.

Welcome to private air travel.

Edgar was already onboard, and we sat side by side in what were basically honey-colored kidskin couches with seat belts, like deluxe baseball mitts for people, with Gerald and James a few acres away. The plane left at Edgar's signal.

Louise is absolutely right: life isn't fair, the rich are evil and my only defense is that I was being kidnapped.

A smiling, relaxed flight attendant offered us menus, angora blankets and a choice of warm cashews or—no, I stopped her right after the cashews and she said, "I'll bring you a large bowl, and don't hesitate to request refills."

Edgar was observing this, entertained. "I should mention," he told me, "that I find the use of this jet reprehensible and I'm advocating to end my family's private travel entirely and to have this plane recommissioned for use in transporting medical services and emergency food supplies to nations in crisis."

"I'm with you on that," I said, but my words were garbled by my mouthful of cashews and my experimenting with the control panel, which governed a choice of first-run movies, a raised footrest and task lighting.

"But meanwhile, there's something else I should bring up. There's a private stateroom at the rear of the main cabin."

We both nodded, like the gutter rats we were. We should be flying MRI machines, mosquito netting and surgical gowns to war-torn lands, but instead I followed Edgar down the aisle, passing Gerald, who was playing video rugby on his iPad, and James, who murmured, "Well, aren't we the dirty little mile-high whores. Your Highness."

We waved to Edgar's security team, and Ian said, "I win the bet. It took the two of you under three minutes to head back there."

"We'll be viewing your activities on the stateroom monitors," said Lucky, and then, "No we won't. Unless there's nothing on Hulu."

"We're glad you're with us, Carter," said Terry. "Unless we have to kill you."

I called out to the flight attendant, "Extra cashews for everyone!"

The stateroom was small but still would've rented for many

thousands of dollars as a New York studio apartment. There was a compact marble bathroom and a king-size (I didn't say anything) bed, and the walls were padded silk embroidered with a repeat of the royal crest. Edgar shut the door behind us.

Our first night of sex had been hyperemotional, frenzied and an Internet sensation. I'd changed my numbers and passwords and, under the guidance of Edgar's palace tech crew, downloaded the most updated anti-malware protection to discourage further hacking. I hadn't posted anything on any platform since Edgar and I had gone viral. Not being on Twitter or Instagram or whatever else was disconcerting, like missing a phantom limb; sometimes my thumbs twitched, sending air texts into the twilight zone. But maybe a time-out from social media would be healthy for me; I became my mom, lecturing myself, "Put down that phone and get some fresh air. Or use the time to read a book or have more sex with Prince Edgar."

We were in the sky somewhere over the Atlantic, with porthole windows available only to really ambitious seagulls. Private air travel is decadent, but it's one of the hushed spaces where the rich and famous can be truly alone. This also explains their sprawling estates, bunker-like home theaters and gargantuan armored limos, all of which create a buffer between the privileged and the rest of us. Maybe privacy is their most-prized and vigilantly guarded luxury.

But before I could pursue this line of thought, Edgar had removed his blazer, folded it neatly and dropped it on the floor. I tugged my sweater off over my head, leaving my face flushed and my hair crazed. There was a bed between us for about two seconds. We lay down facing each other and I traced Edgar's upper lip with my forefinger because I knew it would make him smile.

Edgar ran his own forefinger along the side of my neck because he knew it would make me tremble.

We kissed hungrily but then moved apart, because we had time.

I unbuttoned Edgar's shirt and slid my hand inside, as he moaned. His hand went to the zipper of my jeans; my hips lurched, and I made a sound that I wondered if James, Gerald and the security team had heard, but the door was solid, and if I couldn't make noise I should just grab a parachute and once I was in the water, let the Coast Guard rescue me.

I touched Edgar's hair, questioning if there was anything I could do to make him look less incredible. There wasn't. He leaned in for another kiss, a major one, a lasting one, as our hands moved everywhere, and being on a plane made squirming out of our clothes even sexier. I have no idea how airplanes work or what keeps them aloft, but I quickly learned that soaring through the clouds, surrounded only by air, by nothing, by a miracle, makes being naked unbelievably exciting, and I decided that astronauts' spacesuits are designed to be cumbersome so they won't keep ripping them off and drifting ravenously toward each other en route to Mars.

Edgar had the sort of gangly, leanly muscled, lightly freckled body that I adored; sex with Callum had been great but ridiculous, because he was so cartoon handsome and gym-built that I felt like either his tote bag or a piece of exercise equipment. Sex with Edgar was much more intense and human and raw; he was all over me, as if sex was one of the few places where he didn't have to behave himself, and I stopped worrying and did whatever I wanted, daring myself to treat a crown prince like a hot guy I'd picked up on a street corner.

We did everything two guys can do and then we did it again,

until the stateroom was strewn with sheets and pillows and what I think was a sable coverlet. You can tell sex is good when you make an unholy mess; great sex looks like a crime scene, as if thieves have turned the place and each other upside down. Personally, I know I've had an amazing time when I abandon my usual instincts to straighten everything up or use a detergent pen to pretreat stubborn stains.

Finally we lay in each other's arms, panting and exhausted, with our hands still exploring each other, until we whimpered because we'd worn each other out, and everything ached and felt wonderful and we both had the beginnings of some passionate bruises and beard rash. Edgar didn't cultivate scruff the way Callum had, but his beard grew quickly and felt like, well, like a man's beard against my skin, which is probably the real cause of male homosexuality.

"We have to stop," said Edgar, licking my ear.

"Yes, Your Highness."

There was a pause: had I gone too far and mocked Edgar or insulted him?

"I could have you beheaded."

As we dozed, I thought about hunting down a robe, activating my phone and texting Abby, who would love to hear about Edgar's plane. I caught myself: I had only the tiniest, earliest sense of Edgar's life. He was an international symbol of LGBTQ pride and a figure of . . . I wasn't sure what, exactly—limited but valuable power? Regal influence when it came to causes and whatever riding boots he chose to be photographed wearing? Or did he embody nothing besides entitlement, luck and undeniable stardom? And what did that make me? A new friend? A hanger-on? Or a glorified fan—a fan with benefits?

I was glad we were headed to England so I could experience
Edgar at home and at work, whatever the work of being a crown
prince might consist of. I had no concept of what I might be in
for, but I wasn't dating just some bright, great-looking, promising
new guy. It was more like having incredible sex with English history, and a key player in the English economy, and a controversial
chapter in any book on queer representation, where Edgar's
mainstream status would be compared with the profiles of scrap-
pier, embattled heroes. Which brought up the most critical and
thought-provoking question of all: who would play me in the
movie version, and in the sex scene on the royal jet, would there
be frontal male nudity, and would I have approval of a body
double?

I couldn't wrap my brain around any of this, so I shut my eyes,
put my hand on Edgar's chest and fell gratefully asleep. We were
awakened by the clunk of landing gear in operation and James
tapping forcefully at the door, saying, without lowering his voice,
"Stop groping one another, you repellent little sex rodents. We're
in England. There are laws."

CHAPTER 17

And you've really never been to London?" Edgar asked as we were being driven from the airport and I'd rolled down my window to take in everything, like a basset hound tasting the breeze with his ears flapping.

"Not since I was seven years old, with my family. My parents wanted to make sure I appreciated everything, but all I remember is a blur of statues and brown buildings, and thinking the money was fake because it wasn't American."

Now I was devouring one landmark after another, the war memorials and department stores and curving rows of limestone townhouses; being a child of the Jersey suburbs, I was searching for Harry Potter getting swarmed by wraithlike Dementors, Julia Roberts dropping by a postcard-quaint Notting Hill, and any of the James Bonds zipping across London Bridge in an Aston Martin. I could hear my mom recounting the history of Hugh Grant's hair and my dad treating the entire city as an illustrated lesson plan: "Did you know that Big Ben was silenced during the Blitz so the chimes wouldn't attract Nazi warplanes?" Abby, of course, would be clutching a guidebook annotated in glittery hot pink magic marker with locations of bakeries, theaters, museums and the homes of Kate Winslet, Adele and Robert Pattinson, along with wherever Orlando Bloom went for a daily run.

I couldn't decide if being with Edgar made me less of a tourist, or as if I was visiting Disney World with Walt himself, or if I'd become one of those fifteenth-century sheltered French or Austrian princesses being shipped overseas to make a politically expedient marriage.

Of course, I was all of these things, but I cautioned myself sternly, *Expect nothing. This is a week off, a fun vacation abroad, and that's it.* The second I rated this trip as anything beyond a fling, I'd be fooling myself and attracting the most savage emotional crash. This would be my mantra: protect yourself at all costs. Ruth Ginsburg's voice advised me, "Be careful, bubbelah, but don't be a jerk. Have a good time and tell the queen I say hello!"

Okay, I gave myself exactly five seconds to inwardly scream, *I'M IN LONDON WITH PRINCE EDGAR AND WE JUST HAD SEX ON HIS PRIVATE JET AND NOW WE'RE HEADED TO HIS HOUSE! FUCK ME! LITERALLY!*

"And here we are," said Edgar as the uniformed sentries kept the onlookers at bay, the huge wrought iron gates swung open and the car glided smoothly across an immense courtyard, right toward:

BUCKINGHAM PALACE!!!

"Stop shouting," said Ruth.

I had to quit delivering the breathless voice-over for a docu-series called Carter's English Adventure, and I couldn't continue leaning on Ruth. But calming my inner spokespeople wouldn't be easy. My life was a mash-up of live-action fairy tale, queer rom-com and a video game encapsulating elements of both. Abby always told me to keep saying yes, and I was holding on for dear life. Edgar was helping me to stay somewhere in the vicinity of grounded, but what if he was a flickering hologram, a projection of my fantasies who'd vanish once I removed my virtual reality headset?

The car halted outside the stately front entrance as the security team drove in behind us and additional staff members retrieved my luggage, greeted Edgar in respectful, low voices and opened the massive oak doors. This was something else I wasn't accustomed to: the sheer number of ultraefficient people who facilitated Edgar's every move. He was like a serene A-list movie idol forever inching toward a soundstage as he was being fussed over by a small army of handlers, assistants and hair and makeup people. Edgar dealt with this constant attention in a spirit of gratitude and common sense, rather than annoyance or vanity. Being famous can be a skill and a contact sport. Edgar had a champion's ease.

"Shall we?" said Edgar, gesturing to the palace interior, as James said, in my ear, "There are cameras everywhere. Don't take anything."

The entryway was grand, with a tile floor and plenty of gleaming, carved woodwork, but it was manageable, so I thought, *Fine, it's like a really nice old hotel in, say, Canada. I can do this.* Then another set of doors was opened, leading to a majestic, towering great hall that went on forever, giving me full-on vertigo; at first I couldn't grasp the exact size of the room or how many fireplaces and mirrors and marble columns it contained, along with potted palms, statues of Greek gods and porcelain vases over six feet tall. It made me unsteady, and Edgar obligingly touched my elbow, giving me a time-out to breathe.

How do people live like this? I know that palaces are designed to impress and intimidate, and to establish royal authority, but what was it like to be greeted by this every morning, to breeze through it, to get home at the end of a long day and drop your stuff somewhere on the premises, to grow up here? Was it normal, like anyone's house, if anyone's house could hold the entire state I grew up in?

"This will be your room," said Edgar, and it took me a beat to get that he was joking, because I was so goggle-eyed and weak-kneed and gaping. Stepping into a palace is like walking on the moon or the ocean floor; it takes not just getting used to but a different center of gravity. It also smelled wonderful, a mix of old-world mustiness, time-tested polishes and waxes, abundant floral displays and what I can only call architectural magic. It hit me: this was like living inside Saint Patrick's Cathedral, which was one of my fondest dreams: a cathedral with comfortable seating and fewer pointed sermons about Satan's wrath. An associate event architect's paradise.

"We'll do the full tour," said Edgar, "but first let's get you settled. With my grandmother in residence, the team thought it best that you have your own quarters."

"The team" included James, Marc, Alison and a roster of people with their own offices and agendas. My relationship with Edgar had been fed into some communal database, and I bet there were poll numbers, Venn diagrams and weekly projections, which I wouldn't be granted access to; I'd guess how I was scoring from the pep talks and rueful sighs. Edgar led me past drawing

rooms and parlors and arboretums as he kept up a running com-
mentary: "It's a lot to take in, but basically the palace is a square
constructed around a courtyard, with public spaces and gardens
and God only knows what. I've been told there are seven hundred
and seventy-two rooms, and as a child I kept a notebook, because
I was determined to visit every one of them, as if they were plan-
ets or mountain peaks, but I gave up after fifty-eight, when James
found me sobbing in some antechamber, insisting I was in Edin-
borough."

A distinction: if Edgar and I were mapping the tract home I
grew up in, we'd have been done with the eight rooms in minutes
and begun lazing in the carport or finished basement, watching
cheesy horror movies, scarfing barely thawed frozen snacks and
masturbating, which are New Jersey's officially recognized state
hobbies.

I also suspected that, if my mother and I were left alone in the
palace, we could scope out, critique and diagram the whole lay-
out over, say, a long weekend, rearranging the furniture for con-
versational flow. We have a gift for speed-browsing and have
decimated five malls in a single afternoon.

"Here we are," said Edgar, after we'd trekked down a long,
wallpapered hallway with brass sconces and multiple oak doors;
sections of the palace resembled sets for murder mysteries, or an
interactive version of Clue, which had originated in England as
Cluedo (something my dad had told me while beating me at
Scrabble).

As we entered a bedroom suite, James was unpacking the last
of my sad luggage and placing my clothing in drawers and an ar-
moire after airing my sweaters and touching up my shirts with
an iron.

"James," I told him, "thank you so much, but you don't have to do that."

"I'm afraid I must, if I hope to get any sleep. Cheap, wrinkled clothing from chain stores can haunt me."

"James is a perfect storm of anal compulsive behavior," Edgar explained. "He's what happens when you cross a Roomba with a Royal Marine. He's what we call a power nanny."

"And if I weren't here His Highness would be having sloppy intimate relations with the sort of person who owns a raspberry cashmere hoodie from Uniqlo. Oh, I'm so sorry, that's already happened."

I loved becoming part of Edgar and James's conversations; they were a slightly more queer version of Kirk and Spock, or Luke Skywalker and Yoda after a few martinis. (I could conjure James instructing Edgar to use the Force, to fold a fitted sheet).

"I hope this will be all right," said Edgar, with genuine concern, even though the suite boasted a four-poster bed, a sitting area, a dressing room, a spa-like bathroom and enough additional furniture for a high-end antiques auction.

"I don't know. Is there a futon?"

"I warned you," James told Edgar. "Americans aren't comfortable without things that fold up or down."

"I'm two doors away to the right," said Edgar. "But for now, I think we could both use some rest. If you need anything, there are call buttons beside the bed for the household staff and James will be sleeping on a cot in the hallway."

"My own cot?" said James. "You spoil me."

"Come along and let's leave Carter in peace."

As James left, Edgar grabbed me for a quick, steamy, welcome-to-my-house kiss, which threatened to become something more until we heard James call out, from the hallway, "The antibiotics are in the wicker basket."

"Until tomorrow," said Edgar, smoldering as if he was a notorious highwayman leaping out my window onto his steed.

With Edgar gone I poked around, as if there'd be a mini-bar or a coffemaker, and I read a text from my mom: "I'm so jealous. Please give Edgar my best and don't eat in bed because even in palaces they have bugs. Don't embarrass me."

If the Ogdens had a coat of arms it would depict a Swiffer crossed with a can of Lemon Pledge and the motto "Don't Embarrass Me," in both Latin and Hebrew.

I had a text from Abby as well: "If you don't tell me everything I'll have you edited out of my wedding video. Bali and Dane still fabulous. Kiss Edgar and act shocked if he thinks you're gay."

I put on a T-shirt and tapered sweatpants, the kind straight guys wear to the office. I slipped beneath the many layers of high-thread-count, down-filled bedding, not disturbing any of it, because I was a guest. I would be an illustration in a textbook on invitee correctness, which meant acting as if I wasn't there. I reminded myself, *Just breathe, you're a human being in a nice room in a big house*, as the rest of my brain screamed with laughter.

I had trouble getting to sleep, because of the time change and because I wanted to crawl down the hallway to Edgar's bed, but I admonished myself to demonstrate effortless self-control. Of course the more I clenched my eyes shut and tried to will myself asleep, the more I wriggled around and heard my stomach growl (I'd only had three bowls of cashews on the plane, because I'm not an animal). The call buttons beckoned, but I didn't want to wake anybody up, so I left my room in search of a kitchen or pantry or royal vending machine—Edgar had told me there was a palace ATM in the basement, shattering the myth of the royals never carrying cash. But a home ATM isn't exactly a foosball table.

I crept along hallways and down a mammoth staircase where brass rods held the carpeting in place; I longed for an illuminated map, like the mall directories for pinpointing the Banana Republic outlet and the Sunglass Hut. It crossed my mind: did the palace have a dungeon? A pub for family members? Its own post office overseen by a kindly robot in a tweed vest, like something at the North Pole in a wholesome holiday movie?

I came upon a grand dining room and leaned against a wall, which opened: it was a concealed servants' entrance. I found myself in a more practical, cream-colored brick hallway with industrial lighting fixtures, as if I was onboard a submarine, or in the steam tunnels beneath Grand Central Station.

I pushed open a heavy steel door to a kitchen capable of feeding everyone in England, or five American teenagers. It was both historic and immaculate, with a walk-in freezer, white subway tile and battered metal tables for food prep. From my event work I knew this area would normally be filled with diligent personnel in white aprons, Crocs and hairnets, the backbone of any gala.

I investigated a tanklike refrigerator and helped myself to a pitcher of milk. There was an opened carton of wheat crackers in a nearby cabinet. As I sampled a cracker a voice cried, "Thief! For shame!"

I froze. A small but sturdy woman stood in the kitchen doorway, wearing a sensible cotton nightdress and well-worn slippers, with her hair wrapped in a coiffure-protecting satin turban. She was Queen Catherine, Edgar's grandmother. I recognized her from countless photos and Edgar's ten-pound note.

"What are you doing here, you malignant reptile?"

Oh no. Jesus. I'd crossed the Atlantic to meet this woman, and I'd planned on showcasing myself at my most polished, as humble and civilized and an irresistibly articulate and well-groomed companion for her grandson. And here I was, in sweats, bleary from the flight, with God knows what in my hair, and Queen Catherine was insulting me and shooting lasers from her eyes and about to hoist a cleaver from a rack on the wall and slice off at least one of my larcenous hands.

"I . . . I'm so sorry, I'm Carter, I'm a guest of Edgar's . . ."

I was saying this with a partially chewed cracker in my mouth, crumbs of which were spewing out and onto the floor. Not my best look, with my words barely intelligible. I was like a greedy raccoon, caught in the glare of a homeowner's flashlight as I rooted through the recycling bins.

"You're him," said the queen. "You're that dreadful person in the photograph who humiliated my grandson, myself and the Commonwealth. And here you are, stealing foodstuffs from my larder."

"I'm sorry, I'll put it right back and I'll pay for whatever I've eaten—"

"Stand up. Let me see you."

I'd been crouched, rifling through a lower cabinet. I swallowed the rest of my cracker, almost choked, stood and moved closer to the queen, but not too close, because I didn't want to come off as disrespectful and because while Catherine was eighty-two years old and seemingly unarmed, she was a powerful physical presence, like the most superior, battle-ready, potentially lethal pitbull, off its leash.

"You resemble the photo, only you're wearing more clothing

and you've misplaced your cheap paper crown. You look like an American homosexual."

Was this a slur? A compliment? Would "an American homosexual" appear beneath my chin in my Scotland Yard mugshot?

"I . . . I do?"

"You look oddly innocent, even cheerful, and yet absurd. You're not unattractive and you haven't yet become as large and misshapen as many of your fellow citizens, particularly the politicians. Your hair strikes me as strenuously curated, your skin is acceptable, your dental work remains one of your homeland's rare virtues, and your feet are inexplicably clean."

I was barefoot, which made me feel naked. But I wished I'd recorded the queen's reference to cleanliness, to forward to my mom.

"I'm trying to imagine what my grandson sees in you. Are you some breed of double-jointed sexual prodigy?"

"Yes. Cirque du Soleil. Vegas."

I was so scared that I'd aimed for a joke, lacking any other option. There was an extended silence, and then the queen approached smiling, but thought better of it. Her disdain remained absolute but my approval rating had shifted some microscopic iota.

"Come closer."

I walked slowly, in case this was a trick and she was luring me toward a hidden trapdoor, where I'd plunge into a palace subbasement and land among the skeletons of previous interlopers. To postpone this fate, I held out the box of crackers.

"Would you . . . ?"

"You dare to offer me a cracker, which belongs to me? Have you lost your mind and all sense of decency and decorum? Yes, I would like one."

I handed her a cracker, carefully and at arm's length, not making any sudden moves. As Queen Catherine nibbled:

"This cracker is dry, flavorless and ancient, which I prefer. I'd been told, by Mr. Bracegirdle and Ms. Talbot, that Edgar had sought to issue an invitation to you, a morally objectionable creature. At first I refused on principle, but I reconsidered. I was strategic: if there was a fractional hope of Edgar seeing you for whom and what you truly are, and thereby recognizing your utter unsuitability and sending you packing, then he must witness you among his people, and in his home. Where you will diminish and crumble, much like this cracker, and be swallowed by cold, harsh reality."

She sipped from my glass of milk, which I'd left on a countertop.

I was about to either slink away in abject defeat or compose an outraged speech on behalf of the American dream, gay civil rights, and esteemed associate event architects who'd changed the course of history, who I'd invent, when the queen added, "Or not."

"Your Majesty?"

I'd Googled: Edgar was Your Highness, Catherine was Your Majesty and the rest of us are just zip codes.

"You assume that I'm some unspeakable, intractable ogre, rooted in the fossilised prejudice of centuries long past. Perhaps because you've glimpsed my slippers. But I have only one real desire, and that is for Edgar's happiness and that of his brother. So I'll ask three simple questions, and should you answer acceptably, I shall countenance your presence for the next several days."

"Go ahead. Ask me."

I could do this. I was a Trivial Pursuit grand master. I'd watched so many pageants where Miss Nebraska had sailed through the personality quiz on what she'd tell her younger self (she'd recommend "Don't worry so much" but what she really meant was "Sleep with the judges"). I'm good under pressure. And if Edgar could face off with Abby and Miriam, I could handle Nana.

"Will you be able to avoid any and all further embarrassment to the Crown?" the queen began. "Because Edgar cannot afford additional infamy."

"I'll try. I promise. Because I would never want to do that."

"Excuse me, but does your T-shirt read 'Honey, Just Don't'?"

The shirt had been a birthday gift from Adam.

"Is that your next question?"

"Certainly not. My next question is: Are you a person of integrity? Do you believe in doing what is just and necessary, no matter the cost?"

"Yes. Unless I know in my deepest heart that being ruthlessly honest will only hurt the other person and that their new haircut will eventually grow out."

"Finally: do you love my grandson?"

"What?"

"You heard me. My late husband Richard loved me deeply, and this provided an essential balance to every challenge. If a human being is loved, they have strength. If Edgar isn't loved, on his own merits, I fear for him. And should you only pretend love, from lesser motives, I will see you not only removed but demolished. Edgar has undergone more than his portion of tragedy, and I will not permit another heartbeat of sorrow. So I ask: do you love him?"

I hadn't let myself get anywhere near this question. Edgar and I had been flung together and were making our way. I'd made awful mistakes. Love under any circumstances is the greatest risk, the most highwire undertaking, and I'd fooled myself in the past. I wanted to be in love, this yearning defined me, but I'd spent far too long, my entire life, arguing myself out of it. I wasn't worthy, I wasn't anyone's type, my trapezius muscles were nonexistent, I drooled when I slept, I still hadn't found the right pair of jeans, I was a minefield of quirks and obsessions and excuses.

The queen was waiting. My mom would tell me, "Of course you're worthy of love, even if the sideburns were a mistake we all lived through, because the left side never really kept up. Haven't I taught you that everyone deserves to be loved, except serial killers, people who eat smelly food on the subway, and anyone who hits a child, even a child who keeps kicking the airplane seat in front of him? But you can't lie to Queen Catherine, because she's been around the block, and she'll know. She's lost her daughter, her son-in-law and her husband, and she hasn't shattered, at least not in public. She's tough, and her grandsons are all she has. So do this: picture Edgar's face. Then imagine you'll never get to see that face ever again. You'll know."

I did this. I wasn't sure if I believed in love at first sight, or even after only a few weeks; it's so unlikely, the equivalent of learning another language from a single conversation, or memorizing a library at a glance. But—Edgar's face. Smiling.

"Yes," I told Queen Catherine. "I love Edgar, but I haven't told him, not yet, so please respect that. He's a wonderful man, and I came here to see if I can make him happy, which I probably can't. But I am sure fucking going to try."

I'd just said "fucking" to Queen Catherine. What was I thinking? Had I broken some ultimate taboo? But I wanted her to understand that I'd meant what I said. And there was something about the queen, something feral and watchful and shrewd; she'd heard the word "fucking" before. She'd used it. We weren't on equal footing, but we'd both made our positions clear. Game on.

"We shall fucking see," said Queen Catherine.

CHAPTER 18

Edgar had a full schedule of meetings the next morning, but by noon we were in a car on our way to Wembley Stadium, just outside the city.

"Are you keen on rugby?"

In these politically forward, stereotype-busting times, I should reply that, as a proud queer man, I'm as capable of following sports as anyone else. Except I hate them. All of them. I don't like having anything thrown to or at me, or running around a field chasing a small object, or a slightly larger object, or staking my self-esteem on defeating another team or individual in the course of a bewildering competition that causes head injuries. And of course I think that certain athletes are combustibly hot, especially when as naked as possible, but like opera and ballet, I feel sports should exist only as still photography.

I don't hate sports because I'm not man enough or because I never played catch with my dad or because I've never given them a chance. I hate sports because I'm sane and have taste and know that going to the gym is about being able to wear a T-shirt to brunch afterward. Of course I'll aggressively cheer for a victorious female soccer team led by lesbians and honored with a ticker tape parade. But that's as far as I go.

"You know, I don't think I've ever been to a rugby game."

"Match. A rugby match."

"Or that either."

"But you're sure you'll hate it."

"I'm sure that I'll like anything as long as I'm sitting next to you."

We both burst out laughing.

"I was fairly certain you'd be resistant, and I actually adore rugby, but I'm scheming, because I adore you as well, and I want England to share that. But just right now, due to an incident in Manhattan involving a photograph of two fellows in bed, which I've entirely forgotten, England is somewhat divided. On the subject of you."

"Listen to this," said James, from the front seat, checking his phone. "It's from a squalid, wholly objectionable gossip website which I'm addicted to. And they're taking a poll. Is Carter Ogden A) A gold-digging nonentity, B) An amateur porn star, or C) A Soviet agent. How shall I vote? Oh, wait, there's an additional choice, D) An Associate Event Albatross."

I'd been veering away from these sites and royalty-oriented YouTube channels and the TMZ-style cable shows that I'd once mainlined. But Adam and Louise had sent me the GIFs of King Kong, with my head, clambering up Big Ben with Edgar in my paw; Edgar's and my heads transposed onto a *Dancing with the Stars* tango; and *Drag Race* contestants blessedly supporting us by saying things like "Hate the hate, not the boys." My mom has always told me, "Don't feed the trolls," but when an exceptionally nasty, bigoted tweet got the better of her, she'd log on with, "Carter Ogden is a terrific man and why don't you just fuck off right back to your Klan rally, shithead."

Like everyone else, I'd always guessed that celebrity dish never drew blood and that the stars, wannabes and bottom-feeders hoarded the clicks, because while all publicity isn't really good publicity, at least it's free publicity. But now that I was playing for the other team, even as just a water boy, it was hard not to get defensive and to keep my hand from wandering to the keyboard, despite the fact that any kinder comment ("I think Edgar and Carter are hot, even if I'm the only one!") was invariably met by a raging flood of anti-LGBTQ, anti-Semitic, anti-royal family sewage.

"Here's how to deal with the Internet," Edgar explained. "Never read anything more than once. Don't fall down a comments k-hole and waste your afternoon. And remember that while nothing really goes away, something always lands a few seconds later to replace it. So when somebody says I'm getting chubby, or that I'm dealing crystal meth, or that I'm, and these are my favourites, 'rubbing my gayness in the world's faces' or 'shoving it down everyone's throats,' I pray that Kim Kardashian will have another baby or another divorce, or introduce another buttock-firming miracle cream, or appear nude atop a Ferris wheel, to take the heat off of me."

Fair enough, but the real reason I might return to monitoring the online mood was to chart a course toward pleasing Queen Catherine and making Edgar proud of me. The pendulum might be swinging, because my mom just sent me someone's tweet reading "Carter is cute in a nonthreatening, prom-date-placeholder, basic gay way." I'm getting there!

"Today," said Edgar as the car approached the stadium, "will also be our first official appearance together, so I should prepare you."

"There are rules," said James. "The royals are to be presented with dignity and restraint at all times. So you must stand slightly behind His Highness and never overshadow him or suggest you're his equal. Avoid all overt displays of physical affection. Don't be photographed eating, picking your nose or repositioning your crotch. Always appear to be fascinated by whatever His Highness is saying or doing. You may wave politely to spectators, whom the security detail will hold at bay. Should you speak to anyone other than His Highness, restrict your remarks to the weather, the noble spirit of athletic competition and the glorious nature of the British people."

"I apologise for all this," added Edgar. "But it's efficient, and I'd like the world to see us at our finest."

"Hold on," I said. "Does this mean I can't buy one of those huge foam rubber 'We're Number One' hands, or paint my face in team colors, or drink beer from a gallon plastic cup, like people do at American football games?"

"We can leave Mr. Ogden in the car," said James. "We don't even have to crack the window."

As we were being escorted to our seats, Edgar asked me, "Are you certain you're up for this? It's quite a bit to ask."

I was anxious, like the lesser partner of a Hollywood power couple nearing the red carpet at the Golden Globes. This was a moment of pure fame, divorced from any achievement or worthy cause. I'd borrowed one of Edgar's navy cashmere topcoats, and he was wearing a down-filled vest, so we were going for a young-hedge-fund-managers-just-before-the-indictment vibe.

"Let's do this," I said, and I was about to take Edgar's arm until I caught myself, remembering why this wasn't the right idea and was, in fact, the opposite of the right idea.

Edgar was greeted with a roar of appreciation from the crowd as we took our place in a middle section of the bleachers, acting like two friendly, down-to-earth guys who just happened to be surrounded by a security team, who were wearing plain clothes to blend in.

"Just breathe," Ian said in my ear. "Only not too loudly."

"Pretend you're straight," Clark said, from over my shoulder. "Get drunk and fall down."

The stadium was packed, and the enthusiasm grew more bois-terous as Edgar's beaming, waving image was projected on the enormous Jumbotrons with a nervous and intimidated-looking American beside him, a cross between a dutiful Republican wife and someone who really needed to use the bathroom but was too jittery to ask for directions.

"You're doing splendidly," Edgar whispered to me, without turning his head. "Steady on."

Just before the match started, Gerald showed up with his wife and twin two-year-old sons, all in matching plaid wind-breakers, mufflers and caps. They began waving vigorously to the crowd even before anyone saw them, holding their babies aloft and manipulating their tiny hands to make them wave too.

"Hello, chaps," said Gerald as he and his family sat beside us. "Carter, this is my wife, Maureen."

"The Duchess of Longshire," Maureen added quickly, extend-ing her mittened hand as if she expected me to kiss it. Maureen was very pretty in a perfected way, with a sheaf of expensively blonde hair, expertly displayed. She was still in her twenties but wore the masklike makeup of an older woman, as if she'd chosen the face she wanted from a catalogue and had it permanently installed, with a whitened sheen that looks ghostly in person but flawless in high-definition video. She was smiling brightly, as if she wanted to sell me something and then kill me.

"So nice to meet you. Although of course I've seen the photo. So awfully sorry."

As the match got underway, I activated my high school technique for comprehending quantum physics: I stared really hard and opened my eyes as wide as I could, as if sheer focus could do the trick. But just as with physics, this didn't work. The game was like football only with less headgear and padding and a kind of rugged soccer ball. I kept an eye out for wooden paddles until I remembered that was cricket. Every so often something would happen and the team members would run around in random patterns, the ball would get kicked and half the crowd would leap to their feet and cheer. Edgar cheered for both teams, since he couldn't show favoritism, but he was truly into the game itself, so I kept telling myself, *It's fine, some very nice people enjoy eating ground glass.*

"You're hating every second of this, aren't you?" Edgar whispered to me, smiling.

"No, no, it's great, I was just thinking about how Ralph Lauren once had a line of cheaper sportswear called Rugby, but he shut it down."

As the game kept going, I tried to anticipate when Edgar would stand and cheer, but I was always a beat behind, while Gerald and Maureen were holding their babies over their heads and shaking them as if change might fall out.

"Here's what you need to do," Edgar confided. "Imagine that every man on each team is secretly in love with a man on the opposing team, and after the next goal, envision all of them ripping off their jerseys and making out passionately on the field."

Finally! Without helmets or shoulder pads I could see that the players were major hot stuff, and more brawny and rambunctious than America's billionaire quarterbacks, who often seem doughy and just a few Big Macs away from beer-bellied middle age.

I began pairing up the players, placing favorites in steamy locker room grind sessions or motel room marathons, inventing chest hair patterns and "You're buggerin' me right proud" rugby porn chatter.

Then it happened: a goal was scored and I saw a full-field orgy, with all the players naked and sweating and going at it ecstatically, in couples, threeways and pileups. My imagination took over, and I was hired as a sex referee, running onto the field to get a closer look before making a call, like "Touchdown!", "Bravo!" or "Great use of hands!" I was so into my version of the match that I jumped up beside Edgar and cheered every decibel as lustily, or maybe moreso. As we joined the stadium in banshee howling and fist-pumping, I got so overheated that I grabbed Edgar and hugged him.

As I instantly pulled away, horrified at what I'd done, I caught myself staring at Edgar in apologetic alarm on a Jumbotron. He clapped me on the back as if we were frat buddies, and then someone on the field got into a shoving dust-up with someone else, the crowd got distracted and vocal and on another Jumbotron I saw a woman holding a hand-lettered sign reading "I'm sitting near Prince Eddie and his strange new friend!"

"I'm so sorry!" I wailed, once James had ushered Edgar and me into a nearby private tent after the match. "I did what you told me to, about picturing the players having sex, and I got carried away. Was that a huge fuckup?"

"Of course not," Edgar assured me, "and it was my fault for transforming the match into an X-rated free-for-all. And this is all very new, but we should remind ourselves to be careful."

He was being nice and we both knew it.

"But with so many of these rules and precautions," I said, "I'm not sure I get it. I mean, you're out, which is so great, and you're single. And most of all, you're a symbol for queer kids and queer adults all over the world. You're the guy. You're our hero. You're the out prince."

Edgar was clenching and unclenching his fists, with a clouded look on his face.

"Thank you," he said, "but I'm not sure you fully grasp what you're saying. The implications. The responsibility. Every moment of every day."

"Edgar?"

He held up a hand, controlling himself. What had I done?

"When I first came out, I wanted to believe that I was doing something logical and human and completely positive, and I hoped that the world would respond in kind. I wasn't naive, but I was eighteen years old, which meant I was so sure of myself, of everything. I was doing what had to be done. I was telling the world, 'This is who I am.'"

"And I admire you so much—"

"Wait. Because I need to say this. It wasn't an easy time. Before that my private life had been exactly that: private. Although of course everyone would speculate the moment I was even introduced to a girl close to my own age, and the media would contrive a bedpost-rattling love affair. There were contests and betting pools: 'Choose a bride for young Prince Edgar.' And it had to stop. I knew I was gay, and my family knew, but it was made clear that anything more public presented a real danger. My grandmother proposed that I lead a kind of double life—she listed numerous examples, in royal families, in our own family, since time began. But I asked her, was that what she really wanted? For me or for anyone? A life of endless deception?"

"Did she get it?"

"Eventually. For the most part. She wasn't any sort of homophobe or puritan, but she was concerned. Not so much for the royal reputation, but for my safety. So I raised the question: what did she think my parents would've wanted me to do?"

"Oh my God."

"She was at a loss, which never happens. With tears in her eyes. Because my mum and dad had been, as much as possible, free spirits. They'd cultivated friendships with artists and actors and writers. They were curious. And in fact, the flight they were on, it was en route to an enormous music festival, a fundraiser for AIDS research and health care."

"I didn't know."

"And part of the tragedy, for Nana, was that royal couples are instructed to fly separately, to avoid such a catastrophic result. But my parents had scoffed—they were very much in love, and they'd wanted to experience the world together. And Nana has always blamed herself, for not being stricter, for not saving at least one of them."

"So when you wanted to come out . . ."

"All she could forsee was further heartache. But she was aware, of how proud, and how accepting my parents would've been."

"And when you did it, all I remember is total celebration. I was a senior in high school, and I saved your cover of *People*, and I kept showing it to everyone and telling them, look, he's smiling. He's so cool. It made such a difference."

"But you were already out, weren't you?"

"Yes, and my family was great, but I still felt, I guess maybe the way you did, that being out wasn't just about me. It had to be about all of us. And you were our rock star."

"And a spokesperson. And a lightning rod. The planet's most well-known official homosexual. Because unlike so many figures in the arts, I wasn't perceived as an outlier, or a bohemian. I was the good boy, the scrubbed face, Prince Perfect. But there was also an enormous backlash. I've rarely addressed it, because I've never wanted special treatment of any kind. And the Palace preferred to minimise all of it, the good and the bad. But along with the most thrilling support, there was a firestorm of hatred. For every housewife who cheered me on and just wanted me to meet the right bloke there was a fundamentalist or far-right politician or neo-Nazi who reviled me. There were death threats, and there still are, which demand heightened security. My appearances remain limited, especially in other, less tolerant countries. James insists."

I should've caught on to these repercussions. But I'd clung to Edgar's image of carefree openness. I'd expected him to be a queer heartthrob, an out citizen of the world, a leap forward.

"And now here I am. The role model. The lab rat. Which is a position I take seriously. If I make a misstep, it's viewed, fairly or not, as a mark against gay people everywhere. And I'm not just talking about the conservative response. I receive just as many, if not more, accusations and insults and taunts from other gay people. I'm too vanilla. Too acceptable. Too straight-seeming. I'm out but not out enough, or not in the correct manner, or never sufficiently standard-bearing. The out sellout. The assimilated android. And again, I'm not complaining, I know that I'm far beyond lucky, and that my being out is nothing compared to a kid being bullied, or beaten, or abandoned by his family, or hurled off a building or stoned to death in accordance with another nation's legal system."

"But today was just a rugby match . . ."

"But it counts. Everything counts."

Edgar stared at me with a weary anger.

"Carter. I don't want to discourage you or speak from some haughty celebrity high ground. But this is a major part of why I invited you here, and into my life. Up until now, you've been anonymous, which I envy. You can wander. You can experiment. You can meet hundreds of men and have every kind of sex and stumble home the next morning and discuss it with your roommates."

"Well, not hundreds of men . . ."

"You know what I'm saying . . ."

He sat on a folding chair, shaking.

"Should I go?" I asked him. "Back to America?"

"Would you like to?"

I thought about this. Should I continue blundering, and making Edgar miserable, and shaming my LGBTQ peers? Would I relish becoming an even more public target for the Internet's scorn? I'd met a wonderful person, but Edgar was far more complicated than that. He was a leader and a grandson and, at times, a nervous breakdown in progress. Could I handle that? Was I strong enough? But something had changed with this conversation; there'd been a shift in the balance of our relationship. Edgar was slumped on his chair, steeling himself for another scandal and another bad choice and another goodbye. He needed me.

"No, I don't want to leave," I said. "Unless you'd like to have me deported. Or unless your grandmother creeps into my room with a dagger. But I'm not going anywhere, and do you know why?"

Edgar looked at me with a yearning hopelessness, as if he was drowning and I was in a lifeboat a few feet away, checking my phone.

"Here's why."

I walked over and kissed him.

"You are so not playing fair," he said.

"I know."

And this time he kissed me.

CHAPTER 19

The next day Edgar and I had lunch with a gaggle of his friends, which included schoolmates from Oxford, three titled cousins, a video artist and a poet. There was an unspoken physical code: if the group thought a stranger was hovering to sneak a photo, they'd gracefully block the angle. They didn't interrogate me, but I could tell I was on probation. They were raucous and teasing and they had something in common with my New York posse—a protectiveness. Adam and Louise and I could say anything to one another, the funnier and more slashing the better. But if anyone outside our circle made even the mildest snide remark, we closed ranks. I was glad Edgar had friends like that. I just wished he had an Abby, although she was already on the case.

During the afternoon, Edgar took me to the National Portrait Gallery, the House of Lords and Westminster Abbey. At each stop, a private viewing had been arranged, as if Edgar and I either owned these buildings or were considering a summer rental. It was an amazingly personal way to visit landmarks, but it also felt closed in, as if we were touring a communist country and being restricted to government-approved exhibitions.

"Think of it this way," Edgar said. "Imagine we're checking out the alarm system before breaking in and stealing a Rembrandt. And no one would ever suspect me."

"Everyone would blame me!" I told him.

"So it's a perfect crime."

Following dinner at the palace, we made a great show of retreating to our separate bedrooms. But after five minutes of contemplating Edgar's shoulders, I brushed my teeth again, did a few push-ups, gave myself a smoldering I-could-be-a-model-if-all-the-real-models-died look in the mirror, and stepped out into the hall, coming scarily face-to-face with Queen Catherine, who was wearing a flannel robe and carrying a small plate with what looked like a brownie. Was she shadowing me? Didn't she ever sleep? Most monarchs would have staff members bring them late-night delicacies, but Catherine liked to do things herself.

"Where do you think you're going?" she demanded.

"Um, I was looking for . . . an extra pillow?"

"You are seeking my grandson's bedroom in hopes of a torrid sexual encounter."

"And that."

"I'm not a prude. I've enjoyed a robust physical life. But there's far more to a successful relationship than merely, what is that phrase you younger people use? Hooking on?"

"Hooking up."

"Which sounds like some uninviting form of knitting or crochet. Yes, lovemaking has its appeal, but it's far from the entire equation. And from what has been reported, your attendance at a rugby match earlier today resulted in a squalid and extended display of sexual excess."

"It was a hug!"

"One too many. So you shall return to your solitary chamber and review your priorities, along with enumerating the higher pursuits which you and Edgar might share."

"We went to a museum!"

"Congratulations. Were you awarded a doctorate?"

"You're just going to stand here, aren't you? To make sure Edgar and I don't have sex."

I feinted to the left, but the queen deftly countered. I tried to duck under her elbow and nearly lost an eye.

"You're not going anywhere, strumpet," she gloated.

Strumpet? Now I was a strumpet? Was she strumpet-shaming me? And doesn't "strumpet" sound more like a French dessert or some bold-new-taste American corn chip?

"Well, I am tired," I admitted, innocently. "So maybe I'll just turn in."

"A wise decision."

"Good night, Your Majesty. Sleep well."

"And you. What was your name again?"

"Carter."

"Martin."

I closed the door and counted to fifty, slowly. I inched the door open and was confronted with an uncompromising royal eyeball. I'd become the last cheerleader left alive in a horror movie.

I shut the door and FaceTimed with Abby, who was lounging by her honeymoon resort's infinity pool.

"So she's like the hall monitor?" Abby asked, laughing.

"It's not funny! I'm her prisoner!"

"But you and Edgar still like each other?"

"We do. Today was—major. Remember when he came out and you made me that mood board of all the famous gay people?"

"And I ranked them," she recalled. "By who I thought you should hang out with, like Neil Patrick Harris and Rosie O'Donnell. But we still weren't sure about SpongeBob."

"But from talking to Edgar," I said, "I realized something. Everyone on that board didn't only come out. It's like they added the words 'Openly Gay' to their names whenever they're written about or introduced. Which I love, but I guess—it's a weird position to be in. Edgar's still working on it."

"But do you remember what I told you, back then? About coming out?"

"Of course. You said that anyone who comes out should get their choice of a free car or a trip to Disney World. And right now, I'm sort of getting both. As long as I don't make any more stupid mistakes."

"You will," said Abby, cheerfully. "But when will you get that it's okay? Especially if you've met the right person?"

"Stop. Don't jinx it. Knock on wood. I mean it."

Abby obligingly knocked on Dane's head as he lay beside her wearing a NY Yankees ball cap, listening to a game on his earbuds.

"I love you," I said.

"Of course," said Abby.

I'm not positive, but in my dream later that night, I could swear I heard the queen's supervillain laughter, cackling, "Keep it in your pants, New Jersey sexboy!"

made every effort not to be cranky over breakfast the next morning in one of the palace's smaller dining rooms, which meant that Edgar and I were seated only twenty feet apart at either end of an unwieldy mahogany table.

"She lurked last night, didn't she?" said Edgar. "Nana. In the hall."

"Does that happen a lot?"

"Only when she thinks I'm about to slip out and have a good time. She's like, what was that devil doll's name—Chucky? The one who keeps popping up and mauling babysitters?"

"I think she's worried about us, but especially about me."

"So today we're going to prove Nana and everyone else wrong. We're going to provide a serious and important demonstration of our most caring and responsible selves."

"Please don't make me try and understand Brexit. Because the closest I can get is if New Jersey broke away from New York and floated out to sea while Connecticut laughed."

"We'll attend to that later. I'll be gentle. Today we're going to do some good."

This sounded daunting. I try to think of myself as at least social justice–adjacent, and I've volunteered to plan fundraisers for Hetrick-Martin, which is New York's LGBTQ high school, I've advised on poster art for a great trans candidate's city council campaign, and I've done charity walks and registered voters. I want to offer whatever skills I have, but I'm intensely minor compared to Louise, who tutors at-risk gay kids three times a week, and Adam, who's active in Broadway Cares and, with DuShawn, delivers hot meals to people living with HIV and other chronic illnesses.

"We'll be opening a new wing of a children's hospital," Edgar explained in the car. "I've spent years flattering billionaires, getting them to pay for thirty beds, twelve new nurses and a protected outdoor area where the kids can get some sunshine. You'd think rich people would be instantly forthcoming, but it's an older facility in a low-income neighbourhood, so persuasion has been necessary."

The St. Garvin's Hospital for Children was a collection of red brick Victorian buildings resembling a small-town college. There was a huddle of press and mobile TV units outside the entrance, along with a decent-size crowd of onlookers. Edgar answered every personal question with a reply centering on the hospital, while I stood slightly behind him and to the left, practicing a smile that was interested and alert without being goofy. Dr. Sarman Vatshul, the medical director, led us inside.

"The children are so excited to see you," said Dr. Vatshul as health care workers and patients lined the halls and Edgar posed for selfies; he had a gift for making each person feel heard, rather than patted on the head and dismissed.

"It doesn't quite make sense," James murmured to me, "but His Highness brightens everyone's day. He's not a vote-hungry politician, or even a film star with some superhero bilge to promote. It's about service."

We reached a large, open room where about thirty patients had gathered, all under ten years old. Some were in wheelchairs and others used crutches, with three children on gurneys. Their parents and siblings stood along the walls; photographers had been allowed in, and of course everyone had their phones out.

"Children," announced Dr. Vatshul, "please join me in welcoming our very special guest, His Royal Highness Prince Edgar."

Edgar grinned and quieted the applause and cheers. "Thank you, but today is about you, so let me ask—is everyone enjoying the new wing?"

More cheers, although one little boy announced, "It's all right, but there should be candy!"

"Absolutely brilliant," Edgar agreed. "There must always be candy. And I will consult with Dr. Vatshul. But have you all had a hearty breakfast?"

Everyone nodded, as Edgar said, "But it's not really hearty without chocolate chip cookies, is it?"

On cue, James, the security team and I opened five large boxes of cookies still warm from the palace kitchen. I've never felt more popular, like a vivacious spokesmodel handing out prize money on a game show.

"These really are good," said Charles, splitting a cookie with Ian.

"These are for the children," I scolded, splitting a cookie with Lucky.

"Just this once," Dr. Vatshul warned the kids, most of whom started hoarding, and I didn't blame them.

"These are prescription," Edgar protested.

"And now," asked Dr. Vatshul, "would we like His Highness to tell us a story?"

"Something about cookies and starships and magic?" Edgar suggested.

"Who's that?" said a little girl in a wheelchair, with three limbs in fiberglass casts, using an unfettered arm to point to me. "Who's the cookie man?"

"That is my friend Carter Ogden," said Edgar, "who's one of our helpers today. He's come all the way from America."

Some of the kids were impressed by this; others not a bit.

"Is he your boyfriend?" asked the little girl.

"Is he your kissy friend?" asked an even younger child, with a dinosaur sticker on her cheek.

"Your Highness . . ." Dr. Vatshul began.

"He's my very good friend, and he plans all sorts of parties and events, so he's especially happy to be here amidst all of these balloons."

I nodded vigorously, gung ho but mute.

"Can he tell us a story?" demanded a boy whose head was bandaged and immobilized by a halo of screws and steel rods.

As Dr. Vatshul looked uncertain and Edgar looked at me, the children chanted, "CARTER! CARTER! CARTER!"

"Let's ask him," said Edgar. "Carter, how about a story?"

I was stricken—I didn't want to hog the spotlight, but I couldn't be rude either, especially not to a roomful of hospitalized kids, one of whom shouted, "We want the boyfriend! Make him talk!"

I was remembering a period of over a year when Abby, at fourteen, had been diagnosed with leukemia and received a bone marrow transplant from a donor matched through an online service. She'd been bedridden and dragged from one specialist to the next as my terrified parents had struggled to keep her spirits up. I was twelve; I'd been scared and weirdly fascinated by Abby's gaunt appearance, the pain she was in and the fact that she might die. Asking about any of this was off-limits.

I'd felt invisible and guilty because I hadn't been a possible donor, and I'd searched for a means of helping her feel better that no one else had thought of, and of not just being in the way. I'd decided that what Abby needed was to continue our gown hunt, so I'd canvassed the waiting rooms for bridal magazines and emailed her sketches, along with YouTube videos of the latest wedding ceremony dance routines. My parents had been wary, but their children were headstrong, and during our wedding sessions Abby ignored the IV tubes and the bruises and the nausea from the follow-up chemotherapy, especially when the nurses posted their own wedding albums.

That was when Abby and I had bonded forever, and when her wedding gown had become a symbol of renewed good health and a life with a future. That's also when I started to intuit the significance of event planning and celebrations; these occasions, and the fuss, sometimes mean much more than someone's depleted savings account and a rented inflatable bounce house or backyard-size carousel.

Abby had fully recovered, and the ordeal inspired her own career path; she'd experienced firsthand what seriously ill kids go through and was set on helping them. She believes that sick kids are frustrated by lies, pity and gloom: "A sick kid wants to know that their illness isn't their whole life. A sick kid wants someone who listens, and maybe music and a few troll dolls with hot pink hair they can comb." Although, being Abby, when her own hair had fallen out, she'd sheared her troll dolls as well, as I scissored off the fingertips of surgical gloves to make doll-size turbans.

Which meant that I wanted to entertain the kids from St. Garvin's, without coming off like some condescending rainbow jerk.

"I'd be happy to tell a story," I offered. "If that's okay with everyone?"

Edgar smiled with a slightly appalled anticipation, and Dr. Vatshul held up his hands in surrender—the children were in charge.

"Okay," I began, "so, once upon a time—wait, is that too corny?"

The children shook their heads no, that was fine.

"Good, here we go, so once upon a time there was a handsome prince—can anyone point to a handsome prince?"

The kids laughed and pointed to Edgar, who waved his hands no but finally acknowledged the accolade.

"And one morning the prince decided that he needed to help the whole world."

"Excuse me," said one of the parents, a mom in a peach-colored sweater set and a bowl haircut. "Is this going to become a political statement in any way? Because that wouldn't be appropriate."

"Not at all," said Edgar, "it's just going to be a delightful story, isn't that so, Carter?"

I wasn't sure how helping the world necessarily tumbled into politics, but I said, "Of course. So the prince set off to help people, and his first stop was in a far-off land called America. And while he was there, do you know who he met?"

"An American!" shouted one of the kids.

"A pony! A talking pony!"

"Spider-Man!"

"Yes, that's absolutely right, he met Spider-Man, and they became good friends. And one day, while the prince and Spider-Man were flying around in their magical help-mobile—"

"What's a help-mobile?"

"Is it like an ambulance?"

"Is it like a Prius?"

"Do you have a help-mobile?"

"A help-mobile is a cross between a helicopter," I ventured, "like the prince flew when he was a brave soldier, and the Batmobile if it could fly."

The children looked at each other, unsure, until one boy asked, "Wouldn't that be the Batplane?"

"Totally different. Ask your mums and dads."

"And can't Spider-Man already fly?"

"Spider-Man can swoop around using his web, which is great, but it's not technically flying."

"No, it's not, Devin," the little girl with the dinosaur sticker told the boy. I loved that little girl.

"So they were flying around," I went on, "and helping people—"

"With groceries?"

"And doctors' appointments?"

"And finding Dad's car in the parking lot?"

"All of those things! Such good ideas!"

"Did Wonder Woman help them?"

"Was Spider-Man the prince's boyfriend?"

"Just asking," said another parent, a man in a windbreaker and khakis, "do we really need any references to Spider-Man's sex life?"

"Spider-Man and the prince were just good friends."

As I said this I felt a twinge of disappointment in myself: Had I just scurried past the creation of a heroic gay couple? Or would that be getting way too PC? There have been more and more LGBTQ superheroes in comic books, although only a few have made the super-leap into movies or cable shows. I considered telling the kids about my great-aunt Miriam's favorite superhero, Doctor Strange, although she'd fretted, "I'm not sure if he's Jewish, or if that's really a good name for a doctor. But if he took my insurance I'd love him."

"And then one day," I continued, "Spider-Man and the prince were flying over a schoolyard, and they saw a little girl with blue hair and green skin. And even though she was really smart and her skin and her hair looked great together, she was being bullied by some of the other kids because she could fly. Because sometimes when you're different, other people don't always understand. And one of the other kids, a mean little boy who wished he could fly, he grabbed one of the little girl's wings and bent it."

The children gasped.

"And the little girl tried to be brave, but when she went to fly, she couldn't. So the prince and Spider-Man had to do something. But if they were going to get the little girl to just the right doctors, the help-mobile wasn't fast enough. So the prince whistled, and do you know what appeared?"

"Iron Man!"

"An Uber!"

"Two trillion billion butterflies!"

"A dragon!"

"A dragon! That's right! A pink and purple striped dragon with huge wings. And what do you think the dragon's name was?"

"Dragonmaster!"

"Superdragon!"

"Optimus Prime!"

"Berniece!"

"Yes! The dragon's name was Berniece! After her mum. And while Berniece looked scary, she was actually really nice and traveled around the world educating people about dragon culture and the inaccuracies in *Game of Thrones*. And the prince and Spider-Man carried the little girl onto Berniece's back, with Berniece's full consent, and they held the little girl so she'd feel safe.

"And the dragon flew thousands of miles to find the very best wing-fixing specialist in the whole world, and do you know who he was? Dr. Vatshul, right here at St. Garvin's Hospital for Children and Bent Wings! And soon the little girl was feeling better, and she was able to fly all around London, with Berniece beside her. And the little girl thanked the prince and Spider-Man, but they said, 'We were just helpers. The real heroes are Dr. Vatshul and all of the amazing health care workers here at St. Garvin's!'"

The kids and parents and staff members clapped and cheered, led by a very pleased Edgar, who put his fingers in his mouth and whistled. Dr. Vatshul was pretending a professional distance, but I could tell he was tickled.

And then the adorable little girl with the fiberglass casts

asked, "Did the prince and Spider-Man get married? Like my Uncle Bob and Uncle Baxter?"

This little girl had a tenacious, very specific look on her face that reminded me of Abby in her hospital bed when she'd forced me to choose between a looser bouquet of lilacs and freesia, as opposed to something more formal with roses and lilies in a lace sleeve. She'd explained, "And you have to answer, because the first bouquet's saying, 'Hi, I'm a trailing-ribbons-in-my-hair, barefoot, lute-playing New Hampshire meadow bride,' while the other one says, 'I'm a traditional Park Avenue bride with an iron-clad prenup who means business.' Pick!"

"I think they should get married!" the little girl proclaimed. "And they should get presents!"

She'd clearly undergone more than one procedure and was signed up for many months of physical therapy. She'd most likely been in some horrific accident and wanted not just my answer, but proof of romance and joy and an exultant ceremony far from the hospital's sterile sameness.

I didn't think, or I decided not to think. I had to make that little girl grin, and support her hopefulness, which I saw as my own, and if this meant a dreamy gay wedding, that's what I'd contribute. That's what I do for a living. That's what Ruth Ginsburg had legalized when she'd voted in favor of marriage equality on the Supreme Court. I had a vision of that little girl, Ruth and me in the hallowed *Charlie's Angels* justice-seeking trio-of-hot-babes pose.

"Yes," I told the room, "the prince and Spider-Man got married, but their ceremony and reception were a benefit to buy defibrillators and patient monitors for St. Garvin's. And then they teamed up with the Flash, Ant-Man and Captain Marvel to plant the beautiful garden right outside these windows, and they filled the cafeteria with treats that didn't taste like hospital food at all!"

These details, especially the last one, prompted the kids' loudest ovation yet. I looked at Edgar, who seemed stunned but happy, which was the best possible effect I could have on him.

Within the next fifteen minutes the following headlines were blasted across social media, in many languages, all over the world:

ROYAL COMPANION SAYS PRINCE EDGAR
HAS SEX WITH SUPERHERO

AMERICAN WHOEVER-HE-IS TELLS KIDS
SPIDER-MAN IS QUEER

PRINCE EDDIE INVOLVED WITH SPIDER-MAN
AND ASSOCIATE EVENT IDIOT

QUEER TAKEOVER OF LONDON CHILDREN'S HOSPITAL
CONDEMNED BY AMERICAN PRESIDENTIAL CANDIDATE

COPYRIGHT ACTION BEING CONSIDERED AGAINST
ROYAL BOYFRIEND SMUTMEISTER

LEAGUE OF CHRISTIAN MOMS INSISTS
SPIDER-MAN ONLY DATES PIOUS WOMEN

PALACE MUST RESPOND:
WILL PRINCE EDGAR RETURN TO REHAB?

CANCEL CARTER OGDICK

There were also photoshopped images of Edgar and Spider-Man having sex, a cartoon of me breathing fire onto children, and an animated video of Edgar and Spider-Man, naked and riding a winged unicorn while sprinkling glitter onto the Tower of London.

Adam sent me a spreadsheet dividing the millions of tweets into the following categories: American Homo Tells Sick Kids Porn Story, Royal Family Asunder, Prince Edgar Should Never Be King, Batman Issues Statement Claiming "I Always Knew," Queen Catherine to Meet with Prime Minister Over Gay Sexgate, and Carter Ogden Shut the Hell Up.

My mom texted me thirty-eight times with variations on "I know you meant well. Call me. Oy."

My dad emailed me, "Is Spider-Man the fellow who swings from buildings on some sort of webbing, which isn't scientifically possible?"

Abby texted me, "I know what you were going for and it's good you brought cookies."

Louise posted a photo of herself wearing a T-shirt reading "Free Carter Ogden!"

DuShawn started selling tank tops on eBay airbrushed with the word "SPIDER-QUEER" in rainbow stripes and vowed to use any proceeds for my defense fund.

"What in God's name were you thinking?" Edgar yelled at me back in my room at the palace. I'd never seen Edgar this furious before. He'd been anxious and apprehensive and agitated, but he'd never yelled. I hate yelling. In my family we just simmer and slam doors and make extra appointments with our therapists to discuss our fear of conflict.

"Gay Spider-Man? To sick children? With the press in the room? What did you think was going to happen?"

I'd had major fights with Callum, but they'd been strategic, with me acting ultracontrolled and insisting I wasn't hurt, I was just puzzled that any human being could be so evil, causing Callum to run through all the gestures he'd learned doing TV shows, like "I Give Up!" or "My Brain Is On Fire!" or, finally, "Sinking To My Knees In Anguish Because I Just Found My Wife's Body On *Law & Order: SVU*!"

"I'm sorry," I pleaded. "I know, I'm an insensitive, self-involved American pea brain and I'm the worst thing that's ever happened to you! But in my defense, those kids liked the story, and I was just trying to—I don't know—some of those parents were being so snitty and homophobic, and I was thinking, 'Well, what story do I wish I'd heard when I was a kid?' and come on, I did make you Spider-Man's husband, which is seriously hot!"

Edgar's face grew contorted and bright red and as he came toward me I was positive he was going to kill me and that I wouldn't scream or struggle, but accept my fate, and I was sure Edgar would ask James to shove my body down a laundry chute and then dump it in the Thames, and when I never came home my friends and family would be a little sad but secretly relieved that they didn't have to deal with me.

Edgar kept getting closer and he couldn't even form coherent sentences as he spouted, "You demented douchewipe embarrassment to the entire LGBTQ-plus Jewish communities all over the world . . ."

That was when he grabbed me and started kissing me and before I knew it we were having our most incredible sex yet, all over the bedroom and the dressing area and the bathroom, and when James tapped on the door and asked if we'd be joining Her Majesty for dinner, Edgar yelled, "After we finish fucking!"

A few minutes later, as we lay at a contorted angle to each

other, naked on the bed, Edgar stared at the ceiling and said, "I don't know. I just don't know."

"But do you want to know something even worse?" I asked, also studying the ceiling, as if it might collapse and solve everything, or open a portal to another dimension where I hadn't done anything blameworthy.

"What?" Edgar asked. "Tell me what's worse."

"Not only have I shamed the royal family for all eternity, and forced my mother to have to explain everything to all my other relatives, and been canceled by people in countries I've never even heard of—in fact, places that might've declared themselves countries just so their newly formed governments could cancel me—but this year . . . I'm turning thirty."

I'd been aggressively ignoring this birthday for the past five years, not just because I'd be ancient but because it loomed as a deadline: I would be thirty years old and have accomplished nothing. I would be thirty years old without a boyfriend. I would be thirty years old and I'd start to gain the ten pounds that I'd read accumulate with every decade of a person's life after thirty. I'd be a thirty-year-old associate event terminal loser and I'd have to accept that this was my life.

"So what?" said Edgar. "I'm turning thirty as well."

"I know," I said. "We have the same birthday. January twenty-second."

"We do? Why haven't you told me this?"

"I don't know, maybe I was saving it. Maybe it seems weird, as if we're related. Maybe if things were going well, I thought we could celebrate together. Or maybe . . ."

"Maybe what?"

"Maybe the fact that we share a birthday makes me hate you."

"Why the hell do you hate me?"

"Because first of all, you look great and you're only getting more handsome, so fuck you. And second, you don't have to worry and punish yourself and climb over the railing of a bridge at midnight on January twenty-first. Because you already have— your life. You've got this incredible job where they can't fire you."

"I beg to differ—"

"I know, you could abdicate or whatever, but basically you're like the pope or a Supreme Court justice or a seventy-eight-year-old soap opera star—being royal is a lifetime appointment. You know who you are. The world knows who you are. And sure, there are speed bumps, like for example, meeting me, but still: You're there. You're you. You've made it. So turning thirty means nothing."

He flipped onto his side to face me, saying, "You are such a complete and total piece of shit."

"What? Why?"

"It doesn't mean anything? Of course it does, and of course I've been obsessing. Because, fine, I'm royal and there's a road map, but that's the entire problem: I don't just want to submit and salute and acquiesce. I want to take everything I've been given, the money and the access and the opportunities, and do something with it. The thought of which makes everyone in my family, and my country, shiver and recoil. They prefer me to remain inert and pleasantly comatose, to not take sides on anything, and to feel continuously and only grateful at having my face imprinted on so many cheap souvenir paperweights and shot glasses. Which I could embrace and even wallow in; it would be so easy and restful to merely relax into uselessness, to float amiably down the royal river to my eventual, unmourned death. And

I'm on my way. I've done nothing. Because what I've been moronically hoping and praying for is—someone. A person. A partner. To share the ride and give me a boot in the pants. To goad me and question every action and inspire me. Which is a lazy man's solution. But why do I crave that and dream of it so desperately? Because I'm about to turn thirty. And I'm alone."

"You're alone?" I repeated, indicating certain bodily fluids glistening on various parts of both our torsos.

"I'm sorry," Edgar said. "I didn't mean it like that, I just—I don't know what to do, with myself or with you, or with how I feel about you, or with any of it. Because eventually we're going to be required to leave this bed."

"Okay," I said, feeling suddenly and bizarrely a tiny bit less abysmal. "Let's try to be more, I don't know, upbeat. Because we share a birthday, which means we're both Aquarius."

Edgar groaned, the way so many people do when astrological forecasts enter a conversation. Maybe that's why I have so many friends in the arts—it reduces the groan factor. Do I believe in astrology? No, but like everyone else, I'll skim my daily horoscope, assess its probability and forget it within seconds. It's soothing. It's almost always peppy, rife with "Your horizons are expanding" or "Be on the lookout for love." It's a therapeutic breath mint.

"I know what you're thinking," I told Edgar, "but hear me out. I'm not going to do your chart or make you get an ankle tattoo of your rising sign. But do you know what the primary characteristics of Aquarians are?"

"According to . . ."

"According to a candle wax and weed-stained paperback that I found at the bottom of the closet in my first dorm room. Aquarians are ingenious, creative and adaptable. Plus original and humanitarian. And our symbol, the Water Bearer, is based on Ganymede, a Phrygian youth who was so beautiful that Zeus fell in love with him and whisked him off to heaven to serve forever as the cupbearer to the gods."

"So what you're saying," Edgar concluded, "is that we're both hot waiters."

"Maybe," I replied. "But think about the other part. We're in a huge mess—fine, a huge mess that I caused—but we're ingenious, creative and adaptable."

There was a long pause, and I wondered if Edgar was asleep or silently begging Zeus to come get me, preferably in an airtight container.

"Ingenious, creative and adaptable," he finally said, putting his finger on my mouth to prevent me from issuing any further cosmic tidbits. He smiled, which might be encouraging, and said, "Yes, we are."

CHAPTER 21

"You are relentlessly repugnant," Queen Catherine informed me.

Edgar and I were dining with Her Majesty, the three of us spaced miles apart around the largest mahogany table in the palace—the grand behemoth. "He has repeatedly apologised . . ." Edgar chided.

"And I did show respect for dragons . . ." I chimed in.

"No! You do not speak!" the queen admonished me. "You shall never speak again, not only in my presence but anywhere on Earth! You have not earned the power of speech! I shall have your lips sewn shut!"

Could she do that? She was the queen, and we were in her country. I glanced at James, who was standing by the door, and he mimed sewing.

"This Caleb creature . . ." the queen continued.

"His name is Carter . . ." said Edgar.

"This Porter amphibian is the throne's greatest enemy since the Viking attacks in the ninth century. Except this Carstairs demon is more purely malevolent, an amoebic plague without intelligence, forethought or decent shoes, a form of ditheringly irrational chaos."

When the Queen of England is throwing this degree of shade, it's hard not to feel, well, like an insect trapped under a magnifying glass in bright sunlight.

"From your barely concealed dishevelment," the queen noted, "I presume the pair of you have succumbed to your most primitive desires and ignited a cheap physical release. Which has undoubtedly offended and degraded our entire palace staff. Am I correct in this, Mr. Claverack?"

James shut his eyes and grimaced, as if recalling something too traumatic to bear, perhaps an incident on a foreign battlefield or an especially painful version of Jingle Bells on a Christmas variety show. He tried to speak but couldn't.

The queen brought it home: "There is but one feasible recourse. This rancid crustacean must depart within minutes and never return. And the two of you will cease any and all future contact. In short, this relationship, if it can be dignified with that many syllables, must and shall end immediately."

I'll give her this: She's good at it. She was playing 3D queer chess and winning.

"Nana . . ." Edgar ventured.

"Did I ask you to speak?"

"No. But I have a counterproposal. I agree with you, and much of the world, that Carter's remarks at the children's hospital were ill-advised. But he'd been asked to speak spontaneously, and after the event, donations to the hospital increased tenfold.

I'm told that while some benefactors wished to uphold the hospital's honor, others liked Carter, and I'll quote an email which was accompanied by a gift of fifty thousand pounds, from a woman who said, 'Carter Ogden is a breath of fresh air.'"

Edgar hadn't told me about any of this. Had I done some good?

"And while I can't condone Carter's words, he's guiding me in redefining, or at least adjusting, my role in this family. He's helping me relate to our country more directly and with greater humour and emotion."

"Excuse me, Edgar. Have you suffered a drunken fall from your horse and undergone subsequent surgery? Has much of your brain been removed?"

"Hear me out, Nana. All I've ever wanted is to make you, and my parents, and this country proud. But I've been floundering. I haven't found my voice, so all of my preoccupations, and my dull little speeches, they've been disciplined but routine. I can see it in peoples' eyes—they glaze over, thinking, 'Ah, more royal prattle, listening is optional.'"

"They don't need to listen! They're calmed!"

"Which isn't nearly enough. If all I am is careful and dutiful, I'm worthless. I'm not making an impact or building on your decades of fine work. I'm a shadow. So what I'm asking is this: Let me explore. Let me learn whatever I can from Carter."

"Learn from this fetid slug? This clot of American phlegm? This associate event pothole?"

"Bitch," I whispered, under my breath.

"What did you say?"

I mimed sewing my lips shut.

"Nana, let me prove to you that Carter isn't just an ignorant, destructive, mewling infant."

Slandering me was now the royal family's favorite pastime. I was their Jenga.

"I have an idea, and I've made all the necessary arrangements. There's a way to present Carter in a less pressured, more congenial format. A means of telling the world, 'Here's Carter, and he's not so bad.'"

"*Not so bad*"? James caught my eye, silently signaling, *Hush, Edgar's on a roll.*

"He's a person, he's fun, he's a functioning adult."

James gestured to me: *No! Shut up! This is working!*

"'He's a person'? 'He's fun'?" the queen sneered. "Is he a new enzyme detergent or roll-on deodorant?"

"He could be. I've gone over my campaign with Marc and Alison, and they've approved. So please, Nana, trust me. I can do this. Carter can do this. It's brilliant. It will make everyone say, 'Carter Ogden is a bit of all right. Carter Ogden isn't—Carter, what was that word your great-aunt Miriam called that inebriated fellow who bumped into her on the dance floor? A putz? Imagine it, Nana, if that was on everyone's lips, as they turn to one another and toast our family, if the nation could speak as one and proclaim, 'Carter Ogden—not a putz!'"

"And just what is this inherently unworkable notion?"

"You'll see. Because for perhaps the first time in my life, I'm working on instinct. I'm thinking, as it were, outside the throne room. I'm being ingenious, creative and . . . and . . ."

"Adaptable," I murmured.

"Adaptable!" said Edgar. "So let us surprise you."

I had no idea what Edgar was talking about, and I wasn't being asked for my opinion. But I loved hearing him bargain like this, improvising and coaxing. He reminded me of me when I was thirteen and begging my parents to let me take the train into New York by myself, or when I'd borrowed Callum's leather jacket when he was out of town and lost it at a dance party. I'd told him it was stolen by a Republican senator. He'd bought my story. It's all about believing whatever you're saying, especially if it's insane.

Queen Catherine shut her eyes and inhaled as if she was vaping the universe. She opened her eyes. She glanced to either side, consulting invisible ancestors. She sighed and gave her form of permission:

"Get out of my sight."

CHAPTER 22

We were brought in a golf cart to the set of *The Great British Baking Jubilee* the next morning at seven a.m. When I asked Edgar how he'd come up with this idea, he told me, "I imagined I was you, handed an assignment which called for friendly media attention, a nonpartisan, immersive activity, a colourful backdrop and a live audience which exists to applaud. I'm an associate event prince."

I was floored by his process; this was an innovation worthy of me, someone who'd branded a morticians' conference at a Pennsylvania Marriott by stuffing the gift bags with black water bottles embossed with a skull and crossbones, along with temporary tattoos reading "Kill Me Now." I'd also provided a link to a hookup app called Dying to Meet You. Morticians, it turned out, love to party.

While I'm only an occasional fan of *The Great British Baking Jubilee*, my dad DVRs every full season, and while he's watching he'll text me every few seconds: "Betty's adding currants to her scones! She's living on the edge!" "Eleanor is shaving lemon curd onto her aspic—I can't watch!"

The show's billowing white tent is erected on the grounds of various National Trust manor homes and ruined cathedrals that only my dad knows the details of ("That's where Ethelred the Unsteady married Helen of Bramwich!"). He has strong opinions on the show's longtime host, Agatha Benwhistle ("She really understands tarts") and her current cohost, a younger loose cannon named Miles Tanney ("He went to culinary school, so he thinks he knows everything about marzipan. As if."). He duplicates the recipes and poses each lemongrass loaf or elderberry compote atop a velvet ottoman in our living room to catch the sunlight from a picture window, posting photos on Instagram at Professor Yummy Jubilee.

So I was well-prepared when the show's production manager led Edgar, James, the security team and me backstage on the lawn of Hallinghurst Castle, and when I sent my dad photos he texted back, "Drooling. Jealous. Bring back a spatula!"

"Your Highness," James asked, "while I know it's an inexplicably popular program, is this really a proper environment for a royal appearance?"

"Did anyone catch the episode on sweetbreads?" asked Ian. "There were real eyeopeners."

"Who gives a damn?" argued Clark. "Compared to the olive and garlic rolls."

"I adore this show," said Maureen, joining us with Gerald; they were slated, along with Edgar and me, to act as surprise guest judges on today's episode. "I've had our chef copy the mango and cardamom tea cakes." Gerald and Maureen were, as always, overdressed in coordinated outfits. In their forest green blazers, pink gingham shirts and, oh my dear Lord, ascots, they looked like prissy Mercedes-Benz sales reps, or Hansel and Gretel as cruise ship social directors.

"When I told Maureen that you and Carter were going to be here," said Gerald, "she insisted we chaperone. I went along, because you chaps can't afford another epic mishap."

They had a private chef. We had epic mishaps.

Gerald and Maureen were keeping a close eye on Edgar, and I suspected something: if they could somehow rejigger the line of succession, Gerald would get to be king. They were like conniving understudies, wishing the star every success while spiking his latte with antifreeze.

Or maybe I was being paranoid. But while Abby and I would kill for each other, there was a polite distance between Edgar and Gerald. I'd never heard Edgar say a bad word about his brother, but they didn't hang out together, aside from their royal obligations. This made me even more protective of Edgar; I was starting to feel responsible for him. Which felt good.

"This is a terrific opportunity," said Edgar. Because this was the season finale, the show was being aired live. The proceedings were underway, and on the video monitors I saw that the contestants had been assigned to make trifle, an especially English dessert. I texted my dad and got back emojis of applauding hands and cartwheeling chefs along with "TRIFLE!!! You're in for a TREAT!!!"

The tent was arranged with twenty workstations stocked with sinks, mini-fridges, restaurant-grade stoves, counter space and drawers of pots, pans and utensils. The contestants, recruited from all over the country, could bring a limited number of "lucky" knives, whisks, sifters and measuring spoons. Everyone was wearing the show's signature aprons, which, as the baking progressed, became daubed with ingredients. The show combined cutthroat competition with heartwarming individual backstories, as everyone bustled painstakingly to complete their trifles before the one-hour deadline, with the hosts dropping by each workstation to offer passive-aggressive tips like "Ah, so we're moving toward clotted cream" or "Won't that be marvelous, if it doesn't congeal."

Staff members with clipboards and headsets summoned us for the climax of the telecast. I texted my dad, "It's happening!" and he replied, "If you don't bring me an apron don't bother coming home."

"Won't this be a lark!" trilled Maureen, checking her makeup in a mirror held by her minder for the umpteenth time, and it occurred to me that Maureen's head could become a future *Baking Jubilee* Cranberry-Pistachio Baked Alaska challenge.

"And did Edgar mention," said Gerald, "this is Nana's favourite program? So I'm sure she's watching."

"You see?" Edgar told me. "Just being on this show will make Nana worship you. Along with the entire world. It's the ideal event."

"You're both so brave," said Gerald.

"Contestants, and viewers all across the globe," said Agatha Benwhistle, standing at the front of the tent beside a long, Last Supper–style table covered with a white cloth, "the time has come." Agatha was somewhere in her sixties, stout and wearing a forgiving corduroy tunic, wide-legged purple pants and comfortable shoes with rubber soles. Her hair was a silver thatched-roof bob, and she spoke in a good-tempered, booming, beloved headmistress's voice; she was devoted to English baking, often posted photos of her three basset hounds wearing the turtlenecks and booties she knitted for them and never humiliated contestants. Her worst assessments were "Well, you'll live to bake another day" or "At the end of the day, it's only a smoked walnut flaxseed muffin, not an ailing grandparent."

"I can barely contain myself," said Miles Tanney, who was half Agatha's age, with a background as a bubbly podcast host (*Smiles from Miles*), commercial spokesperson (for everything from kebab skewers to garden hoses) and YouTube influencer (with videos where he organized closets "by necessity and mood"). His giddy cheerleading was a great foil for Agatha's earthy straightforwardness.

"Oh, Agatha," Miles gushed breathlessly, "today's episode will become culinary legend!"

"Perhaps, but just for now, let's allow our cat out of the bag, shall we? Because to rate our final trio, and to award our highest honor, the season's Grand Jubilee Golden Rolling Pin, let's welcome our esteemed and very special guest judges—Their Royal Highnesses, Prince Edgar and Prince Gerald; Maureen, the Duchess of Longshire; and a friend of the family, Mr. Carter Ogden!"

Edgar embraced Agatha, while Miles managed to bow, wave his arms and crouch in wonderment as if we were giraffes he'd spotted in the wild, enthusing, "Welcome, royals and friend! What a surprise! What an occasion! As I'm sure our contestants will agree, today is a *Great British Baking Jubilee* pinnacle par excellence!" He pronounced "excellence" as if it was floridly French and the equivalent of a magician's "Abracadabra!"

"Thank you so much for inviting our little group to become part of this superb program," said Edgar. "We're so lucky to be here amidst all this extraordinary baking talent."

"Just so," said Gerald, and after trying to come up with another remark, repeated, with emphasis, "Just so."

"I live for this show," said Maureen. "I even watch it in the bath!"

"And Mr. Ogden?" said Miles. "Are you familiar with the *Jubilee?*"

"I think it's wonderful, and it's my dad's favorite show of all time!"

The crowd in the tent liked this, and Edgar and I smiled at each other—so far, so good.

"You must send your father our best," said Agatha. "Hello, Mr. Ogden's dad! And now let's get to it, shall we? We have three contestants who've survived an especially grueling season—let's not even mention our unfortunate detour into organic braided strudel. But they've remained staunch and true, moving ever closer to the finish line. So let me introduce Angus McReedy, our lorry driver from East Sussex; Harriet Nordstadt, author of fourteen introduction to hand-embroidery pamphlets for children and a gifted trombonist; and, all the way from Great Torrington we've got Anora Persad, who brews her own nonalcoholic ales, hangs wallpaper and volunteers as a firefighter."

The contestants were exchanging jittery but pleased glances, stunned by the royals' presence. They took their places behind the table as jumpsuited staffers gingerly placed their entries in front of them. To my great relief, none of the contestants nor the rows of audience members were paying even minor attention to me.

Trifle, as far as I could tell, was a layered dessert consisting of just about anything combined in a large clear glass container; the trifles were colorful, complicated and reminded me of rare squids or jellyfish squeezed into cylindrical aquariums. Think parfaits on steroids, or brandy snifters packed with pudding, cream cheese and sponge cake.

"Let's begin with Anora, our firefighter and alemistress," said Agatha. "Tell us about your trifle."

Anora, sweet-faced and anxious, said, "Well, ma'am, I've always loved a good trifle, and since my family is from Trinidad, I'm honoring them with melon balls, candied yams, butterscotch treacle and shredded coconut, with a drizzle of caramel and rum."

"Your Highness?" said Miles, handing Edgar a silver spoon.

"I must tell you," said Edgar, as if confiding a sexual fetish, "I wait all year for Christmas trifle. If you'd allow me, I'd devour everyone's trifles on the spot. But Anora, yours looks delicious."

Edgar dipped his spoon, snaring several layers, and tasted. He beamed. "This is heavenly! I can taste the yams, the butterscotch and the sublime coconut! It's a symphony! Well done, Anora!"

Edgar wasn't faking any of this; the man loved trifle. And I loved the man.

"Although I'm not sure we need the caramel," Agatha commented, having dipped her own spoon. Agatha was supplying balance: "While caramel is always welcome, it occasionally becomes a lingering guest who's misplaced his car keys." After each of us had tried a trifle, we'd rotate and taste the others.

"Your Highnesses?" said Miles, handing spoons to Gerald and Maureen. "May I present Angus, who's recently had a hip replacement following a workplace mishap, but who's never stopped baking."

Angus, an older man with a cane and a curlicued moustache, said, in a rugged accent, "I've tried to create a sophisticated trifle, using malt bouillon, diced almondine wafers and a suggestion of raspberry gelatin, mingled with mascarpone, which I've tinted to resemble stained glass. It was me mum's recipe."

"It's unusual," Gerald decided, after a brimming spoonful,

"perhaps a mite academic. But a worthy effort, even with reserva-
tions."

Oh, please, Gerald, I thought. *Stop puffing yourself up as if
you're the Global Trifle Authority.*

"I'm enjoying it," said Maureen, who'd of course only nibbled,
to appear ladylike and avoid excess calories. "The mascarpone
matches the amber stripe in one of our guest bedrooms, so good
job on your colour palette."

"Colour palette"? Really? Okay, now I was just being snarky.

"And Mr. Ogden," said Agatha, "would you please do us the
honor of sampling Harriet's trifle?"

Harriet was tall and narrow, with a nature guide's can-do
pluck. "I've given this much thought, and I'm so pleased to meet
His Highness and Mr. Ogden, because I've always dreamed of
creating a rainbow trifle. So I've used blueberries, strawberries,
lemon rind and celery, along with my signature crushed ginger
biscuits, splashes of fresh peppermint and homemade grape jelly
from my pantry. And for a final touch, I've added a candle accent."

The trifle was ringed with lit rainbow candles and looked like
the happiest pride parade float. I was determined to love it, because of Harriet's toothy smile, her politics and her trombone
habit.

I dipped my spoon between the candles, tasted and swallowed.

"The mix of flavors is surprising and completely delicious," I
said, meaning every word.

"It's like a rainbow in my mouth. Congratulations, Harriet . . ."

Hold on. Had something caught in my throat? Had a ginger
biscuit been waylaid? No. I wasn't about to gag, I couldn't. I went
for a mild cough, covering a burp.

"Carter?" said Edgar, concerned.

"Mr. Ogden?" echoed Agatha.

"The aftertaste is even more appealing, it's . . . it's . . ."

Oh my God. I can control this, I can force my body, especially my esophagus, to brace itself, or at least wait till I'm off-camera. Except something's rising. Why am I thinking about that scene in one of the *Alien* movies where the fanged creature bursts out of that guy's shuddering chest?

"Carter?" asked Miles, worried. "Is there a digestive issue?"

"No, not at all, I love Harriet's trifle . . ."

I was trying so hard. I was commanding my stomach to stop contracting and my body to stop sweating and shaking. But there was an ice-pick pain radiating from my gut into my throat, and my shoulders heaved as the trifle climbed higher and higher, clawing its way and unstoppably returning to my mouth.

"Carter, you're white as a sheet," said Edgar. "Is there a doctor standing by?"

"This is hard to watch," said Gerald as I clutched at the table-cloth, to at least stay upright, while making uncontrollable gag-ging noises at a cement mixer volume.

"Perhaps it's an American response," said Maureen, turning away.

"I . . . I . . . I'm fine, I just, I just . . ."

I've always hated vomiting, because it's gross and because it turns my body against itself. As a child I'd sworn that I'd never vomit, that I wouldn't let it happen, not to me. *Do not vomit*, I shouted inwardly. *YOU ARE NOT A PERSON WHO VOMITS.*

And then not just a spoonful of trifle, but everything I'd eaten in the past week, or maybe since birth, rocketed volcanically up my throat and out my mouth, splattering Harriet, Agatha, Miles and all the royal judges, because my head kept whipping back and forth like a malfunctioning sprinkler system. I couldn't stop vomiting, and the second I thought, *This must be everything*, my gullet upchucked more, until I expected to see my lungs and spleen hitting the ceiling of the tent. Whatever gag reflex I had was long gone; I was an open tunnel, a vomit superhighway. I might very well be birthing an island or a new continent made entirely out of regurgitated trifle, which was also now drenching the camera lens.

As I staggered, and Edgar tried to yank and steady me, I fell headlong, dragging the tablecloth and upending all the trifles, causing the candles in Harriet's trifle to set the tablecloth on fire, which was when everyone in the tent began screaming and running for the exits as the cameras swung wildly and the bodyguards sprinted to find fire extinguishers while hoping not to slip in my barf. It was like watching a mob fleeing from Godzilla or a marauding triceratops, not knowing which way to turn, with parents being swept away by my tidal wave of trifle, reaching out helplessly for wailing babies. Right before I passed out I knew only one thing:

For the rest of my life, whenever anyone didn't like something, a politician or a movie star's performance or a holiday sweater, their opinion would be punctuated by a clip of me vomiting trifle.

"Might I?"

It was Maureen, an hour later. I'd refused an ambulance because I was so mortified, and I was lying on a cot in a holding area, a few yards from what remained of the *Baking Jubilee* tent. The fire had been quickly contained and the show's finale was in the process of being rescheduled. The sweat that had soaked my body was starting to dry, and Edgar had been tending to me with fresh towels and ice chips. A local doctor had checked me out and said that I'd most likely had food poisoning, either from an ingredient I hadn't known I was allergic to or from one of the trifle's dairy products spoiling under the hot lights. Edgar was off finding me some crackers, which were all I'd ever eat for the rest of my life, when Maureen walked in.

"Hey," I said, pulling myself up on an elbow.

"Don't. Just rest. You've earned it. You poor boy."

"Your Grace?"

"Maureen, please. Oh, Carter, when I saw your face going so deathly pale, my heart just broke."

"I'm so sorry, and look at your blazer . . ."

"My blazer is fine; a spritz with club soda and all was well. But you're my concern. Because, and I know you won't believe this, but I know just how you feel."

"Maureen?"

"Gerald and I have been married for five years, and it's been lovely. Strenuous but lovely. It was the year before the wedding that almost destroyed me."

"How?"

"I was an ordinary girl from the Cotswolds. My dad ran a small construction business, and my mum was his receptionist. They'd sacrificed so much to send me to university—not Oxford with Gerald, but nearby. We met at one of those awful parties where everyone's drunk and sprawling and pretending not to notice there's a royal in the room. And Gerald was so out of place, because he's not really a party person, as perhaps you've gathered. He was sitting in the corner of a couch, barely sipping some frightfully adult cocktail, in his grey flannels and cardigan, as if he was someone's dad, or a faculty assistant, and he looked so morose that I took pity. I like a project."

Maureen was being surprisingly genuine.

"But once things grew more serious, I had to make a decision. Because I simply wasn't prepared for the onslaught. After our first public appearance, at the dedication of a footbridge, I wasn't merely criticised, I was flayed alive. I was too common, my ankles were too thick, I was a gold digger with two rhinoplasties and a breast augmentation. I was pretentious and dull, and above all else, I'd never be as kind or as glamorous or as saintly as Gerald and Edgar's mum."

"What happened? How did you turn things around?"

"Laboriously. And, to this day, never in full. I think when people realised that Gerald wasn't buckling under, and that he'd made his choice, there was a sort of truce. But I was still unbearably plain, and not up to the task, and then there was the most fearsome obstacle of all."

"Queen Catherine?"

"Who hated me on sight. She thought I lacked spirit, whatever that might be, perhaps because she kept me in a constant state of terror, and would mistake me for a palace assistant and call me Mabel."

"Been there. Am there."

"I've still made only the slightest dent. After Gerald sat her down and said he was marrying me, with her approval or without, she shrugged, and decided that it doesn't really matter, since Gerald will never be king. So she's become, well, almost cordial. I've made my peace with this, but that's why I wanted to speak with you, especially after today. Because you don't have to do it."

"What do you mean?"

"I mean—this life. It isn't for everyone. Think about the future. Right now, you've still got a chance at escape. And I know how much Edgar means to you, I can see that, but what I'm saying is, this isn't just about affection. It's about you."

"Me?"

"Don't be trapped by the occasional dazzle and the attentive staff and some image of yourself as a sunlit, gracious royal, carefully posed beside Edgar on a magazine cover. That's only publicity, and whatever pleasure it holds fades, rather quickly. And then it's just the two of you, behind barbed wire and brick walls and armed guards, making a life, as best you can. Think it through."

Why was Maureen telling me this? Was she being straightforward and helpful, as a battle-toughened veteran, or maneuvering to eliminate me? Her face was, as always, masklike, and I wondered what would happen if she ever cried.

"Maureen—do you regret marrying Gerald?"

She uttered the tiniest sigh. "No. Of course not. But at times, I regret marrying everything else."

"Triscuits or saltines?" asked Edgar, carrying boxes of both. "Maureen? I thought you'd gone back to London."

"On my way. I just wanted to check in with our boy here, who seems to be on the mend. Please feel better, Carter, and think about what I've said. I'm one of the few people with a firsthand perspective. And Edgar, do take better care of Carter. No more rainbow trifle."

She touched my hand and left.

"What is she talking about? What did she tell you?"

"That I should rest and drink fluids and try not to barf on her shoes again. She was fine. Very sweet."

This was the first time I'd deliberately lied to Edgar. Through my exhausted haze, I managed to sit up on the edge of the cot.

"Carter, I've come to like Maureen, but the one thing she's not is sweet. What did one of the tabloids call her? 'The Pink Piranha'?"

"Okay," I said, resolving not to dance around my most recent fiasco. "I know that today wasn't my fault, sort of, but it's part of a pattern. I can't keep embarrassing you and forcing you to look chipper and put a smiley-face spin on everything and tell me I'm doing great. It's not fair to either of us, but especially not to you. Or to all those queer kids watching us and thinking, 'You know, maybe being straight isn't such a bad idea after all.' I just, I'm . . .'"

I was grasping for some adequate phrase, to let Edgar off the hook. I couldn't look in his eyes.

Harriet was standing a few feet away. "Mr. Ogden?" she asked. "And Your Highness? May I have a word?"

"Of course," said Edgar, although there was nothing I could say to make amends with Harriet after what I'd done to her.

"Mr. Ogden, I'm so sorry about your physical distress, and I need to apologise for the trifle."

"No no no, it's not your fault, and your trifle was fantastic, you deserved to win . . ."

"But don't you see? I did win. Because I've had the opportunity to meet His Highness, and even more importantly, the fellow he cares about. That's why I chose the rainbow. My partner, Edith, she's an optometrist, we've been together for twenty-one years, and things haven't always been . . . unhindered. Our families barely speak to us, and just last week, this bloke was walking past Edith's storefront, and he saw the small rainbow flag in the window. He marched in just as Edith was giving an eye exam to

Rebecca, a woman from our church, she's been coming to Edith for years. And the man was clutching the flag. He spat on it, tossed it on the floor, and called Edith and Rebecca, and I'm quoting, 'a couple of ugly dyke bitches.' And he stomped out."

"Oh my God . . ." I said.

"I'm so sorry . . ." Edgar added.

"And that's why you mean so much, and why Edith has been showing me all the photos of the two of you together. Edith?"

A woman Harriet's age, only shorter and redheaded, in a Levi's jacket and a long skirt, had been waiting outside.

"What a pleasure," said Edith, shyly. "You've made our day."

Edgar and I were about to cry as Harriet and Edith asked for a selfie, and I tried not to breathe on them.

"Oh my," said Edgar, after the couple had gone.

"They're so wonderful. And everything they said, we don't deserve it. I don't."

"But Harriet and Edith thought otherwise. And Carter, I know we shouldn't keep at this just for the optics as queer mascots. That would be madness. So there's something I should tell you."

Here it comes. He's being a gentleman. Letting me down easy. Even though we're both Aquarians. Or maybe because we're both Aquarians, which can be an overdose. We'd been ingenious and adaptable and all the rest of it, and the result was clear. We should burn everything we had on. He'll say it's not me, it's him. We'll both be so caring.

"When I saw you barf, with that rainbow of partially digested trifle geysering from every opening in your body, I only had two thoughts. First I told myself, 'Do not laugh. That would be so inhumane.'"

"Thank you."

"But beyond that, as you went through the day, putting your-self out there, and all for me, I was just . . . Well, it was all very touching, but in truth I barely noticed what you were doing. Because all I kept seeing was you. I couldn't stop. Because of a simple fact that has nothing to do with palaces or event planning or buckets of contaminated trifle. I've been thinking about every-thing we fought over the other night, and how I blathered on about finding a partner, as if you weren't right there beside me."

"Edgar, it's okay, I get it, we both have goals, and I don't want to stand in your way of meeting just the right guy, someone who deserves you—"

"Will you please be still?"

"Fine!"

"Good Lord. All right. I've never said this before, not in this manner. I thought I'd never have the opportunity. And now I'm stammering and flouncing and trying not to say it, because I'm petrified that you don't feel the same way."

"What way?"

I could hear Ruth Ginsburg whispering in my ear, "Shut up. You need to hear this."

I could hear Louise growling, "Incoming neo-capitalist emo-tional manifesto. Beware."

I could hear Abby telling me, "Pay attention, doofus. I wish you could send me whatever he's about to say on your phone."

"I love you."

CHAPTER 23

He loved me. Edgar loved me. I'd just vomited rainbow trifle on international television, I could barely stand up and he loved me.

After he said it, Edgar refused to let me answer or say anything whatsoever. He told me I shouldn't say it back, not yet, and not because he expected me to. He said we had time, and then I wobbled to the car, we drove back to the palace and Edgar put me to bed in my own room, ordered me to get some sleep and left.

Of course the second he was gone, I FaceTimed Abby on my tablet; since the *Jubilee* she'd been texting me nonstop, but I'd been too distracted and fatigued to respond.

"Finally!" she said. "I saw the baking thing and I could tell exactly what was happening—sometimes food poisoning takes a few days, but I've seen cases where it kicks in within seconds, and it can wipe you out. Did they give you IV fluids with electrolytes? Even sports drinks can help. Are you okay?"

"I will be, and the doctor was great, but this isn't about the *Jubilee*. It's about what happened afterward. It's an Abby Alert."

"Oh my God!" said Abby, her face lighting up. I remembered that she and Dane were on the last night of their honeymoon, and they were strolling back to their beachfront villa in the moonlight, both wearing sarongs and straw hats.

"I'm sorry!" I said. "It's your last night in Bali, so we can talk later!"

"No," Abby insisted. "This is major, and Dane's cool with it, aren't you, babe?"

Dane, who'd enjoyed more than three cocktails sipped through huge straws from guavas, gave Abby and me two thumbs up. As he entered the villa, Abby sat on the front steps. "So?" she asked. "Did he say it?"

Abby and I had invented Abby Alerts years ago, while she was sick. We'd sworn an oath, that whenever a guy said that he loved either one of us, we'd report back as quickly as possible. When Callum had said it, I'd called Abby from outside a Fire Island dance club, and while we'd both cheered, Abby mentioned that she'd just seen Callum, who was playing a divorced dad with a great dog, say "I love you" to a young widow with two adorable kids in a Lifetime movie. "So just remember," she'd warned me, "he's good at it." When Dane had told Abby he loved her, after a Central Park softball game, she'd been wonderfully discombobulated, telling me, "I mean, I knew he loved me, we've been going out for a year, but with straight guys it's so cute, because they have no idea how to say it, so Dane sounded like a little kid, blurting it out, as if he was going to punch me on the shoulder. But then he kissed me and he's really good at that."

So this was a necessary, sacred call. I described exactly where and how Edgar had made his declaration. Abby got very quiet.

"Whoa," she finally said. "So he was basically covered with your puke and then he said 'I love you.' Which is both the most disgusting and the most romantic thing I've ever heard. Oh, Carter. Now just blank everything else out, the barf and the Internet and who Edgar is, and just tell me: when he said 'I love you,' what was the first thing you thought?"

"I thought—that I'd heard him wrong. That he'd said something else, like 'I'm sorry' or 'There's something on your chin' and that my idiot brain had turned it into 'I love you.' And then it hit me that he'd really said it, and I froze and I thought, 'I am in so much trouble.'"

"You're in trouble? Why?"

"Because . . . because . . . because up until that second, I was winging it. On Valentine's Day I'd asked God and Ruth Ginsburg for guidance and true love and now all of a sudden, it was happening. Answered prayers. I'd met this amazing guy who's ridiculously out ⟨ ⟩y league and all I can think about is—no. I can't do this. It's too much, it's too real. It's the ultimate hall of fame triple-platinum lottery jackpot opportunity for me to fuck everything up. Because that's what I do."

Abby was staring at me, with clouds scudding across the Balinese night sky behind her, and I could tell she was deeply pissed off. She was about to say something, but she held up her hand, to stop herself from being too harsh. And then:

"Carter, if I could reach through this phone I would grab you by the throat and strangle you till you were dead. So you listen to me. You are not just a smart, handsome, fabulous man with so much to offer, you're even better than that, because you're my brother. Edgar is after the most awesome package deal. Why hasn't it sunk in that Edgar is thinking, 'I'm in love with the perfect guy and also his irresistible pediatric surgeon sister'? He's all about free medical advice. It explains everything."

"Abby . . ." I said, smiling.

"You need to be fucking clear about something. This is the guy. And if he's going to become the king of England, well, boo-fucking-hoo. You found him. He found you. You both got so lucky. And you are not going to fuck this up. You are going to believe in it. You're going to show Edgar and yourself and the universe that this can work. You can't run away or talk yourself out of it. You're going to do the opposite. You're going to go for it."

"But . . ."

"What part of 'Fuck you, it was bad trifle, get over yourself and have an incredible life with the guy you love' don't you understand?"

The next day Edgar called Cassandra and promised her the use of the royal crest as an endorsement on her website if she gave me two more unpaid vacation weeks.

I was intent on using these weeks to prove Maureen, Her Majesty and all the haters wrong. I'd convince everyone, and myself, that this was for keeps. That I was ready. That I'd been tested by the rugby match and the children's hospital and the *Jubilee*, and I'd never make such rookie mistakes again. I would unveil not just a revamped, slightly more aware version of myself, but a completely new product. Someone confident, polished and adult, someone who belonged at Edgar's side, or at a respectful distance behind him, on the world stage.

Over the next two weeks, here's what happened:

Edgar had a tuxedo custom made for me, explaining, "It's not for special occasions; it's a uniform." I'd always loved the suave, man-of-destiny notion of myself in a tux, but I'd made do with rentals and thrift-store bargains. With a tux draped, cut and sewn to my exact dimensions, I was a roguish financier lighting a cigarette atop the Eiffel Tower or 007 tossing his diamond cuff links onto a blackjack table at Monte Carlo. I was someone who made out with Edgar, both of us in our tuxes, in a side room during a ball at the Australian embassy.

I found that the secret to holding my own at, say, a country house dinner party was to never obscure or lie about my background; as an American interloper, I could ask the other guests questions and be bad at croquet and glance at Edgar across the room, especially his ass in riding clothes.

The key to defeating Queen Catherine's nightly surveillance was to face her down and say, "Your Majesty, if you'll excuse me, I need to go and perform fellatio on His Highness. Someone has to do it." The first time I did this she was speechless, then threw up her hands, hissed, "Charming," and let me pass.

Touring the Chelsea Flower Show was actually fun; the displays of enormous dahlias and wisteria and fuchsias, micro-calculated to arrive at their peaks, were like horticultural musical comedies. I like fanatics, and if you mess with their succulents, English gardeners are capable of using trowels as switchblades.

Edgar and I could make a political statement just by showing up, and especially by dancing. We practiced, and two men in white tie waltzing in a ballroom at an event to promote international human rights can make an impression on a snide Russian oil baron who wants to cultivate foreign investors. I checked with Louise and she approved, calling our waltz "a subliminal protest action and a decent start."

My renewed campaign confused Gerald and especially Maureen. She'd expected me to be persuaded by her admonitions at the *Jubileee* and flee the country and any future with Edgar. She'd meant well, but she'd also wanted to clear a path, for Gerald's ascension to the throne. Whenever I'd run into her, at a formal dinner or a charitable tea, she'd say things like "Still at it?" or "We're praying for you," which weren't precisely votes of confidence. While Maureen could be congenial and almost an ally, at heart she was a political spouse, plotting Gerald's rise. I was careful around her; being cheerful and polite were my own tactical maneuvers, for safeguarding Edgar.

Late one night, while we were in bed, Edgar tossed my sweatpants at me, saying, "Come along." Barely dressed, I followed him up three flights of stairs and into a darkened room. He pulled back the curtains, and a full moon illuminated furniture hidden beneath sheets. He uncovered a well-worn, chintz-upholstered sofa and beckoned for me to sit beside him.

"We're here," he said. "This is it."

"Where are we?"

"The nursery. Where I'd have fun with Gerald and our parents."

This was the place Edgar had told me about during our first dinner at IHOP. This was his sanctuary when the world became too much. When he needed to be alone.

"It's—it feels like we're floating," I said, peering at the walls, which were painted with a mural of animals in striped vests and top hats playing musical instruments. "As if when we go outside, a hundred years might've passed. Or we'll be on a mountaintop or a pirate ship."

"Yes. Sometimes I've thought about tidying things up, but I haven't. I've been waiting. To show it to you."

He looked at me, to see if I could handle this. To see if he could become this open, and connected to his past, and free.

"I love it."

Which wasn't me saying "I love you," but still an important step; we were trusting each other more and more.

"Look," Edgar said, finding something behind a cushion. "He's still here."

He was manipulating a hand puppet of a threadbare lion.

"Hello, Carter," said the lion. "Will you have sex with me?"

"Now I understand everything. You had a gay puppet."

"You belong here," said the lion.

CHAPTER 24

"Holding it together?" asked Edgar, as we sat side by side having our hair and makeup tended to in a greenroom at BBC Studios. We were wearing similar but not identical blazers (his navy versus my gray Harris Tweed). We had tissues tucked into our collars to protect our crisply laundered shirts from the foundation that was being sponged onto our faces and set with powder. Our hair had been trimmed, slicked and sprayed, and we'd definitely trounce the poodles at the Westminster Dog Show.

"You resemble strange evangelical cousins," said James. "The sort of people who come to the door with Bibles and won't leave."

"You look so handsome, Your Highness," said Edgar's stylist, an ultra-competent woman who wore very little makeup herself and kept her hair in a ponytail.

"As does Carter," said Edgar, thanking my stylist, a great guy with a shaved head and multiple piercings, who said, "Next time I'll give you matching Mohawks."

"It's a mite scary," commented Ian to the security team. "They look like those twins in *The Shining*."

"Or hired assassins," said Terry.

"But in a good way," Lucky assured us.

As we waited off-camera with the Palace advisors, Edgar told me, "You're going to be splendid. The country will forget all about me."

"The country will embrace both of you, God willing," said Marc.

"People just want to see if I'll barf. And what color."

"They've already increased the estimate to three hundred million viewers worldwide," said Alison, who'd masterminded the interview. "Polls have Edgar's approval rating at ninety-two percent, with Carter hovering around seventy percent, which is a vast improvement from earlier in the week."

I'd been staying off social media to dodge such statistics, but I was glad my numbers were rising. Adam had texted me that, according to CNN, "Almost no one thinks you're a Scientologist who's trying to convert Edgar, not anymore," and Louise had liked our attending an Amnesty International banquet (we didn't get into the disconnect of having former political prisoners speak at a $25,000-a-plate dinner).

The studio buzzed with grips, camera operators and production assistants going about their tasks. The set was flimsy, with its green screen backdrop, which would project an abstract rotating globe, but with proper lighting and close-ups, everything would be transformed into must-watch morning show prestige.

Caroline Chadwick, our host, was already seated and having her microphone clipped to the neckline of her sleeveless, tomato red sheath, the choice for newswomen everywhere who want to appear professional but svelte. Caroline, who's England's foremost news/entertainment/chat personality, was approachably glamorous; she was you, if you had access to stylists, round-the-clock day care, publicists, a driver and interns who'd been forbidden to make eye contact.

Edgar and I were brought to chairs opposite Caroline, and I'd been trained, by my associate event background, to sit on the tail of my jacket so it wouldn't scrunch up, to push my shoulders back and to not put my hands in my lap. The key to talk-show appearances is to stay relaxed and completely artificial at the same time.

After a stage manager's countdown and Caroline's pounding theme music, the lights became blinding and Caroline swiveled to the camera, chirping, "Good morning, everyone, and welcome to *Caroline and Company*. And what a divinely special morning this is. Because today, as promised, my guests are His Royal Highness Prince Edgar and his much-talked-about American companion of late, one Carter Ogden."

As Caroline filled in the most up-to-the-minute data on what she called our "burgeoning affiliation," Edgar touched my arm and murmured, "Here we go."

"Good morning, Your Highness and Mr. Ogden. It's marvelous to have you here for your very first live-on-the-air, in-depth interview as a couple."

"It's our pleasure, Caroline," said Edgar. "We always enjoy your program, and thank you for asking us."

Using a host's first name warms things up; it's why politicians tell newscasters, "Hank, that's why I'm in favor of nuclear power plants near schools."

"Let's get right to it," said Caroline. "Your Highness, how would you characterise your relationship with Mr. Ogden?"

"Carter is not only a dear friend, but someone I've had the

privilege of getting to know. He's impressed me beyond words, and he delights me. And I'm sure your viewers will feel the same."

"And Mr. Ogden? Your thoughts?"

"I admire and respect His Highness, especially because he's been introducing me to the English people, who've overwhelmed me with their kindness, generosity and great good humor. And yes, I've come to enjoy trifle as well."

We all laughed; my *Jubilee* trauma was the elephant in the room, so I'd climbed on its back and waved merrily. I could tell from Edgar's grin that he liked my approach.

A few days ago, when Edgar had asked me about doing this interview, I'd been skittish, and he'd said it was my call. But I'd thought about how well we'd been getting along and about how much smoother our public life had become, so I decided, *Why not?* I loved that Edgar wanted to be up front about our romance, and his team had ratified that Caroline's show would be friendly turf.

Marc and Alison had been raring to prep me, but I didn't want to worry everything to death. Wouldn't it be great if Edgar and I could be an everyday gay couple, even in the spotlight? Of course, I'd coached fathers of the bride, Easter brunch cater-waiters dressed as bunnies, and mermaids floating across the indoor pools of Tribeca real estate showings, for years; I was savvy about positioning a brand. Only this morning that brand was An Appealing and Affable Gay Royal Couple.

"But Your Highness," said Caroline, "can you be more specific? Our viewers are dying to know—how do you forecast your future with Mr. Ogden?"

Caroline had become my great-aunt Miriam, wheedling for intimate details and, on behalf of parents everywhere, grandkids.

"Our future will depend entirely on Carter, but I'm hoping it will be bright. I'm not the easiest companion, I'm afraid."

"Carter, is this true?"

"Well, Edgar has much better manners than I do, and he's far more dedicated to helping just about everyone. Yesterday he hosted an event for the Royal Clean Water Initiative, which he founded. Before meeting His Highness, I'd had no idea that over a third of the world's people don't have access to something as basic and essential as clean drinking water. Edgar's traveled to over twenty-two countries, where he's helped to dig wells, install plumbing and secure funding for pipelines."

From observing Edgar, I'd become a pro at redirecting a personal question toward a larger issue. It's how a movie star turns a gossip reporter's third degree about a recent breakup involving a drunken street brawl and a trip to the emergency room into a plug for her new documentary on koala habitats.

"Carter is an invaluable asset," said Edgar. "He's wonderful at talking to people and drawing them out. He has an accomplished background in event architecture, and he's accessible and open-hearted, traits which I'd very much like to emulate."

Edgar reached out and took my hand. For a royal, this was an unprecedented signal. Edgar was openly gay, but today he was proving it. The moment would be forwarded and paused and praised and condemned, and it made me love Edgar even more. Sure, for most couples, holding hands is no big deal, and Edgar wasn't angling for a Nobel Prize in LGBTQ PDA (Public Displays of Affection). But as Harriet and Edith were aware, the world isn't always a safe or inclusive place, and Edgar's gesture was seismic. As for me, I'd been anointed as the royal boyfriend, and for right now, that was swoonworthy enough.

"Your Highness," said Caroline, "I appreciate your many good works, and it must be gratifying to have met someone to share your causes. But we're all romantics at heart, so I'm speaking for fans everywhere when I ask, are you committed to one another? And I promise that we aren't adding winged cupids over your heads or shimmering orchestral glissandos in the editing room."

Edgar looked at me with such affection and trust. He'd told me he loved me and doing this had changed him. He wasn't the guarded, wounded man I'd first met, the guy who'd been hurt before and had conditioned himself to loneliness. He'd made the leap. He'd dared to be happy. Abby was right, about everything.

"Yes, we are, Caroline," said Edgar. "Deeply committed."

"And Mr. Ogden?"

"Yes. That's why I'm here, and that's why I'm grateful to have met someone who—well, as my great-aunt Miriam told me at my sister's wedding—he's a catch."

As everyone in the studio laughed and Edgar blushed, Caroline added, "Well, I think that's all brilliant, despite my next question, which I'm afraid I must ask. Your Highness, are you aware of cell phone footage that surfaced a half hour ago, and has gone viral, of Mr. Ogden passionately kissing another man?"

Time stopped. What was she talking about? Edgar was still holding my hand, but his was trembling.

"I'm not certain what you're referring to, Caroline," Edgar told her, keeping an even tone.

"Let's see the clip, where Carter seems quite smitten with someone who's been identified as Callum Turner, an American actor."

Edgar and I both turned as the screen behind us showed Callum and me, outside a restaurant, kissing.

"Well, that's quite simple, then," Edgar explained, visibly relieved. "Yes, Carter was involved with that chap, but it was some time ago. I'm sure this is from that earlier period."

"It's time-stamped from last night," said Caroline. "Just a few blocks from the palace."

No. No. I hadn't done anything wrong. Had I?

Last night Edgar and I had reluctantly agreed to stay in our own rooms so we'd be well rested for the interview. I'd had trouble getting to sleep, because I kept thinking about the show, with so many people watching, and how much I wanted to please Edgar. As I was lying in bed and giving myself an Abby-style you've-got-this pep talk a text came in, followed by a call. It was Callum, who was in London shooting a small role as a henchman in the next Bond movie; with his hair slicked back and the right mirrored sunglasses, Callum could pass for a glowering Euro-thug. He was nearby and wondered if I was up for a drink.

I knew it was a bad idea, but I was antsy and I could use some fresh air. Callum and I couldn't be more over, so what was the harm? And if I was being ruthlessly honest, I was itching to preen a little and to see if Callum would ask about Edgar so I could act super-casual as Callum tried to come off as unimpressed.

I pulled on my clothes, snuck out of the palace and walked to a café. Callum was waiting at a table in the back, and yes, he looked good. No one can slouch in a battered motorcycle jacket and jeans like Callum. That had been part of our problem; I could never tell if he was brooding or auditioning a new headshot.

"Hey, Carter. Look at you."

"I can only stay a minute."

"One drink."

"One Coke."

Callum gossiped about the movie and how excited he was, because "People haven't seen me do evil." I almost said, "I have," but resisted.

"So tell me about what's-his-name, your new dude, Prince Edward?"

"Edgar."

"Edgar, right. Skinny. But he seems cool. Is he a good guy?"

"The best." I was ashamed, because I wanted to brag, but I didn't need to punish Callum with my happiness. And my prince. I knew I should leave. Except I hadn't been out of the royal orbit for weeks, or talked to another American in person, so I told myself, *Five more minutes.*

"So is it, like, serious?"

"I think so. I hope so. I'm adjusting, but it's going well."

"Good. Great. I'm happy for you. Shit."

"What?"

"You probably can't tell, 'cause I was covering it, but I've been thinking about us. And when I see pictures of you with Prince whoever-he-is, it kills me. And I hate myself for that. I just want you to be happy. Really."

"Thank you. And I get it. Are you seeing anyone?"

"The vice president of the United States. Kidding. A couple of guys, nothing major. Not like us."

In his own confused, Callum-centric way, Callum was struggling. I wasn't sure if he still had feelings for me or if, because I was off the market, I was a challenge. Callum loved being adored by everyone, but he was so transparent that I could never hate him. He was sweetly stuck on himself. And by "a couple of guys" that meant there were at least four.

After more show business schmooze and Callum prying for

more information about Edgar, which I skated over, we left. As we were standing on the sidewalk and I was saying, "Great to see you, and congratulations on the movie," Callum put his hand on my neck and kissed me. I pulled away, but I didn't want to make a big deal of it, or smack him, especially because during the kiss, I felt nothing. Not even nostalgia. I was thinking about kissing Edgar and how much I missed him, even after only a few hours apart. The kiss may have lasted a moment longer than it should have, because my mind and my heart were elsewhere, and because Callum was holding my shoulder and not letting go.

"Hey, enough," I said, managing to break his grip.

"Just wanted to give it a shot."

"Not cool."

"Sorry."

Callum dipped his head and raised his eyes to reflect the streetlamp; this was one of his tricks, stolen from the use of key lights on movie sets, which add sparkle to an actor's eyes. Callum was his own best cinematographer. Then he gave me a wry half smile, the one he'd once used on a can of Diet Sprite, and sauntered off, maybe worried that he was losing his touch and should cut back on the carbs.

There had been sidewalk tables with a handful of stragglers, but I'd had no idea anyone was paying attention, not to me. Edgar was the famous person, and he wasn't here.

I hadn't told Edgar or Abby or anyone else about my encounter with Callum, as it had been brief and embarrassing and I'd already erased it.

"Mr. Ogden?" said Caroline.

"I . . . I . . . nothing happened," I said, because I was innocent. "It was nothing."

"You lived with Callum Turner for three years," Caroline continued, ramping into steely district attorney cross-examination mode. "And now he appears in London. Other patrons at the café have reported a highly amorous conversation and overheard Prince Edgar's name."

"We were just having a drink! Callum is shooting a movie!"

"And you were together for over an hour."

"Carter?" asked Edgar.

"And as the footage reveals," Caroline said, savoring the accusation, "the kiss is quite lengthy. And sensual. And Carter, when our staff contacted Mr. Turner, he said your relationship remains very real and that you'd been avid to see him. He said you seemed worried and offhand about His Highness. He chose the words 'restless' and 'unsatisfied.' He said you were keen on reconnecting with him, because the two of you had never really broken up."

God damn Callum. His ego was that fragile. And I'd fallen for it. Callum liked to think that because of his relentlessly Instagrammed cheekbones and ranch-hand-in-a-Tylenol-ad jawline, he had no competition. Until now.

"He also provided us with an album of photos, hundreds actually, depicting the intensity of your romance. They're on our website. He said you belonged together. And that His Highness was, in his phrase, 'a rebound deal.'"

"No he's not!" I said vehemently, to end all of this and expose Caroline's distortion of the facts. "And you have to understand, that's exactly the sort of thing Callum would say!"

"Carter?" Edgar repeated. His face was ashen, because he didn't know what to believe. How had I let this happen? And how could I fix this? And why was I being blamed for Callum's ugly scheming?

"Callum is lying," I said, speaking as clearly as possible. "He's jealous and he cheated on me and he made me feel terrible about myself."

"A provisional theory," Caroline smirked.

"Edgar, please, you have to believe me. I would never do this to you. Because I know how it feels when someone gets bored or horny and starts lying about everything, and I stuck with Callum for way too long, and it almost destroyed me. So that's not who I am. Yes, I went for a drink, and he grabbed me, but that's all that went on. I would never want to hurt you."

"That's a pretty speech," said Caroline, hungering for more fireworks.

"It's not a speech!" I practically yelled, my voice strained and desperate; I was telling the truth, but the more I underlined everything, the more I sounded trapped.

"Your Highness?" said Caroline. "Any response? To Mr. Ogden's somewhat far-fetched and unlikely tale?"

I have never hated anyone as much as I hated Caroline right then, Getting louder or standing up wouldn't help my cause, because Caroline would turn it against me and ask Edgar if I'd ever been violent. I could feel my face reddening as I clutched the armrests of my chair, digging grooves into the fabric. I wasn't sure when Edgar had let go of my hand, but he seemed miles away. He wouldn't look at me.

Edgar shut his eyes, in pain. He opened them and attempted to breathe.

"All right," he began. "Carter, when we started seeing each other, I asked for only one promise, one absolute assurance. That I be able to trust you."

"Understandable," murmured Caroline supportively. "Crucial."

"And now . . ." Edgar said, although he was fighting it, "and now I'm not convinced that I can."

"Edgar?" I said.

"I believe what His Highness means is . . ." interjected Caroline.

"I know what he means!" I howled at her.

"Mr. Ogden," she replied, every bit the offended sparrow, "I will request that you modulate your volume."

"What I mean," said Edgar, "is that I may have done something I swore to myself I'd never do ever again—for the sake of my own mental health, and my service to this country. But now I . . . I've allowed myself, and this is entirely my doing, and I take full responsibility, but I've let myself be compromised. To be placed in a position of, I believe the word is, vulnerability."

"Which is a good thing!" I insisted. "You need to be vulnerable! Everyone does! Even princes! Especially princes!"

"Why?" asked Edgar.

"So you don't shut down," I pleaded. "So you don't cut yourself off, so you don't condemn yourself to being suspicious of everyone you meet, and eliminating them, and ending up alone."

"Your Highness," said Caroline, "If I might suggest an alternative bridge to personal fulfillment, based on my recent bestseller, *Rewiring Your Love Clock* . . ."

"Shut the hell up!" I yelled.

"I beg your pardon!" she said. "But many fine people, millions of readers worldwide, have found my book to be miraculously helpful. Adrienne Lestercroft, a bank manager from Leeds, posted a five-star review on Amazon just this morning, terming the book, and I'm quoting Adrienne's own tribute, 'a masterwork of reenvisioning one's own inner loveways . . .'"

"I DON'T GIVE A DAMN!" I rasped, as if a fire-fueled demon had entered my larynx. Caroline was hijacking my life to sell her book, and Edgar was growing smaller and smaller, huddling in the corner of his chair as if he could will himself to disappear.

"Mr. Ogden!" cried Caroline. "Are you threatening me and my devoted readership?"

"No! And I'm sorry for yelling, but Edgar, please, we need to talk, somewhere private, we can get through this, it's really not a problem at all . . ."

"It's not?" asked Edgar, sitting up straighter.

"Your Highness?" said Caroline, her nose all but twitching from the scent of blood.

"Carter," said Edgar, "I have told you things and formed an intimacy . . . that I may be regretting. I have no idea what the truth of this Callum Turner situation, and these charges, may be, and that's the dilemma. I don't want to be here. I don't want to sit beside you and question everything. I don't want to leave myself open to any further heartache and disgrace and—pancakes!"

"Pancakes?" asked Caroline incisively, as if she'd just flung open a trunk and found the murder weapon.

"No!" I told Edgar. "I won't let you do this. I won't let you turn me into a liar and the bad guy and the reason you're about to torch your own life. That's not fair. I'm a mess and the worst baking show judge ever, and I don't even want to think about what my hair is doing right now, but I am not your enemy!"

"I don't care!" Edgar said, and now he was shouting. "I don't want to care! About any of this! And about doing this stupid interview!"

"Your Highness," said Caroline, deeply insulted, "may I remind you that the Palace agreed to your appearance, and Mr. Ogden's, and that I have an award-winning reputation for my comprehensive communication skills—for example, my two-part special evening edition with Mariah Carey—"

"I DON'T CARE ABOUT MARIAH CAREY!" Edgar bellowed, standing up. "I don't care about protocol, I don't care about calculating my royal profile, I don't care about love . . ."

He turned to me. His face was wild, and I was so frightened, not by his anger, but because I knew what he was going to say next.

"Which means . . . which means . . . that I can't care about you!"

His body was flailing; he was about to either spontaneously combust and fill the airwaves with a zillion floating shreds of convulsive royalty, or leave. He lunged at me but at the last second yanked himself back. He moaned in an unearthly combination of a Neanderthal's war cry and a wretchedly teething baby, shook his arms to the heavens and hurled himself out of the studio, followed by a frantic James and the security team.

"Oh my," said Caroline, shocked but pleased by the chaos she'd incited and the ratings that would accrue. "Mr. Ogden?" she asked serenely. "Any final thoughts?"

"Any final thoughts?" I said, staring at her incredulously, in disbelief at the height, or the depth, of her sheer gall. I marched directly to one of the cameras and said, "Only one. Everybody knows that Caroline's book sucks and that she wrote that Amazon review herself. And beyond that, I have no idea what I'm doing here, on this show or in England or anywhere else! Because I'm from New Jersey, and I'm going home!"

CHAPTER 25

'd shut off my phone and my tablet and I was wearing a sleep mask. My family, along with Louise and Adam, had been trying to track me down, but I couldn't deal with anyone, not yet, not even with Abby, as I slumped in my middle seat in economy on the plane back to New York (I'd put the ticket on my last functioning credit card). There was no way I could doze, or slow my pulse to a normal range, or cajole myself into believing that in the history of the universe, a gay couple splitting up on live global TV was a blip, a speck of LGBTQ info-dust, and that the whole gaypocalypse had undoubtedly stopped trending on every social media platform hours ago. As I'd passed through Heathrow wearing sunglasses and a knitted wool hat pulled almost to my chin, I'd glimpsed headlines on the newsstands and video monitors: "Edgar Denounces American Man-Slut"; "The Prince And The Pipsqueak"; "Royal Raunchgate"; and "GLAAD Condemns Carter Ogden Because Cheating Isn't a Gay Civil Right." A haughty woman on TMZ was saying, "If my man kissed some-body else, I'd be all, 'Bye, Carter. See you in hell!'"

What just happened? Had I betrayed Edgar, or had he over-reacted, and why, before I'd started ignoring my devices, hadn't he reached out to me in any way? What was I guilty of? Why had I gotten together with Callum, and let him kiss me, and why hadn't I been more conscious of my surroundings? And above all else, was anyone, especially me, surprised that I'd twisted my greatest chance for love into the most epic and public cataclysm?

I couldn't begin to sort anything out, but one aspect was cer-tain: I'd made this happen. All those months ago I'd sat in St. Patrick's and prayed for love and the largest possible life. My prayer had been answered, but with an expiration date.

Because I was Cinderella Ogden. Because I should've known that sooner or later my prince would catch on to how unlovable I was, how inadequate in every way, and he'd leave. So I'd sped up the inevitable. Ruth Ginsburg was about to tell me some-thing, but I'd stopped listening, especially to figments of my imagination; Ruth was gone, which was something else, on a very long list of truths, I'd be forced to accept.

"Excuse me, sir," said a flight attendant, tapping my shoulder, "would you like to purchase a beverage?" As I shook my head no, he whispered, "And I'm so sorry about you and Prince Edgar. I thought you were adorable together."

"I'm not going to judge you," added the voice of a second flight attendant. "Because Callum Turner is seriously hot, and I bet you're feeling like crap right now. So if you'd like a cocktail, we won't charge you."

With my sleep mask still in place, I heard another voice from two rows over: "Is he that cheating guy? The one with the prince?

I know the drill. Two divorces and fifty-eight stitches in the back of my head from my ex's golf club."

As more passengers and crew members joined this open forum on my love life, the first flight attendant clapped his hands and said, "People? Come on, let's leave the poor guy alone. He's been through a lot."

I was grateful for this but refused to cry until someone asked, "But why did he have to kiss that other guy?"

'd planned on taking a cab from JFK, but when I got to the luggage carousel, there was Abby. She'd made an educated guess about which flight I'd be on, and she opened her arms and I let go, let it all out, and she held me for a long time.

"Come on," she said, hefting one of my bags and leading me to her car. She drove us to New Jersey, pulling into the Piscataway IHOP parking lot. At first I resisted; weren't IHOPs now cursed forever? Abby scoffed, and soon we were sitting in a booth, because this was, if not a solution, at least a temporary salve; maple syrup-flavored topping was my drug of choice.

"So," she began as the waitress brought our pancakes, "I've watched the whole thing on YouTube maybe one hundred times, and here's my thinking: you didn't do anything wrong."

"But—"

"No. Sure, Callum was a total prick and you fell for it, but that's not a crime. But then he lied, and Edgar should've believed you. He knows you. Why didn't he trust you?"

I sighed. I was assembling my thoughts, telling Abby, "Because Edgar can't trust anyone. And the awful part is, I understand why. He lives in this bubble where everyone's after something, and his family and the whole world keep telling him who he should be. It's hard to feel sorry for him, because of all his money and fame and whatever, but I saw it up close. I'm amazed he can even get out of bed in the morning."

"Which is why you're so good for him! I picked up on it, at my wedding. He called you out on your self-esteem stuff, and you made him laugh and loosen up and act like a person instead of a cardboard cutout welcoming tourists to Royalty World. And when you danced together, I was so thrilled, because, of course, my wedding gown had made you fall in love."

For the first time in what felt like centuries, I smiled.

"Okay," Abby continued, taking her cue from my smile, "so how do we fix this?"

I put down my fork, because there was only one answer: "We don't."

"Excuse me?" said Abby. "You've met the perfect guy, he adores me, and everything was going gangbusters, like total gay Bachelor put-a-ring-on-it finale, until this tiny little obstacle, this one minor hiccup. And you're going to give up?"

"Abbs, it's not just about Caroline and her morning-show massacre. If anything, I should thank her. Because being on that show, and the whole Callum shit storm, and Edgar's reaction: it proved something."

"Like what?"

I didn't want to say this, but I had to. It was the first well-reasoned, rueful but accurate, adult decision of my entire life. "It proved that Edgar and I are—impossible, and we always were. That interview was an ultimate red flag. I got caught up, and maybe Edgar did too, in our whirlwind courtship, in the fairy-tale craziness, in the prince and the peon trope. It sounds good on paper, or in some gay teenager's journal with doodles of doves flying around with rainbow banners, but it could never work. Edgar could never really let me in: he's too scared, and everyone around him is too invested in keeping his life just the way it's supposed to be, according to the ye olde royal nodding-and-waving-from-a-balcony handbook. And maybe he won't always be alone, maybe he'll meet someone who checks all the suitable-spouse boxes, like Maureen, and they'll become a palace-endorsed team. But that's not me, and it never will be."

"But . . . but . . ." Abby was formulating a defense. "But maybe you haven't tried hard enough, either of you. And maybe Edgar needs to stand up to his family, and you need to stop being so sane and mature and willing to take, like, romantic early retire-ment. You're only thirty years old—"

"Twenty-nine. I'm still twenty-nine. For a few more months."

"Which is way too young to be giving up! And didn't Edgar tell you he loved you? Doesn't that count for anything?"

"Of course, and I'll always remember it. My Disney prince Hallmark epiphany, with upchuck. But I don't know if he even meant it, or if maybe he was feeling sorry for me, due to the barf, and . . . and I never said it back."

"Which is on you. So this isn't over. It can't be. Carter, I have a patient, this little girl with a heart valve replacement. She's go-ing to be okay, although she was on a ventilator and she needs months of recovery. But she found out that I was your sister, and do you know what she keeps asking?"

"Why did I let Callum kiss me? And why did I tell Caroline to fuck off?"

"No. All she's been asking about is a royal wedding. Because she wants to know what you're going to wear."

"You're making that up."

"I'm not, swear to God. I was going to introduce you, because she'd be over the moon. But not if you're wedding-phobic. Not if you're a total dickless coward."

"I'm not a dickless coward! I'm being realistic! I'm saving my-self, and Edgar, from making an even bigger mistake! So we don't keep going and, I don't know, have an even more vicious light-saber battle on *The Today Show* or mud-wrestle each other on pay per view!"

Abby stared at me; we'd reached an impasse. But I was right, because I felt clear-eyed and older and grim. I felt like an almost-thirty-year-old grown-up. I finished my pancakes, and even though Abby makes a lot more money than I do, I paid the check. And granted, an IHOP bill isn't a second mortgage, but I made my point. When it came to my life and my future and pan-cakes, I was in charge. Abby drove us to our house. She'd warned everyone to back off until I was ready to begin the healing pro-cess, which meant that as my mom opened the front door she said, "At least your skin looked nice on TV," and my dad com-mented, "You should be grateful you're not Gaveston, the male lover of Edward II, who in 1312 had him excommunicated and run through with a sword."

Miriam was waiting in the living room. "This is what happens when you hang out with those royals, because they like horses more than people. I thought that Edgar, that Little Mister Crown Prince, I thought he was different, but he's a cold fish, which is a meal only people in Connecticut enjoy."

I stayed in my childhood bedroom for a week, staring at the

posters for *The Light in the Piazza*, *Avenue* Q and a community theater production of *Anything Goes*, in which I'd played a tap-dancing sailor. I slept fitfully and ate only brightly colored, packaged foods. The Palace had issued a brief statement asking for people to respect His Highness's privacy at a difficult time, and Gerald and Maureen held a briefing on the steps of their estate, cuddling their twins as Gerald told the assembled media, "I love my brother and he's been granted a fortunate reprieve," as Maureen echoed, "I've no interest in defaming or disparaging anyone, but as to Mr. Ogden, I'll only say this: the man can't hold his trifle."

I went back to work, deflecting Cassandra's hugs, her condescendingly sympathetic remarks ("I hope you've learned something") and her requests for me to "get in touch with your grief-core and tell me everything." I'd raise a hand and murmur, "Too soon," so she could make compassionate clucking noises.

I moved back into the apartment, where Louise and Adam took over, telling reporters that I'd left town or that they were wielding sawed-off shotguns behind our locked door. They did what friends do, which was to resolutely take my side and to refer to Edgar as a dumpster fire, a lowlife and His Royal Shithead so I could protest, "No, he's not that bad, things just didn't work out," and Louise could say, "He's a pig-faced pile of white-privileged pee stains who never appreciated you on any level and fuck him until the people of England rise up and throw him in the Tower of London, or off the Tower of London," and I could nod meekly and say, "Maybe you're right." Adam and DuShawn acted out the woke, revised climax of a recent *My Fair Lady* revival, in which Eliza Doolittle brandishes her independence and leaves Henry Higgins in the dust, striding out of the theater itself by way of the center aisle.

I was recognized wherever I went, and I developed a sympathy for peripheral figures in heavily publicized scandals, for the escorts and porn stars and naive college students who'd dared to get involved with famous people and had been punished for it. I was contacted about a quickie book deal if I was willing to divulge sex secrets of the royals, which I turned down, even though Abby had speculated, "But what if it got made into an HBO Max original series and I could be played by Jennifer Lawrence?"

I no longer pondered romance as even an abstract concept or a lie repeated to sell paperbacks, greeting cards and weekend packages at hotels in the Poconos with heart-shaped bathtubs. When I was confronted with footage of Edgar running through a park with his security team or in full, resplendent uniform, saluting beside Queen Catherine as she reviewed the troops on a parade ground, I'd either shut it off instantly or stare at it numbly, to dilute its power. There's a particular peril to breaking up with either an actor like Callum, or someone world-famous like Edgar: they're everywhere. It's like falling in love with the "Don't Walk" sign, or earbuds, or the sky.

Which brings me to my family's Thanksgiving dinner, several months after I'd fled England—or, more correctly, been kicked out on my ass.

CHAPTER 26

Thanksgiving was going to mark my return to normalcy, to getting on with life and if anyone brought up Edgar's name, saying, "I met him once I think, at the UN." When I got out to Piscataway, my relatives were doing their best, even Abby, who was still refusing to abandon hope for an Edgar/Carter rematch.

"There you are," said my mom as I walked into the kitchen. "Don't you look nice."

"Our son is a very handsome man," said my dad.

"Have you lost weight?" asked Abby. "Not that you need to."

"You look good, dude," said Dane, who'd been integrated into our family and was catching up with our demented strategies.

"If that fancy-schmancy little Prince-Stick-Up-His-Tuchus could see you now, he'd be sorry," said Miriam, causing everyone to yell, "MIRIAM!"

We crowded into the dining room, around the elegant table; my mother's holiday tablescapes are the true spark for my career choice. Tonight she'd premiered a new set of dishes, painted with bold oversize daisies, to honor my re-blooming. None of this related to the Pilgrims' early meal with their Indigenous guests, but as my mother said, "If those Pilgrims had been Jewish, everything would have looked much nicer."

"It looks gorgeous," I told her.

"Are these new?" wondered Miriam, admiring her dinner plate.

"I found them online," said my mom. "They're from Finland."

Except for boyfriends, imported is always better.

"Pish pish," said Miriam, which was her most profound compliment, finessed with an unspoken, "Do we trust Finland?"

"Before we begin," said my dad, passing out an essay he'd written and then copied on his printer, "I'd like to share my thoughts on the historical facts of this holiday, which was most likely inspired by a religious harvest festival of the Protestant Reformation. Relations between Governor Bradford of the Massachusetts Bay colony and the Pequot tribe were in truth plagued by violence, particularly on the part of the colonists."

"I did not know that," said Dane, taking an essay.

There was an incessant knocking at the front door.

"I hope that's not Governor Bradford," commented Miriam as my mom went to find out who was dropping by. "I would not let him in my house."

There was urgent conversation from the foyer, and then Edgar's security team trooped into the dining room and took up positions along the walls.

"It's good to see you, Carter," said Charles.

"We've missed you," said Terry.

"Even your sweaters," added Clark.

What was going on? For a heartbeat I wondered if Edgar was here, and I was sure Abby was thinking the same thing. But why was he descending on Piscataway? Had he changed his mind about everything? Or was he returning something I'd left behind in my rush to leave the palace—I'd never recovered my favorite body-wash or my workout gloves, all of which I'd quickly replaced.

But instead of Edgar, Queen Catherine entered grandly, in a lime green silk coat dress with matching shoes and bag and a hat with lime green velvet roses, all of which complemented my mom's tablescape.

But what was the queen doing in our dining room, in Piscataway, on Thanksgiving? Everyone was staring at her in silence, which was the first time in recorded history that my family has stopped talking.

"Your Majesty?" my dad finally intoned, holding out an essay.

"She says that she'd like to speak with Carter," said my mom. "And that she couldn't do it over the phone because she doesn't trust technology and she needs to see his face."

How had my mom become the queen's mouthpiece?

"Mr. Ogden," said the queen.

"Yes, Your Majesty?" said my dad, wary but elated.

"The younger Mr. Ogden. There are two grave matters which I must discuss. The first is your complete and utter lack of even the most meager social decency in never thanking me for my hospitality."

"You didn't write a note?" my mom asked me.

"Or send a small gift?" said Miriam. "Some scented hand lotion or a fun oven mitt?"

"Nothing?" said Abby, in disbelief.

"Dude," said Dane.

"I apologize on his behalf," my mom told the queen. "That isn't how he was raised. But once they're out of the house . . ."

"You're like a rabid animal," Miriam all but spat at me.

"I understand," said the queen. "And I never blame the parents. And secondly, I must address the matter of your relationship with my grandson."

"But first," said Miriam. "I need to say something."

"I need to say something" will be carved on Miriam's tombstone, along with, "And that's only my opinion, but it's the truth."

"We've never met before," Miriam told Queen Catherine, "but I feel like I know you."

Miriam was standing beside the queen, telling the room, "Look at us, it's like I have a twin."

She was about to put her arm around the queen but decided, maybe not yet.

"And you are?" asked the queen.

"Miriam Yansky. You may know me from that TV ad, from years ago. I was coming out of a Broadway theater where I'd just seen this big musical, and they videotaped me saying, 'I don't care what anyone says, I enjoyed it.' That ad ran for years, on all the Long Island cable channels."

"And your relationship to Mr. Ogden?"

"I'm his great-aunt, who only wants what's best for him. Sometimes I call myself his greatest aunt, but I'm not sure you have a sense of humor."

"None. But I also want only the best for my grandson. Which is why I'm here. Mr. Ogden, when you departed, under a cloud of no small horror, I assumed that Edgar would breathe an enormous sigh of relief at his liberation from certain tragedy. I know I did. But Edgar, it seems, has become entirely incapacitated."

I was still reeling from Queen Catherine being here, holding a handbag that Miriam was about to stroke to determine if it was real leather.

"He's—incapacitated?" I said.

"He eats nothing. He sleeps much of the day. He attempts to exercise yet returns within minutes. Our family has, of course, provided wise counsel and a list of rehabilitative activities, all of which he's refused. This has continued for months. Yesterday I called him into my office and had him stand before me. I informed him, 'You are a Crown Prince, not some whimpering, lovesick schoolboy. You formed an unfortunate emotional attachment, and you paid the price. But this has caused a neglect of your duties. I'm offering a choice: dispense with this endless unproductive mooning at once, or I shall dispatch you on a six-month goodwill tour of the arctic circle."

"What did he say?"

"He said, and I'm quoting him directly . . ."

The queen paused, genuinely upset. We all leaned toward her.

"He said, 'Don't worry about me, Nana. I'm so sorry for all the trouble I've caused. And I quit.'"

The room grew even more gaspingly attentive.

"Oh my God," said Abby.

"Whoa," said Dane.

"What did he mean by 'I quit'?" I asked.

"He intends to abdicate. He said that his behavior, during his time with you, was erratic, highly sexualized and out of control, and that such an unstable person has no business ever assuming the throne. He said that he was our nation's worst possible option and that it was absolutely necessary to spare our beloved country such a dismal fate. So he intends to abdicate in favour of his brother, Gerald."

I had an incredible yearning for Edgar, and heartache for what he was going through. Abandoning his responsibilities was a last resort for Edgar; he must be in the darkest and most hopeless place.

I had a second, meaner thought: Gerald and Maureen were getting what they wanted. They hadn't plotted this, but they were ambitious, and I could picture them consoling Edgar, maybe over tea and scones at their estate, while sadly conceding that abdication was the only way out.

"Mr. Ogden?"

"I . . . Your Majesty, I'm so sorry, and I know this doesn't matter, but I feel terrible, and I wish I'd never met Edgar, so he wouldn't have to be so despondent."

"Many people, perhaps an entire nation, ardently wish that you'd never met Edgar. But I'm not among them. I believe that you and Edgar shared a great depth of affection. And for your brief time together, I'd never witnessed him so happy. He was transformed. And I can't dismiss or deny that. And that's why I've come here and imposed on your family's goodwill."

"It's no trouble at all," my mom assured her.

"And I have so many questions about the Tudors," said my dad.

"I love your hat," said Abby.

"Sit," said Miriam. "Eat something. You'll feel better."

"But Your Majesty, what would you like me to do?" I begged. I was shocked that she'd said such kind and supportive words about my effect on her grandson. "I've tried contacting Edgar, but he never responds. And sometimes I'm still angry at him for not believing me and for not trying harder to work things out. And I'm not sure we can ever be together, or if that's even a good idea, but I'd do anything to help him, so please, tell me how I can."

"Mr. Ogden, you've already done irreparable damage—to England, and to my grandson. And I have no idea what you should do to change Edgar's mind, so he may serve his country and attain some measure of happiness. I'm at a loss, and that's why I've come here. There's so much at stake. Everything, in point of fact. And it's entirely up to you."

"Me?"

"Edgar intends to address the Commonwealth this coming Saturday to announce his irrevocable decision."

She was diabolical. She'd dumped everything on me: Edgar's despair and his country's self-image and probably climate change, while we were at it. I'd become one of those renegade astronauts in a summer blockbuster, summoned to the White House for a suicide mission to rescue the planet from an oncoming meteor. What was I supposed to do, cock my head, gnaw on a cigar, leave my Montana trailer and say, "Yes ma'am"?

Abby caught my eye, aggressively tipping her head toward the queen, indicating, "Are you listening, Carter?"

As Her Majesty thanked my parents and turned to leave, Miriam surreptitiously opened the queen's purse and deposited a dinner roll wrapped in a napkin. As the queen exited, followed by the security team, Miriam explained to the rest of us, "For the plane."

A second later, Ian popped his head back into the room and told me, "She means it, mate. We could use your help."

CHAPTER 27

As I paused in the doorway to St. Patrick's, I thought, *I am the Judeo-Christian ethic, in one person*. After Queen Catherine left, our Thanksgiving had become a raucous back-and-forth on What Does Carter Owe Prince Edgar, Was The Queen's Demand About Love Or International Diplomacy, and What Should Carter Do And What Should He Wear While He's Doing It. And while I appreciated my family's outpouring of concern, I had to be alone.

So the next morning, after taking the train back to the city, here I am. The cathedral wasn't overpopulated, but I knew the pre-Christmas crowds would soon be kicking in.

I took a seat near the back, inhaled the lingering incense and thought: *Edgar.*

Did I still love him?

Yes. Or at least I'd know for sure, if I saw him again.

Was that enough?

Enough for what? To argue or coax or berate him out of ruining his life? Or, if he wanted to abdicate, should I respect his decision? He was conflicted over how royals could contribute to a greater good, so maybe bowing out and forging another route was the right idea. Or was that bullshit, because I knew he'd be an incredible king, and not just because he was gay, although that was a fabulous dividend, but because he was a compassionate and forward-thinking man who could make a difference?

Did I have any place in his life?

I'd already destroyed him, for reasons we'd dispute, and he wasn't speaking to me. If I could somehow reach him, and advise him, what would I say? "The guy you think cheated on you says to have faith"? "Listen to your gold-digging American slut"?

Was I a gold digger? What if Edgar was, say, a barista or a bank teller, or a guy I'd met online or at the gym? Would I still be devoted, or was I more in love with his money and celebrity and with some imagined, photoshopped Instagram story of myself by his side, performing a gracious, trademark royal wave to our fans behind the barricades before breezing into the hottest restaurant for a cozy dinner with a pop star and her Oscar-winning current husband to chat about everyone's charitable foundations?

No. When I thought about Edgar, he was never hobnobbing at the Met Ball or being applauded at a summit. He was either in my arms or sitting across from me at IHOP, delightedly torn between ordering the cinnamon raisin pancakes or the chocolate chip with extra whipped cream. And I was telling him we could have both.

Was I still angry that Edgar hadn't listened to my side of the Callum situation, or trusted me, especially in front of pretty much everyone on Earth?

Yes. And he was every bit as stubborn and pigheaded as me, only because he was a prince, I was expecting him to do better, to take the high road, to be more royally magnanimous. To do all the heavy lifting.

What did I want most, in my heart of hearts, as my St. Patrick's truth?

I wanted Edgar to make the first move, to apologize, or at least text me. No, that was what I wanted in my snittiest, smallest, pettiest brain. In my best sense of myself I wanted—Edgar. And because of that, I wanted him to be happy. And I wanted his happiness and our love to become the same thing.

How could I make that happen?

Should I max out my Amex, jump on a plane, run to the palace and bang on the doors, yowling Edgar's name as Scotland Yard dragged me away?

Why was being in love so impossible? Was it worth it? Even if by some extreme–long shot, never-gonna-happen, Abby-inspired chance I could corral Edgar and talk him out of abdicating, and we got back together, how could I be sure that, especially knowing me, I wouldn't fuck everything up all over again?

That was when my phone went off, and a woman seated in front of me turned around and glared.

So I left the cathedral and sat on the steps outside. James had sent me a video, which I noticed he'd also forwarded to Edgar.

CHAPTER 28

James had trouble framing himself in the camera, muttering curses as he finally centered the image and said, "Is this right? Can I be seen? Is this damn thing working?"

He was in what was most likely his apartment at the palace; behind him I saw a frighteningly well-made bed and a small oil portrait on a plain white wall.

"Gentlemen," he began. "And already I'm being far too kind. I have something to say to both of you sniveling brats."

He peered into the camera, gave up worrying about it and went on.

"I'm quite a bit older than both of you. In fact, I'm older than much of the solar system. But forty-seven years ago, I was hired as a footman to His Highness's grandfather. I was exceedingly thankful for the job, and then, as now, I revered the royal family. Because they were disciplined, they were well-dressed and they persevered.

"But I was a lad, and during my half day of freedom each week, along with the rare evening off, I sought companionship. Life was quite different then, and there were laws against sodomy and what was called 'gross indecency.' I didn't care, or shall we say, my body and my heart felt otherwise. I learned, from household employees, of meeting spots, of parks and lavatories and pubs hidden behind other pubs, where dancing was rumored to occur. And one afternoon, in a far corner, I met a man my own age, named Albert—it wasn't until our third encounter, at his tiny flat, that we shared our surnames. Albert Cradham was employed as a clerk on Savile Row. He was handsome, or at least I believed him to be—dark-haired, dark-eyed and impudent. He would tease me about working at the palace, and call me Your Lordship and worse.

"We found ourselves, much to our surprise, falling madly in love. At that time, not only was this illegal, but unimaginable—we had no examples. No LGBTQ princes, no associate event consorts.

"I spent every spare moment with Albert, at his flat and strolling through the city, careful to be taken for brothers, or mere acquaintances. But Albert wanted more—he said that we were bonded, and should celebrate our union, such as it was. I was fearful, but agreed, if the occasion could be kept entirely discreet.

"We invited friends from that special pub, and a few fellows from Albert's shop. We had music and a ham and even a clutch of balloons and streamers. There was champagne, which I'll confess to you I'd thieved from the palace cellar. Albert and I were dancing, holding each other close, when the police burst in. Someone, to this day I have no idea who, had reported an indecent gathering, and everyone was arrested, and we were pressured to provide names of additional inverts.

"I was consumed with fear and shame. My supervisor from the palace was alerted, bail was met and I was brought before your grandfather. He wasn't a cruel man, not really; he was simply ignorant, and of his era. He told me the Crown would intervene for my freedom. I begged for Albert to be included in this mercy, and released, but your grandfather refused. He said the offer pertained to me alone, with a condition: that I never see Albert, or any other man of his sort, ever again.

"I had a choice. Albert did not. I was the sole support of my embittered mother and drunken father, and I was desperate that they know nothing of my plight. I'm ashamed to say I agreed to the contract. Albert served, from what I know, two years in jail, and I never saw him again. I never tried to; not only was any such endeavour forbidden, but I assumed I was rightfully despised. I'd loved Albert and abandoned him, which was my real crime. I'd saved myself. Which was my punishment.

"The palace became my only life, and when His Highness was born, and I was assigned to assist in his upbringing, I was gratified. Edgar, your parents were among the finest people I've known, and they welcomed my participation. And when they perished so unthinkably young, I knew that your care had become more essential than ever.

"And of course, I've taken only the greatest pride in watching you mature into a thoughtful and accomplished young man, worthy of your parentage. And when it struck me that you were . . ."

He paused and smiled.

"That you were like me, I was secretly quite pleased. And when you chose to live openly, I was riddled with doubt, yet wanted to cheer. But I couldn't, for one reason: I didn't deserve to. Not after my treatment of Albert. Whom I think of to this day. Every day."

He gestured to the oil portrait, which was of an impish-looking young guy with a mustache.

"When the few visitors to my room have asked why I've saved this picture, I've told them he's a distant but cherished cousin. Edgar, I believe that is what I've told you. Until today, I was too ashamed and too heartsick to admit the truth."

He had tears in his eyes, but collected himself.

"I'd almost had what you, both of you, are about to discard so easily, due to a childish spat. I'm asking you, not for myself, but for Albert, and for the countless men and women who've been denied your opportunities, or been punished for them—let love, and not pride or position, be your only guide. Don't abandon each other. Or I will wring your vile little necks."

Abby's car was already double-parking in front of the cathedral as she leaned out the window, asking, "Need a lift?" As always, she knew where I'd be, and where I had to go, even if it meant racing through the yellow lights.

CHAPTER 29

As Abby kept the motor running outside my building, I bolted upstairs, taking the steps two at a time. Louise had my backpack waiting, and Adam had dug up my passport. I had a reservation on a flight leaving with just enough time to get to the airport and make it to the gate.

"This is so romantic!" said Adam. "When you're running through the airport, jump over stuff!"

"Go," said Louise, holding the front door open. "But spray paint something about the revolution on the front of the palace."

"Am I out of my mind?"

"GO!"

At the last second I dashed back into my bedroom and took the framed photo of Ruth Ginsburg off the wall, as she told me, "I can't wait to see London!"

As Abby exceeded the speed limit to JFK, she asked, "Do you have a plan?"

"No. But I think James is going to be very helpful. I'm going to find Edgar and take it from there."

"Oh, Carter. Should I come with you?"

"Thank you, but no. This is on me. But I'll stay in touch."

"And once you've fixed everything, tell Queen Catherine you want a knighthood. Or like, a manor house. Where I'll have my own room. Rooms. And I have to tell you something. When we were kids and I got sick, I felt so bad, because I didn't want to die, but even more because I had to be around to watch you grow up. So I promised God that if I got better, I'd become a beautiful surgeon."

I almost asked her if while she was praying, she'd used that exact phrase, but of course she had.

"And I also promised that I'd look out for you, for obvious reasons."

"Excuse me?"

"Because you'd brought your GI Joe doll to the hospital, and when I asked why, you said so he could meet a cute doctor. Which I totally agreed with, but I also thought, 'Carter is going to need dating tips.' So here goes . . ."

She pulled up in front of the terminal, kissed me and said, "Go get your prince."

Adam had printed out my boarding pass, and I scrambled to the gate with seconds to spare, joining the latecomers. I made it onto the plane, shoved my backpack into the overhead and began pitching my body forward to force the takeoff to go faster. I'd texted James, who'd be meeting me at Heathrow, and who was devising a way to ambush Edgar. If everything clicked, I'd land in London with at most an hour before Edgar's live abdication speech. I could use the flight to outline exactly what I'd say to stop him. I wasn't above begging or threatening to shave my head or promising to create an ad campaign with every sort of LGBTQ person wearing a crown and saying, "I am Prince Edgar." After watching James's video, I'd do whatever it took.

The plane taxied toward the runway. We were third in line. I hated the first two planes but forgave them. I craved only the very best karma.

We rolled to a halt. There was a problem with the landing gear. A problem that the pilot, over the PA system, said could be fixed very rapidly by the ground crew. I pressed my face to the window, debating if I should lead the other passengers in chanting, "COME ON!!!"

The crew drove beneath the plane in a jeep-like vehicle. We waited.

It would be at most twenty more minutes.

We waited.

There was another piece of equipment, which was being rushed over.

We waited.

I wasn't the only person asking a flight attendant if I could get off the plane and search for another flight. I couldn't.

We waited. It would only take another half an hour.

We waited.

The flight was canceled. The pilot said the airline was sorry.

We waited for a gate to become available.

We waited.

I used my phone to feverishly check if there were any flights on any airlines leaving for Heathrow.

There was one. It was overbooked. Did I want to be placed on standby for a possible business seat? I did.

Once passengers were finally permitted to leave the plane I beelined to the other gate, referencing every Olympic gold medalist and prison escapee. My shirt was sticking to my heaving chest and my knees were buckling, but I could collapse once I was on board.

I waited as everyone went through.

The seat had already been taken.

I pleaded to stand or kneel or ride in a pet carrier.

There were no other flights for at least eight hours.

It was over.

CHAPTER 30

By the time I got back to the apartment, by subway, Adam and Louise had the place fully stocked with microwave popcorn, Twizzlers and sympathy.

"That's it," I told them, dropping my backpack on the floor. "I tried, but not hard enough."

"You didn't break the plane," said Adam.

"And if you keep blaming yourself for everything, we're not giving you any popcorn," added Louise, who hugged me, which is something she never does; she once told me that "Hugs are what idiots do instead of voting."

I tried every conceivable method of contacting Edgar, but my texts and calls and emails went unanswered. He was resolute about not dealing with me. I had one number for James, but it went to a voice mail with the recording, "You have reached James Claverack with your concerns. Good luck, dear."

I had no means of getting through to the security team, and I

was in the strange position of cursing myself for not having the
Queen of England's personal email.

I lay on my bed and asked Ruth Ginsburg, who I'd retrieved
from my duffel bag, if there was anything else I could do, but
she shook her head sadly, finally mentioning, "You could change
your sheets."

I had two choices: drink or drug myself into some version of
sleep, or stay up all night replaying everything that had happened
since I met Edgar. Both of these were bad ideas, so instead I did
what lovelorn people always do: I listened to sad love songs, everything from country-western vengeful breakups to Broadway
power ballads to whispery female singers who liked the words
"morning," "hurt" and "rain." None of this helped, because nothing ever would.

Outside my door, DuShawn had joined Adam in softly har-
monising on the score from *The Book of Mormon* to cheer me up,
but they knew: even musical comedy has its limits.

After maybe five minutes of fitful napping it was seven a.m.
and time for Edgar's speech. I could refuse to watch it, which
seemed cowardly. If nothing else, his abdication would truly end
things; it would be a lasting emblem of the damage I'd done and
why, despite James's and the queen's best efforts, Edgar and I
would never see each other again.

Louise, Adam and DuShawn were up, stumbling toward the
couch with their coffee. I fell onto them for one of those occasions when a group of friends becomes a single lump of support
under one frayed, fairly disgusting blanket.

The cable news networks and morning shows were all carrying the speech live, and CNN was as good a choice as any. The
anchor intoned, "There's been no announcement as to the con-

tent of Prince Edgar's speech, and the Palace has refused to confirm or deny rumors of abdication."

Edgar was seated behind a desk in his palace office. He was pale and doleful, in a dark suit, as if serving as his own somber attorney. He cleared his throat.

"He looks thin," said Adam.

"Thanks, Great-Aunt Miriam," I told him.

"He looks like his dog just died," said Louise.

"And his eyes are red," said DuShawn. "He's either been crying or doing cocaine."

The rest of us stared at DuShawn, who said, "Because he's sad."

I wanted to either hug the flat screen or throw it out the window, as if that would block Edgar from proceeding.

"Hello," Edgar began, at first in a whisper, then speaking up. "Hello. I apologise for bursting in like this, and I'd like to thank the media for the airtime. I . . . I . . . I'm sorry, let me just collect myself."

He stood up, with the camera jerking to follow him. After a second of indecision, he shook himself, waggling his head and rotating back and forth as if twirling an invisible hula hoop. The way I'd taught him to, all those months ago, at the United Nations.

"What's he doing?" asked Adam.

"Is he having a stroke?" wondered Louise.

"He's—loosening up," I explained.

Edgar sat back down, his hair now a bit less dutiful, his face flushed.

"There. All right. For the first time in my life, I'm not sure what I'm going to say next. And I'm a prince, so I'm supposed to know."

"He looks better now," said Adam.

"Is he drunk?" asked DuShawn.

We all stared at DuShawn, who said, "Because sometimes it helps."

Edgar barely drank, and he wasn't drunk now. But he was ignoring any prepared remarks on the teleprompter.

"After my parents passed away," Edgar was saying, "and I'd begun the earliest twinges of acceptance, I only desired two things: to be safe, and for life to make sense. And that was fine, that was enough, more than enough, for many years, until—I met someone. The most unlikely, infuriating person."

Uh-oh.

"And because I'm me, I pressured him. I badgered him. And I made him surmise that in order to please me, and this country, he'd be required to change in every respect. To alter so much about himself that I adored. I'm an idiot. As probably everyone but me already knows, if you love someone, you don't try to change them. You honor them. You listen to them. You believe them. You hate them and you love them and if you're very lucky, they change you. And beyond all else, you trust them. I have what are called trust issues, as the result of past betrayals. But that was no reason for me to lash out at a man who'd only been honest. A man who'd never given me the slightest cause to doubt him. A man who'd had no difficulty admitting he was from New Jersey and introducing me to his altogether splendid family, especially his marvelous sister, Abby. When I accused this man of lying to me, I should've reconsidered immediately, because Abby's brother would never lie."

My phone was blowing up with texts and emails and a photo of Abby screaming with happiness, taken exactly one second ago.

"So if Carter Ogden is watching this," Edgar continued, "on his couch with his friends . . ."

"How does he know that?" asked Adam.

"Does the royal family use drones?" whispered DuShawn, peering out the window.

"Where else would Carter be?" Louise said, sensibly.

Oh my God. Oh my God. Edgar was looking right into the camera. Right at me. He was making sure I was paying attention. It was like he had me by my shoulders.

"Carter, if you're out there," Edgar said, "I'd like you to know that I'm truly sorry for the way I've behaved, or misbehaved. And that I trust you and treasure you and would like nothing more than to spend the rest of my life battling with you about whether IHOP's maple-flavored syrup is actually tastier than real maple syrup. Because I love you."

"That fucker," said Louise, with tears in her eyes. "It's so not fair. When someone says 'I love you,' you should be given twenty-four hours to consult with your union representative."

Adam and DuShawn were holding hands and singing "Seasons of Love" from *Rent*.

"And finally, Carter," Edgar said, "I'd like to ask you one simple question. A question that everyone, everywhere can understand."

He smiled. Full-on, abashed, heartfelt and my downfall. Edgar's smile was already a proposal, but he went on. He looked into the camera and asked, "Carter Ogden, will you marry me?"

By the time I started breathing again, after Edgar had signed off and all the news teams were jabbering about what they were calling "His Highness's surprise proposal, to say the least," Louise was dangling my backpack, Adam had my passport and Du-Shawn was handing me the framed photo of Ruth. Within seconds, I heard Abby's car screeching up to the curb downstairs.

CHAPTER 31

James was standing beside the car outside Heathrow, holding a cardboard sign reading "Peasant."

"That's me."

"Get in."

The flight attendants on the plane had been delirious, slipping me extra chocolate chip cookies and mini-pillows: "What are you going to tell him?" "Are you going to do a prenup?" "We took a vote and think you should honeymoon in Turks and Caicos," "You have to post a picture of the ring," and "Prince Edgar made me cry! I smacked my boyfriend and told him, 'Why can't you be like that?'"

When I let myself think about any of it, I ricocheted between inwardly jumping up and down, superstitiously repeating Miriam's mantra of pretending to spit on the floor while saying "Poo poo poo" and drafting what I was going to say to Edgar. I didn't want to sound rehearsed, so I kept wiping my brain clean and only skimming Abby's barrage of texts about matching tuxes ver-

sus Edgar in his Royal Marine uniform and me in a rainbow sequined cape.

"Thank you, James," I said in the car. "Your video was heartbreaking and incredible and everything Edgar and I needed to
hear."

"I'm a saint. Remember that when I ask His Highness for a pay
rise."

Marc, Alison and the rest of the staff were lined up, waiting
for me in the great hall just beyond the palace entryway.

"We were all shocked," said Marc. "But mostly in a good way."

"Have you any notion of your response?" asked Alison. "Because I've prepared a range of press releases."

"I'll let you know. But thank you."

The security team joined us.

"Aren't you glad we let you have sex with His Highness?"
said Ian.

"Did you bring us anything from America?" asked Lucky.

I quickly distributed the mini bags of chips, peanuts and
Oreos I'd pocketed from the plane, and the guards cheered.

I was about to ask for Edgar's location, but I knew where
he'd be.

I bounded up many carpeted staircases, only slipping twice,
just to make everyone gasp and speculate, "What if on his way to
give His Highness an answer, Carter suffered a concussion?"

I reached the top floor. I adjusted my clothes, to appear dignified and worthy of a milestone occasion, but I settled for being
slightly less creased from the flight. I strode down the hall to the
nursery, the place where Edgar was most himself.

I knocked, and Edgar's voice answered, "Yes?", as if he was in
a meeting and didn't want to be disturbed.

Inside, all of the furniture had been uncovered. The room had been thoroughly dusted and polished, the woodwork gleaming, the air smelling of lemon and pine. All the curtains had been opened, with sunlight streaming through. This was no longer a haunted retreat, but a welcoming, comfortable aerie, alive with history and the promise of hanging out, snacking and wearing sweats. Edgar wasn't forgetting the past but building on it.

Edgar was standing near a window. He wasn't smiling, not yet. He was torturing me.

"Your Highness?" I said.

"Can I help you?"

"That was so incredibly embarrassing. Proposing to me in front of the entire world."

"That's why I did it."

"I thought—I thought you were going to abdicate."

"I considered it."

"What stopped you?"

"James's story was extremely powerful. And I weighed the loss of never having my face imprinted on a ten-pound note. And then I thought about you."

"Okay, but before we go any further, I need to say something, about Callum—"

"I get it. He's very attractive. In a cheap surfer dude sun god sort of way."

"And I was so scared."

"Scared of what?"

"Of everything. Of doing that interview. Of your grandmother. Of letting you down."

I'd never admitted this, to myself or anyone else: I'd gone to see Callum deliberately, in a spasm of self-sabotage. I'd wanted to prove that I wasn't cut out for happiness and that I'd always fuck things up. I was daring the universe to contradict me. And when Callum kissed me, of course it was a mistake but I'd allowed it, and maybe even encouraged him, because that's what I did: I was Carter Ogden, misery magnet.

"You were scared," said Edgar, "so you snogged your ex."

"Snogged?"

"It means kissing," he explained. "Just kissing."

"But I shouldn't have done it and I'm ashamed of myself, and I'll never do it again. And if it's any consolation, you're a much better kisser."

"Now you're just flattering me."

He was smiling, just a little. A vicious tease.

"But I'm warning you," I said, "if you and I, if we decide to do—what you were talking about on TV, I'm going to be a total disaster. Your worst nightmare. Your country's worst nightmare."

I was still doing it. Throwing up roadblocks. Promoting handy bullet points of all the reasons for Edgar not to love me.

"And I will continue to be a tight-ass," he countered. "And a control freak. And a huge royal pain."

"With great hair."

"There's that."

Three-quarters of a smile. A hint of the full fireworks. The trailer for the main attraction.

"But Carter, I think that, as always, you underestimate yourself. Because this job, being a royal—you're a perfect fit."

We were still a few yards apart. What was he babbling about? What ridiculous theory was he concocting? What easily refuted nice try?

"How am I a perfect fit?"

"Our life together, our public life, would be a series of events. Events that I'd like to see become more imaginative, more entertaining and more human."

"Are we talking about more vomiting? Because I can do that."

"I'm aware."

"And I have some ideas," I said, without meaning to. "About rebranding the royals. Apps. Collaborations with recording artists and designers. Maybe a video game. *Playing The Palace.*"

"But in this game, the king would always win, correct?"

"Dream on."

What was happening here? Was Edgar making sense? Was he converting me to, God forbid, not just the feasibility of the two of us moving forward together, but of me—becoming a functioning, almost sane, valuable human being?

"But all of it," he said, "the crowns and other people's opinions and the protocol, we can figure that out. Because those things don't really matter. But if they ever start to matter, if they threaten to overwhelm us, I pledge, from my soul—that I will always choose you. I will choose us."

Don't cry. Not yet. Queer up.

It was no use. I was crumbling. He was winning. He was forcing me, through charm and logic and something that might even be called—gulp—the truth, to not just love him more than I'd even thought possible, but to love myself and some absurd, why-the-hell-not dream of our future. He was making it sound doable and enticing and real.

"So I suppose you'd like some sort of answer," I said, still clinging to wisecracking insecurity, "to your big question. But if I say yes, which I'm not saying I am, would I get some sort of title?"

"First you'd become the Duke of Somewhere. Perhaps the Duke of Piscataway. And while I pray that my grandmother will be with us for many more centuries, we will someday mourn her loss. And then, following a coronation, I would become King Edgar and you would become the Royal Consort, Prince Carter."

"Which sounds like a rap star's baby."

"Your answer?"

"Not yet," I said, because Edgar had just provided a legitimate hindrance. "Because there's one more royal rule, isn't there?"

"What rule?"

CHAPTER 32

The walls of the Throne Room are covered in red silk damask, and it's carpeted in red, with the red upholstered throne placed on a raised platform at one end. This is exactly what I'd always wanted my childhood bedroom to look like.

Queen Catherine was seated on the throne, wearing a hot pink dress of stiff linen. Just to make sure I got the point, there was a larger-than-life-size oil portrait of her, in royal regalia, including one of her most stupendously jeweled crowns, a sword and an ermine cloak, in a gilded frame on an easel beside her. On a certain gaudy level, Buckingham Palace is a prime high roller's suite in Vegas.

Edgar and I stood a few feet away. There weren't any chairs for us. On purpose.

"Nana? Mr. Ogden has a question."

"What now?"

"Your Majesty," I said, "no one in the royal family is allowed to be married without your approval, isn't that right?"

"Quite true. And if I had my way, no one in the world would ever be married without my approval. I could save people so much time and trouble."

"So," I said, now standing next to Edgar, "what do you think?"

The queen sighed deeply, monumentally annoyed, as if deciding between breakfast and an execution.

"I think that you are two men from different countries, with extremely different temperaments. And the world will be watching you, at every moment, for any signs of distress or impropriety."

"Or personality," I added.

"Or outrageousness," said Edgar.

"Or fun," I said, looking Her Majesty right in the eye.

"Or trifle," she shot back.

"Nana?"

"You are both causing me such—Mr. Ogden, what was that word your great-aunt Miriam used? Tsuris?"

"It means headaches, in Yiddish."

"Precisely. Miriam is a learned and accomplished woman. This morning she FedExed me a pound cake. But the two of you have given me tsuris, and this will only increase."

Hearing Queen Catherine's version of Yiddish—which became weirdly Irish—was making my day even better, if that was possible.

"And all you're doing," she continued, "is waiting with barely concealed, glint-eyed greed for me to expire, so that Edgar may succeed me, with Mr. Ogden as your scampering playmate, installing flat screen televisions in every room of the palace, and hot tubs."

"Nana, that isn't true. I've told you repeatedly, I forbid you to die. It simply can't happen. Not on my watch."

"Although," I mentioned, "I'm loving the hot tub idea."

"And to have the two of you on the throne," said the queen, "or in Mr. Ogden's case, on a cushion nearby, will be either a gargantuan fiasco, unequalled in modern times, and the end of the monarchy, or . . ."

"Or?"

"Or?"

"Or perhaps—a step forward."

She raised an eyebrow. Which felt like a symphonic crescendo.

"So," I asked, "do we have your blessing? And your permission?"

"Edgar? Do you love this small, inappropriate, fidgeting person?"

"Yes. So very much."

"And Mr. Ogden? Do you love my grandson?"

I'd never said it before, not to Edgar. He hadn't let me. Saying "I love you" can be too easy, the way some overly exuberant people use it as a greeting. If it gets too earnest, it can feel like you're pushing and working to convince yourself. Stop overthinking this, I told myself. Stop having a panic attack. Stop being you. Thanks to Edgar, you're not that same neurotic, pessimistic, occasionally deranged person. Progress happens. Love happens. You and Edgar are happening. You can do this. Say it.

"Yes," I said. "No matter how hard I fight it, and no matter what happens. And I hope the palace has insurance. But I love him."

I turned to Edgar.

"I love you. Deal with it."

Edgar smiled. Full-on. The sun coming up. Roman candles over the skyline. Every fountain in the world gushing toward heaven. Every voice raised in jubilant harmony. Every bell pealing. Edgar's smile.

"Oh, get on with it," said James, standing by a far-off door, but his perfect diction and the room's acoustics lent clarity. "Your Majesty, I'm sorry you have to see this, but it's necessary. It's how these things work."

"If they must," said the queen.

We kissed in the Throne Room at Buckingham Palace. I could hear Miriam declaring, "Let me take a picture." I could see Abby cheering and wrestling me to the ground until I admitted that she'd predicted all of it. Somewhere Adam and DuShawn were singing "People Will Say We're in Love" from that terrific multicultural revival of *Oklahoma!* where the cast had served chili at intermission. I could sense Louise making gagging noises.

"That's quite enough," decreed Queen Catherine.

CHAPTER 33

This was the controversy: is a lavish royal wedding an obscene anachronism, a waste of time and money poured into an over-produced spectacle of regal, prejudiced crap? Or is it, like the royal family at their best, a symbol of unity and joy, a celebration shared by all? And, in the case of a gay royal wedding, is it as-similationist dreck, a hideous example of queer people being every bit as obnoxious as straights? Or is it an LGBTQ triumph, a hugely visible win for our side, kind of like a royal pride parade?

Edgar and I argued about every aspect: Should we have a small, quickie ceremony and build a website for wedding day contributions to worthy causes? Or would everyone, especially gay people, feel cheated out of what could be a highly original blowout?

"You're the associate event architect," Edgar finally decreed. "You figure it out."

I got busy. In my profession, a royal wedding is a dream, a pinnacle, the Nobel Prize for centerpieces. I invited Cassandra

and the Eventfully Yours staff to assist me, in coordination with
the palace and Abby, as my associate event cochair—I appointed
her because Edgar demanded it, and because I didn't want her to
kill me in my sleep. The wedding was scheduled for June, in the
sunshine. My first meeting with Abby, over a hypersecure con-
ferencing app engineered for the occasion, began like this: "Okay,
Carter, you know that every cell in my body is hyperventilating
with bliss, for you and Edgar and me. Because ever since my wedding, I've been thinking about yours. I didn't want to tell you,
because I know how nervous you can be, but I've totally got this."

She went on: "This wedding can't be just about the happy
couple—it's for everyone. It's a world wedding. Which means it's
big. The biggest. Which doesn't mean money, it means poring
over every detail and opening up the guest list. We need bits
from every all-stops-out traditional royal-palooza but also stuff
that no one's ever seen. It's like a UNICEF commercial, a Hallmark Channel Very Special Event and the inauguration of a non-
binary president, if they all adopted a baby. It's everything."

I trusted Abby. She was an intersectional bridezilla—a
bridezilla of tomorrow.

So here I am, on the morning of our wedding. Edgar and I
have spent the night apart, out of respect for the Crown and because we both like the idea of seeing each other in our nuptial
couture for the first time at the altar of Westminster Abbey.
Booking the abbey hadn't been easy, because of the conservative
outcry. Queen Catherine had settled matters by issuing a statement expressing her affection for Edgar and me and explaining
that every royal couple deserves the abbey, and that was that.
When I thanked her she'd gestured to herself and said, "Queen
of England. Done."

Abby and I were in a suite with my friends and family at a hotel near the abbey. I was wearing a custom-made morning suit in navy, with a rainbow-striped vest. I'd worried about coming off as a queer ringmaster, but the tailoring was so precise that even I had to admit I looked tall, dashing and broad-shouldered. "You finally have the body you've always wanted," Abby said admiringly. "Just never take off the suit, because it's built in."

Earlier in the morning, for a personal touch, Adam had added a subtle, royal blue stripe to my hair. He inspected it, concluding, "It's the perfect accent. It says 'I love being a royal and I just couldn't help myself.'" He and DuShawn were dressed in matching jumpsuits hand-painted with images of their heroes, from James Baldwin to Patti LuPone. "You all look fabulous," Louise informed us. "And the proceeds from the Royal Wedding Ken dolls are going to the American Civil Liberties Union."

Edgar had promised to find Louise a new girlfriend, and at our rehearsal dinner he'd sat her beside his cousin Lady Isabelle, who was spearheading a drive to repatriate artworks from British museums to the countries they'd been stolen from. She also had waist-length red hair and a tattoo of a medieval sorceress covering her back, so Louise had been very pleased, because, in Abby's words, "Louise likes drama."

"We couldn't be more proud," my mom told me, "not because you're marrying a prince, although that doesn't hurt, but because you're marrying the man you love."

"But if you're not sure," said my dad, "there are precedents for canceling a royal wedding. In 1528, Princess Hildegarde of the Netherlands—"

"I'm good, Dad, I'm ready. But thank you for the research, and you both look fantastic."

"Is this all right?" said my mom, referring to her flawless pale yellow shantung dress.

"No," I said. "You're a disgrace. You look like you went to the mall and shut your eyes. You're embarrassing everyone on two continents."

"You have such a smart mouth. I hope Edgar knows what he's getting into."

"We can leave now," said a voice. "I'm here."

Miriam had on a gold brocade suit, which she'd worn when accepting an award as Accountant of the Year; she'd had it reconfigured for today with the addition of blooming pink chiffon roses everywhere. She looked great, like a garden party in heaven.

"I love all of you," I told the group. "And I'd never get married without every one of you being part of this."

"Of course not," said Miriam. "It wouldn't be legal."

Dane, who'd been incredibly supportive of Abby's wedding mania, and who was wearing the fashion-forward tux from a Japanese designer that Abby had picked out, led a toast, saying, "What a cool day. I thought just marrying Abby would be kick-ass, but here's to the dudes!"

While I'd wanted to walk to the abbey, as a man of the people, or a person of the people, Abby and Miriam had insisted that I ride in the traditional gilded royal carriage drawn by six white horses wearing feathered headpieces. The streets were thronged, and I'd asked Abby and Miriam to ride with me. They were in their element, waving to the cheering, whistling crowd and calling out, "You look gorgeous, too!" "Thank you for being here!" and "Can you believe this?"

I couldn't decide if I felt like some new, progressive Disney prince or more like Jiminy Cricket, but I was fine either way. I'd feared that, given my history, no one would show up, or people would understandably jeer me, but this wasn't the case. Because while the English people could be skeptical, once they'd established that Edgar was happy, they were all in, at least for today. The shops were brimming with souvenirs, including tea caddies, dish towels, commemorative platters and pillow shams, all with often unrecognizably retouched images of Edgar and me standing side by side. Conservatives assured one another we were just staunch coworkers.

"It's like the best kind of fairy tale," Abby told me, assessing a window stacked with Edgar-and-Carter bobbleheads, "because it's got a fifty-percent-off sale table."

The night before, Edgar and I had sponsored five free concerts at venues across the city, with pop and hip hop stars performing along with local bands, solo artists and choirs, all celebrating the country's diversity. At the abbey, in addition to hymns, we had a children's chorale, a fifty-member all-female a cappella group, the Brighton Gay Men's Chorus and a klezmer band. The pews were filled with dignitaries seated among postmistresses, fast-food workers, schoolteachers and health care aides, all of whom had entered a lottery (Edgar and I had also made sure to invite Harriet and Edith, from the *Baking Jubilee*). We had a no-gifts policy, except for donations to the Royal Clean Water Initiative and a list of global charities.

"It's showtime," said Abby, wearing a dress the size of a taffeta school bus and carrying a bouquet of calla lilies, thistle and English tea roses as we stood at the rear of the church. Abby was my matron of honor, preceding me down the aisle, and I remembered that awful year of her illness. I was so glad she could be here in all her glory.

I followed, with my parents on either side. "I'm crying," whispered my mom. "Because I'm so happy and because I just saw Oprah."

"What a thrilling day," said my dad. "Now you're part of English history, like Sir Thomas More, who presided over the Abbey before he was convicted of treason."

We passed Gerald and Maureen, barely concealing their disappointment over Edgar not abdicating. They'd given interviews championing LGBTQ rights and were building a new tennis court on the grounds of their estate. As I passed their pew, Maureen mouthed, "Congratulations! Fingers crossed!"

Miriam sat across the aisle beside Queen Catherine, who'd insisted on this partnership. I'm not sure if they'd planned it, but the queen was also wearing gold and pink, so the women looked like sisters, or cowinners of a beauty pageant, splitting the title of Ms. Senior Boca Raton. Miriam was clutching the queen's gloved hand, and they both mouthed "Kina hora poo poo poo" at me and mimed spitting on the floor. The queen smiled, something I wasn't sure I'd ever seen before. It was like a benediction, and Miriam turned to her and whispered, "Good for you!"

I let myself see Edgar, in his amazing royal outfit, which combined a military jacket looped with gold braid and a sash dripping with jeweled medallions and ribbons, atop a splendid kilt and lustrously polished boots. He looked so impossibly handsome and sexy that I turned to James, who was by Edgar's side as his best man, and we exchanged the universal gay facial expression meaning, "Oh my GOD!"

The security team, while technically on duty, was clustered nearby, also serving as Edgar's groomsmen. They scanned the crowd discreetly, but as Lucky glanced at Edgar and me, I saw

Terry pass him the handkerchief the team was sharing to manfully dab at their eyes.

Edgar and I faced each other. We were being married by the
archbishop of Canterbury, Rabbi Kottleman from my family's
temple in Piscataway, and Louise, who'd had herself ordained
online at the Church of the Unicorn Renaissance, a nondenomi-
national group that charged ten dollars for a certificate. As Louise had told me, "You need a black woman up there, and because
I'm a Unicorn Goddess I get to say anything I want."

My framed photo of Ruth Ginsburg had been placed on the
altar beside a crystal vase of roses. Ruth needed to be here, and I
might've heard her murmur, "Very nice. And you know, I could've
performed the ceremony, because I'm a judge."

Edgar and I had already initiated a tradition, as we'd cele-
brated our mutual birthday a few months back. We'd thought
about a party, but with the wedding approaching, it would've
been overkill. So we'd had a small cake for just the two of us, in
the nursery. Edgar had told me, "Thirty looks good on you" and
I'd answered, "Fuck you, because everything looks good on you."
We blew out the candles together and sang to each other, which
we agreed was perfect and also too revoltingly cute for any guests
to witness. I was, and remain, deeply superstitious, but I let myself envision the two of us devouring cake and laughing and making love, in this room, every January 22, for many years to come.
I no longer dreaded turning thirty with nothing to show for it;
now I wanted to be equal to the task, and the opportunities, and
the man who was about to become my husband.

We're at the altar. Edgar and I can't stop smiling in joy and
disbelief. As Abby always told us, we'd both gotten so lucky, to
have found each other and to have her in charge of our wedding;

she'd commissioned an official oil portrait of herself with the title Westminster Abby. No, I couldn't stop her.

This day, and our meeting at the appropriately named United Nations, and our marriage, were loony and enchanted, and I had no idea what would happen next, once we left the abbey. But I was exactly where I should be, with exactly the right guy. So for the moment, I let myself stop fretting, second-guessing and doubting. If Edgar believed in me, that was more than enough. So I let myself believe that this was my life, or at least a fabulous beginning. I let myself be in love.

ACKNOWLEDGMENTS

I'd like to thank Cindy Hwang, my wonderful editor, for welcoming this book and for her terrific guidance and enthusiasm. I'm also so grateful for the efforts of everyone at Berkley, including Ivan Held, Christine Ball, Claire Zion, Angela Kim, Jeanne-Marie Hudson, Jin Yu, Bridget O'Toole, Jaime Mendola-Hobbie, Dana Mendelson, Craig Burke, Erin Galloway, Loren Jaggers, Lauren Monaco, Jennifer Trzaska, Brian Contine, Max Felderman, Jennifer Myers, Christine Legon and Colleen Reinhart.

As always, David Kuhn was instrumental in helping this book find such a great home.

For their ongoing support, good humor and forbearance, I'm indebted to Patrick Herold, Dan Jinks, Richard Garmise, Todd Ruff, Dana Ivey, Arlene Donovan, Scott Rudin, Jamie Krone, Scott Berlinger, Albert Mellinkoff, Kim Beaty, Allison Silver, Adrienne Halpern, Candida Scott Piel, William Ivey Long (a true royalist), Christopher Clarens, David Colman, and the Klahr sisters, who are no longer with us but remain a glorious inspiration.

I began writing *Playing the Palace* long before the COVID-19 crisis, but it was rewritten and edited during that awful period, so I'd like to salute the healthcare workers who've been so brave and tireless, along with everyone else who's been staying safe and doing their best to keep our world functioning.

I'll also pay tribute to the English royal family, especially Queen Elizabeth, a group that's fascinated and entertained us all. It's strange that Americans, in particular, are often so obsessed with a monarchy, but the personalities involved can be hilarious, admirable, questionable and delicious fun.

Finally, and with love, I need to thank John Raftis, who's willing to make German chocolate cake frosting from scratch, create the most beautiful garden, explain so many things and keep me sane or thereabouts.

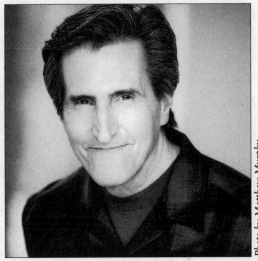

Photo by Matthew Murphy

Paul Rudnick is a novelist, playwright, essayist and screenwriter. His plays have been produced on and off Broadway and around the world and include *Jeffrey, I Hate Hamlet, The Most Fabulous Story Ever Told, Valhalla, Regrets Only* and *The New Century*. He's won an Obie Award, two Outer Critics Circle Awards and the John Gassner Playwriting Award. His novels include *Social Disease* and *I'll Take It*, and his YA novels include *Gorgeous* and *It's All Your Fault*. *The Collected Plays of Paul Rudnick* was published by Harper-Collins, along with an essay collection entitled *I Shudder*. Mr. Rudnick is rumored to be quite close to film critic Libby Gelman-Waxner, whose reviews have appeared in *Premiere Magazine* and *Entertainment Weekly*, and whose collected columns have been published under the title *If You Ask Me*. Mr. Rudnick's articles and essays have appeared in *The New York Times, Esquire, Vogue* and *Vanity Fair*, and he's a frequent contributor to *The New Yorker*. His screenplays include *Addams Family Values, In & Out*, the screen adaptation of *Jeffrey, Sister Act* and HBO's *Coastal Elites*.

Ready to find
your next great read?

Let us help.

Visit prh.com/nextread

Penguin
Random
House

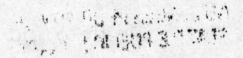